The
Lowlands
of
Heaven

For Chris
Best wishes from
Branch 92.

James

[signature]

June 9, 2011

The
Lowlands
of
Heaven

ෙ

F. J. Dagg

Branch 92 Books

Second edition, January 2011

Web: branch92.com
Contact: info@branch92.com

Cover illustration by Jennifer Rummens
www.jenniferrummensstudio.com

Cover by Robert Goodman, Silvercat,™ San Diego, CA
www.silvercat.com

ISBN: 978-0-615-37622-6

Printed in the United States of America

Acknowledgments

The author is deeply grateful to Mary Dagg, without whom *The Lowlands of Heaven* would not have been, and to Cynthia Dagg Catsman, Cheryl Cohen, Christopher Cameron, Claudia Ward, Renee Phillips, Judith Ann Bishop, Allen Pomianek, Thornton Sully, and Joe Rathburn for their time, insight, and endless encouragement.

For

Mary Bradford Dagg,

with Love

The angels keep their ancient places;
Turn but a stone, and start a wing!
'Tis ye, 'tis your estrangèd faces,
That miss the many-splendoured thing.

– Francis Thompson

Prologue

Laurel, young yet ancient, lost Kate on a golden summer afternoon near the beginning of the 20th century. Had a midday outing begun a second earlier or a moment later, their story might have been entirely different. But on Earth—in this aching world—darkness often prevails.

છ

Late on a shimmering afternoon in early September, John and Carrie Bradford drove along a dusty road beside a winding creek in the Illinois countryside. The summer's heat had broken at last, the day was lovely altogether and though she was in the final month of her "delicate condition," as it was called in those days, Carrie would not be denied a ride in the country. Though the husband and father-to-be protested, the woman won out.

A physician who served the children of Chicago and its outlying communities, John Bradford at thirty-three was tall, slim, and sandy-haired—and much loved by his young patients for his gentle manner. His colleagues, too, held him in high regard—his published articles on pediatrics commanded respect in medical circles well beyond the area he served, and everyone knew he was a man with a future.

When they met, Carrie had just returned from Europe, where she had studied for a year with one of the most prominent violinists of the day, and was poised to begin a career as a touring

1

concert soloist. It was a rare thing for a woman of that era, but given her great talent—and that none of her many suitors had carried her heart—she accepted the prospect of such a life's loneliness. Then, John Bradford came along. That he proposed marriage didn't surprise her; that he proposed only a month after their introduction did, although she had been as sure as he from the start.

So, despite her uncommon professional standing, she bowed, quite willingly, to the cultural currents of her time, and chose to marry not only for her own completion, but for the continuity of family and community. And of course because, with the Irish wit he had inherited from his mother, John could make her laugh. As for music, she was much in demand with local ensembles and was an occasional soloist with the Chicago Symphony Orchestra. It was the best of all worlds.

Late summer, late afternoon in the lush countryside, some miles outside the metropolis, the day ripened. High above, cumulus castles towered, reflecting the dying daylight. Carrie reveled in the sultry scents, the green luxuriance of the woods bordering one side of the road, the glimmer of the creek on the other, the joy of existing.

She tucked away a strand of ebony hair that had escaped from under her white touring gear and turned her eyes—the great blue eyes that had nearly struck John Bradford to his knees when first they met, and commanded him still—to the side where the land fell away from the road, and admired the low sunlight that burnished the surface of the creek and glinted off the steel rails of the tracks on the water's far side.

Music, she thought, would complete the day. Just then the distant wail of a railroad locomotive's whistle reached her. "Eighteen-oh-two," she said, flashing a grin, a challenge, to her husband. The doctor stole a moment's attention from navigating the new Model T over the old country road to return a wry smile. So attuned to the universe of sound was Carrie that she knew the locomotives by their voices, though her tone-deaf husband couldn't distinguish the song of an elite passenger express from a crow's rasp. She asked herself, again, why this plain, simple sound enchanted her so.

John Bradford's thoughts, as they had more and more lately, turned to a son who would carry on the family tradition, a son who with his father's guidance would shine in the grand, new world of the 20th century, this Age of Science. (Everyone knew that the month-old war in Europe—a misunderstanding!—would soon be over and that Progress would then resume.) Dr. Bradford Junior would not have to settle for ordinary practice. His father would be well enough positioned to set his son on a higher path. He might pursue research and become a scientist—perhaps one of those whose name History records.

The train's sound grew louder as it drew nearer on the far side of the creek.

A hummingbird swooped in front of the car, his throat flashing iridescent rose as he darted and turned, at odd moments his crown reflecting the sun in a gold-white flash. To Carrie's delight, the bird zipped and dashed and hovered in front of the car's windscreen as if to halt them, chittering loudly as he did.

"Oh, look at her!" cried Carrie. "She must have a nest nearby."

"Not now," replied the doctor. "They would have left them weeks ago. Anyway, 'he.' It's the males that display those colors."

"Oh, stop a minute!"

John Bradford shook his head. "These roads can be treacherous after dark, love." Indeed, in the eastern sky one star was awake. "We have to get you and the little fellow home."

She shot him a sideways look. "You mean you have to get us *girls* home…"

3

The doctor feigned horror and put on his ancestors' County Kerry accent. "Heaven and Earth! And how could a man be hopin' to stand up to a *pair* o' ye?" It was an old joke between them; still, Carrie's laughter chimed out and mingled with his.

Turning toward the creek, she spied an old, ragged woman with a long, cloth bag stooping in the reeds below. The train's pounding was loud by now, and the woman looked in unison with Carrie to the surging locomotive, "1802" emblazoned on the cab, sure enough. Carrie waved cheerfully over her shoulder to the engineer, who replied with a couple of short, muted blasts of the whistle.

As she turned back, her attention was seized by a tall, pale man walking on the far side of the tracks some distance in front of the locomotive. He was thin—gaunt, even—and he wore, oddly, given the season, a long, dark coat. *Was he...? No. He wasn't there before...*

At that moment, the man raised his head to look directly at Carrie. His ghastly pallor struck her, and for an instant she felt something like revulsion. She chastised herself for her lack of charity and half-raised her hand to him. He lifted his arm slowly and she thought he was acknowledging her faint attempt at a greeting—but no, rather than a wave, his hand closed in a fist. A prickling thrill coursed through her, and her hands went unbidden to her belly. The fell, silent communication endured for the split second before the rushing locomotive cut him from her sight. Carrie, suddenly grave, snapped her gaze ahead, her breath quickening. The glory had gone out of the day.

The Model T came to the old wooden bridge that sloped over the creek. To the doctor, this was a personal amusement park ride—the sudden swing and swoop down the angled deck, tempered by a prudent application of the brake—then the merry rattle over the tracks on the creek's far side. He always smiled at the sensation. The ritual customarily concluded with a wave toward the white farmhouse a little way down the road.

Now, as he turned onto the bridge, three sensations gripped John Bradford in quick succession: the weightless feeling of falling backward in the absence of the brake's expected effect, the electric charge through his belly as he recognized the terrible nearness and speed of the roaring locomotive's black, smoke-gushing mass on the track that ran just before them, and Carrie's questioning look as she grabbed his arm for support as the car accelerated down the steep slope.

He applied the brake again. And again. Time slowed. He remembered their wedding day.

Carrie's hands tightened on her belly, her child. *No... No...*

John Bradford's quivering arm bent the metal brake lever as his mind filled with a vivid image of his mother as she had been when he was small. His wife's scream barely penetrated this odd reverie that accompanied his death. The roar of the locomotive's machinery and the howl of its whistle were even fainter.

⌃

Science—the Sovereign of this Age—instructs that only the material, that which can be perceived by human senses, and measured—is. But there are those who dwell on the fringes—those who, by will or by chance, remain uninstructed.

One such was present that late afternoon, stooping among the reeds of the creek, searching for only she knew what. The long whistle blast drew her gaze up from the marshy water. The shattering impact froze her in place. Then, as the train ground and shuddered to a halt, plowing crushed metal before it, the old woman found her feet and struggled up the bank, slipping in the long, damp grass, one gnarled hand gripping the taller growths for support, the other clutching her ragged cloth bag.

5

She reached the track, hobbled toward the locomotive, then halted as she drew up to the horror.

The sun was nearly down and the light was further dimmed by smoke and vapor as the halted engine clanked and hissed monstrously, blowing off steam in the still air. The train's crew and a few passengers ran forward, not seeing the old woman, transfixed as they were by the smashed tangle of metal. As they milled about, shouting, gesturing, she sank to the ground, mouth half-open, eyes half-closed. And where the train's crew and the braver passengers saw torn metal, and blood, she saw—Light.

Three faint, glowing spheres hovered, clustered, a few feet above the wreckage. One was turquoise, another, pale orange. The third was marbled—blue and gold interwoven—and slowly rotated. After a moment, turquoise rose a little, followed by orange, while the multicolored one floated in place.

Then, with sudden swiftness the two monochrome spheres flew vertically, vanishing from the old woman's sight. One trailed a ghost of a silver thread. Her gaze turned to the third sphere, still hovering. Its rotation quickened, then, like a cell viewed under a microscope, it divided in two, one blue, one gold. The pair hovered—and began a slow, circular dance, touching briefly, pulling apart—touching, parting again.

The two spheres came to rest; then Gold rose in a wobbling spiral as Blue sank, disappearing back into the wreckage.

The old woman's gaze followed the golden sphere as it soared skyward, diminishing with distance. Her trembling hand, as of its own volition, slid into the ragged cloth bag and retrieved a leaf, ground it hard between bony fingertips and palm and raised it to her nostrils. She inhaled deeply—and swooned. After a moment she recovered and settled, cross-legged, very still. Her eyes rolled up, white, and then closed.

And now, she truly saw.

Her second sight, an observer apart from her physical frame, dashed in pursuit of the golden sphere as it mounted to the sky. Soon—though time loses its accustomed iron authority in this regime—the sphere was among labyrinthine clouds, nearly lost to view as the observer soared through ragged mists, now thick, now thin, now thick again, until Gold vanished into a bank of dense, dark vapor.

Second sight, astral body, soul perhaps—the observer pursued, determined, and soon burst into a grand coliseum built of cloud, shot red-gold by the retreating sun, and glided to a halt. Astral body, second sight, soul—many study, some assert, most differ—whatever the right name of this point of awareness, it saw, lying in a far reach of this great glowing vaporous arena, a young girl.

Or, as became clear as the observer approached, the youthful-looking angel into which Gold had resolved as it came to rest, exhausted.

She lay on a bed of vapor, a shelf in the light-drenched clouds so crisp and well-defined as to appear solid. One might have guessed her age to be about twelve or thirteen years, though in fact she was inexpressibly ancient. The smallness and delicacy of her body contrasted with the storm of wavy gold-white, blood-flecked hair all about her, and her great wings with their tattered white feathers and long crescents of vivid iridescent blue at the tips.

Her breath was fast and shallow, her face battered and bloody. Her eyes were closed—indeed one was swollen shut. Dimly, the observer reflected on the strangeness of an injured angel. One of the angel's wings curled around her body, feathers disarrayed. The other dangled from the vaporous shelf at a painful angle, broken.

Then, like a tiny rocket shot from earth, a hummingbird appeared, his feathers flashing bronzed green and rose. He darted,

7

chittering, all around the angel. He moved closer to fan her face, wings thrumming, then pulled back, loosing another volley of chirps.

Sensing the observer, he pivoted as if in recognition, as if there were mortal eyes there to meet his own. The bird chirped, dipped earthward, deep and abrupt, then up again, all the while holding the observer's gaze, his head and neck ablaze with iridescent red. More chirps and another dip, lower, then up again.

The battered angel half opened one blue eye. Though the motion was subtle, though she seemed to look to a world unimaginably distant, the angel instantly commanded the observer's attention. Something passed through her gaze, a knowledge long and deep, outside of time and wordless but for one syllable: *Love*.

Understanding bloomed in the observer—and a dire urgency. In that instant the old woman convulsed as her second sight reunited with her body far below.

∛

Harsh voices and a great hissing of steam again filled the old woman's ears. She staggered to her feet and ran headlong through the crowd surrounding the wreck.

"Baby! The baby!" The crowd froze at the shrill voice. Belying her apparent weakness, the woman pushed people aside and began to tug and dig in the jagged wreckage. In a moment her hands were covered with blood, some her own, some not. The crowd pulled her back as two automobiles and a horse-drawn wagon arrived. She howled, incoherent but for the repeated, "Baby!"

Sheriff Tom Quinn stepped from the first car, followed by his deputy, Micah, from the second. A tall, weathered man in denim overalls stepped from the wagon and followed the officers. The crowd turned to the sheriff, and then made way for him as people do for such men as he. He moved to the center of things and peered into the wreckage, stone-faced.

"Anyone know who this is?" A slight grimace betrayed him. "Or how many?" The question brought their attention to the enormity of what lay before them and they grew silent.

Quinn looked about, picked out the train crew. "You boys got pry bars, anything of that kind?"

They nodded and trotted off. The old woman's howls carried on. The sheriff spared her a glance, then turned to the man who had arrived behind him in the wagon.

"See it happen, Orv?"

The man shook his head. "No, Tom, just heard it. Figured I'd better come see what I could do."

The crowd began to murmur again, and a sharp voice rose above the sound, "What's the old nut raving about? What baby?"

The crewmen returned with crowbars and lanterns, and set to work on the tangled metal. As they revealed the interior of the wreckage, two turned away, ill.

A man hurried from the direction of the train's coaches bearing a black leather bag. "Let me by! I'm a doctor!"

In dim lantern light, the doctor located flesh within the crumpled and jagged metal, drew a stethoscope from his bag, and applied it where he could. After a few seconds, he exclaimed, "This one's alive!" He stood and began issuing orders. "Move that piece…bend that, right here! Carefully…carefully…" He directed the men's efforts a little longer, then stood straight, casting an urgent look over the clustered faces. "Is there a clean place nearby where we can move her?"

Orville spoke up, "My place, quarter mile down."

By now the crew had pried the wreck open enough to reveal Carrie, horribly battered. The doctor called for light, and when a man brought a lantern to bear, examined her more closely. "Good God! She's with child."

Heads turned toward the old woman, now serene, rocking slightly, humming tunelessly, while under the doctor's guidance men lifted Carrie and moved her to the wagon. Orville, with the doctor and a couple of volunteers on board, clucked the horses into motion and reined them toward his farmhouse down the road, the one John Bradford used to wave to after his rides over the bridge.

The sheriff turned to the old woman and regarded her a long moment. "Em…how'd you know?"

She kept rocking and humming, seeming not to hear, her gaze fixed in the far distance. Suddenly her face bloomed in childlike wonder. She staggered to her feet and peered eagerly at the sheriff.

"*Dandelion!*" The crushed leaf was still in her hand. She urged it on the sheriff, pushed it toward his face. "Smell!" She sucked in a great rasping breath. "You'll see the angel!"

Quinn gently seized her hands, pulled out his handkerchief, wiped off the mash and grime, and smiled, grim and gentle at the same time. "Thanks, Em, can't now…another time. Let's get you some supper, what do you say?" He fished in his pocket, and handed some coins to his deputy.

"Micah, get Em a bite to eat and take her home." He paused, then added, "And keep an eye out for Clementine. She's probably out looking for her."

"Will do, Tom."

Em babbled happily and let Micah lead her to the car.

At the farmhouse, the four men moved the improvised stretcher—planks that happened to be in Orville's wagon—into the kitchen and set it on makeshift trestles.

In Micah's car, Em rocked and muttered, "'Twas Ol' Scratch done it. Smelt 'im…" Suddenly she jerked up straight, eyes wide, and declared, "It's broke!"

"What, Em? What's broke?"

"Silver string. S'gone." She squinted, silent a while. "Don' matter… Baby's a'right." She sat back and chewed contentedly on nothing.

In Orville's kitchen the doctor bent over Carrie and applied his stethoscope. He straightened and shook his head. "She's gone…"

Orville drew the bloody blanket over Carrie's bruised face as his gray-haired wife, Molly, murmured a prayer.

"…but I might save the child." The doctor rearranged the blanket, took a scalpel from his bag. All but Molly turned away as he made the incision.

Later, the doctor wrapped a pallid infant girl in a blanket and stepped toward Molly. She crossed herself, then took the child into her arms as the little group drew close to wonder at the tiny survivor, who would be named Kate, and who—if darkness did not at last prevail—would fulfill a grand destiny.

Part 1

Two Worlds

1

A dappled dove soared in a brilliant blue sky, following a river that meandered through an emerald forest far below. A range of blue-gray mountains rose behind her to the east, the forest climbing its lower slopes. The great timberland, lush and dense, stretched from the mountains almost to where the river met the sea, where beyond a shimmering white beach, a sun-gemmed ocean illuminated the western horizon.

A large, sheltered bay lay a couple of miles south of the river, an inverted letter "J" formed by two peninsulas—to seaward a four-hundred-foot-high ridge rising from the river's mouth and running some six miles south, to landward a nine-mile thread of scrub-grown sand just above high water, whose northwestern end broadened into a wide platter sheltering under the lee of the seaward ridge.

Clusters of sturdy cottages stood, a few on the seaward side, more to leeward of the high peninsula's ridge line; yet more on the flat shelter of the low peninsula.

Above the harbor's northern shore stood a village of larger buildings, mostly of red-tile roofs and stucco, some of stone. The plain that stretched from the village to the sea held a wind farm, which at a distance resembled a vast fleet of sailing ships putting out to sea, but was in fact rows and columns, just the least bit uneven, of sail-winged windmills, like those commonly used in some Earthly regions before that planet's Industrial Age.

Two moons graced the sky. One, a thin crescent of gold, sailed high above, and another, larger and of ghostly silver, hovered low over the eastern mountains. The air was like Earth's but sweeter and more pure, and though there was a visible sun—the source of the path that shimmered on the sea—the light that not only illuminated, but was the essence of this place, came as if from everywhere.

Onward sped the dove, following the river, still a way east of the ocean. She was joined by another, and yet another, and by more and more of her tribe, converging from all points of the compass, so that by the time she reached the red-roofed village by the bay she belonged to a great flock, a gathering so grand they cast shadows like racing clouds and their wings trailed gentle thunder.

Where the river met the sea, the birds wheeled as one and reversed their course, weaving among the languidly turning sails of the mills. Onward they raced, surging past the graceful Mission style building that stood at the town's western boundary. Over the building's tall, twin graven oak doors appeared a legend:

BRANCH 92

The flock winged over the little town, and soon arrived at a great stonework building, which announced itself as the

AVIARY

The building's sunward side consisted of row upon stacked row of portals, each sized perfectly for a dove. Into these openings the flock alighted in a great fluttering rush.

The interior of the Aviary might have been the model for Earth's medieval cathedrals, with a few exceptions: a cheerful chaos of sounds—birdsong, chimes, flutes, all blending with the voices that rose from the throng of angels, creatures of human form, seemingly solid, yet made of light of many hues, who occupied the great chamber, for the most part whisking birds in hand this way and that, though a few attended to instruments ranged against the walls. Laughter echoed, and no voice contended, or if it did, it did so without rancor.

No single style of design dominated. The instruments that occupied some of the angels' attention suggested the highest of 21st century technology, but the devices' enclosures and other fittings were here Victorian, there Baroque, elsewhere Rococo. Other accents included Art Nouveau, Greek, Renaissance, and 21st century digital, all defeating any attempt to assign the place to a period. Additionally to the things hand-wrought, plants abounded—-the place was arboretum as well as museum and aviary. Some might be tempted to call it chaos, but all harmonized—perhaps because Time, in this region, is not what it is in others.

A complex of scents filled the space: that of incense, and those of the various blooms, ever changing; water—ocean or river, depending on the season and the wind—and the subtle redolence of the ancient stones of which the place was built, as if the ages bore distinctive olfactory characters. Some said that the older angels could map the birds' long travels by the essences wafting from their feathers.

One vast wall contained many rows of small doors, the inner termini of the array of portals in which the flock of doves had lately ended their long journey.

Screens on the portal doors blinked and flashed, displaying such words as "Desire," "Gratitude," and "Good Wishes."

Narrow brass-railed balconies divided the wall into horizontal sections, each serving a half-dozen rows of portals. Luminous angels briskly came and went on these balconies and on the rolling stairways that served them, maintaining a steady traffic of weary birds into the great chamber. A legend carved in the marble lintel above the portals read:

HEAVEN'S POST OFFICE
BRANCH 92

A sturdy-looking, working-class sort of angel reached the top of one of the stairways. Gerard, one of Branch 92's senior angels, appeared to be fifty or so, of medium height with the build of a wrestler and a ruddy complexion. His hair, brushing his shoulders, was thick, red, going to silver. Taken altogether, he possessed might and gentleness in fine proportions. Gerard read the display on one of the doors, then opened it and removed the dappled dove who had just arrived. He greeted the bird as an old friend. He looked her over, petted her, muttered a few affectionate words in a language unknown on Earth (that is to say, one not known in any recent time), and bounded down the stairs.

Gerard spoke, a hint of a brogue in his voice, to Benedict, an angel of perhaps twenty. "First now, lad, she'll have her message classified and appraised."

Benedict followed as Gerard set off at a brisk pace across the great chamber. "So then, the birds carry wishes and prayers…"

"No," Gerard interrupted.

Benedict tilted his head, questioning.

"Prayer," Gerard continued, "is direct communication between a soul and its Creator. Nothing mediates that. The birds carry the more subtle things…mental currents that might have been expressed in prayer but, for whatever reason, remain unformed or were hidden below the horizon of consciousness."

"Like the burst of happiness that comes from a glimpse of beauty?" Benedict ventured, "Or that kind of concern for a loved one in distress that never really rests, even when you're distracted?"

"Just so. The whole business might be thought of as a sort of safety net…His way of making sure their concerns are heard when they're absorbed in other things."

He paused as he handed the bird off to a young angel behind a counter in an alcove labeled, "Inbound."

After a space, Gerard retrieved the bird and glanced at the small tag now attached to her leg. He nodded. "She's carrying a request…as you'd expect, since those make up the bulk of the traffic. And you'd be astonished at how many of them down there do not really know what they ask for."

Benedict's eyes widened. "No?"

Gerard considered his reply, then explained, "It's not so much that they don't know, Benedict, but that they do not see. As you cannot see your hand in front of you in a darkened room, neither can they, on Earth, see reality complete. And Earth, always in shadows, grows lately ever darker." Silence embraced them for a moment. "Adrift in darkness, they forget. They forget to be grateful…and they often forget to wish their fellows well."

Benedict looked down and considered in silence. His mood grew somber and the frown returned.

"It's…it's just that it seems so…well, complicated. Why doesn't…I mean, couldn't He simply…?"

The elder angel laughed gently. "Of course…and, one expects, does, when it suits His purpose. But remember, son, He has given them free will, and in learning to use it, they necessarily make mistakes. Too, we must be mindful of *our* purpose, which is to serve those below, even if at times we don't fully grasp the meaning of our service. If we face a few constraints…and tests… as they down there face many, then we come to empathize." He held the youth's gaze a moment longer. "And that reminds us that all we do here is only rightly done for the sake of Love."

Gerard laid a hand on the youth's shoulder and guided him

toward the portal marked "Requests," where he handed off the weary dove to another angel. "And now," he said, "when she's through here, she'll get a bite to eat and a nice nest or tree, as she prefers, for a good, long nap. Takes it out of 'em, it does, that long haul."

The sea breeze that flowed over and through the little town penetrated the spaces of the Aviary, spicing the air, as the pair approached the great arched entrance to another large chamber. Gerard paused, surveying the great spaces—with just the least bit of possessive pride. He arrested his errant thought, examined it. No, not pride of ownership, certainly, but the warm pleasure of belonging. The well-beingness of belonging to a very good thing, something larger than oneself, in the company of many good souls. He reflected on his long good fortune.

Gerard's gaze returned to the younger angel. "Be thankful you're here, Benedict. Though Heaven proper is yet some way above, it is still a grand thing to find yourself in its lowlands."

As the two entered the next great chamber, the elder swept a hand over the scene. Had Benedict not been so absorbed in the novelty of the place, he might have noticed that Gerard's mellowness had become tinged with a bit of wry skepticism. "And here, to finish up, is the newest…ah…innovation."

The diverse yet harmonious mix of styles prevailed here, too, but tended more toward the modern; a team of angels monitored the array of great, glowing consoles that lined the walls. Conversation was terse and hushed. To an inhabitant of the 21st century, the scene might call to mind an air traffic control center.

Gerard beckoned Benedict to one of the consoles where a young angel's attention was riveted. Her eyes scanned a glowing screen that looked like a starry sky, except that the stars swam about, myriad glowing dots in graceful, if random, motion as her hands glided over an array of controls.

Gerard spoke in a low voice so as not to break her concentration. "Kaira's looking for a bird to bring up."

One of the many roving angels slid in beside the console and handed Kaira a slip of paper. With a quick look at it Kaira resumed her search of the display. Her hands ceased gliding and began dashing smartly over the controls. She rolled a trackball, and a luminous square enclosed one of the glowing dots. A rapid, high-pitched chiming rose from the console, the box surrounding the glowing dot blinking in rhythm with the chime. Gerard pointed, whispered.

"There now, she's locked on. The bird down there will be sensing a glow high in Earth's sky. They know to fly to it."

Kaira swatted a large, domed red button on the console. A beam lanced down from the top of the display and engulfed the enclosed dot, which bloomed like a sun turning into a nova, then vanished.

"There you are, the bird's near here now, upriver, or along the coast or maybe just outside. She'll find the portals herself… done it a hundred times, she has, as have most of them." Gerard paused, held the youth's eye. "And that, Benedict, is the business of the Bird Works," he said, using the Aviary's popular nickname. "Questions?"

"Well…umm…meaning no disrespect…it seems…I mean, some parts of it seem kind of…"

Gerard let Benedict struggle a short space, then he chuckled. "Unheavenly?"

Benedict nodded, relieved that the elder had said it.

"You're not the first to have thought so. In truth, I prefer the Old Way, myself. But you see, lad, there's nothing, not one thing, that appears below that hasn't been first expressed in the Higher Regions, be it towering tree or tiniest fern, minnow or whale, mouse, elephant…and all things wrought by men." He

21

gestured toward the consoles. "They'll be wanting this sort of thing down there in their near future and, soon after, things even more fantastic...and potent. 'High tech,' they'll call it."

"You don't like it, do you?" Benedict asked.

"It makes me fear for them," Gerard replied without hesitation. "They set out with the best of intentions...but they're so easily tempted. If one of their philosophers says that science might be used 'to ease man's estate,' and another says that it will make man 'Master and Possessor of Nature,' you may count on them, in time, to embrace the latter.

"They've become prideful in their mastery, and the more they succeed in bending Nature—matter, as they see it—to their will, the more they believe there is nothing *but* matter. The more amazing their works, and the more they wield dominion over Earth, the more they tend to forget their Creator. In their pride they begin to doubt His existence...and then they're in danger of mistaking themselves for Him. And that can only lead to grief." He paused, and Benedict thought he looked tired.

"But this is the path they choose to walk," Gerard continued, "and our duty is to serve them, so..." Again, he gestured to the blinking, chiming gear.

Benedict reflected. "I'd like to hear about the Old Way, then," he said at last.

Gerard was pensive a long moment. But he had heard the boy and returned to himself and said, "Oh, to be sure, lad. It's still done, and it's a fine thing to see..." He stopped again, thinking of how Earth's time intruded here, more and more, "... and when we have a moment, we'll..."

And then time halted. Tranquility stole upon the Aviary. Voices stilled. Birdsong faded to silence. The bells and chimes went still. Eyes met eyes, questioning, expectant.

The quality of the light within the great rooms—indeed,

throughout the little town, the entire region, indoors and out—mellowed. A deep golden hue suffused every space, and a timeless peace settled over all. Gerard and the other older angels recognized this condition—they called it a *Shift*—and knew that it foreshadowed change, some significant event just over the horizon.

The silence lingered for a space, until Kaira called out, "Gerard! Come look!"

A light, conspicuously larger and brighter than the others, had appeared in Kaira's monitor. Just as strangely, a smaller light, as brilliant as the other, clung very closely to the larger, at times seeming almost to merge with it. Gerard studied the lights a long moment. Finally, he murmured, "I wonder…" and his brow furrowed as he leaned closer, not sure, despite his long experience, what to make of the anomaly. He waited for the still voice that had guided him, wordless, time untold. After a moment he heard, then decided, and laid a gentle hand on Kaira's shoulder.

"Allow me, dear, if you will." He took her place and ran the controls with practiced ease. The targeting box bracketed the two bright blips—but the expected blink and chime failed.

"Well…?" Gerard demanded of the screen. He waited a half a breath then whacked the side of the console with the flat of his hand, so sharply that Benedict and Kaira startled. *Ting! ting! ting! ting!* sang the chime, and the box blinked as it should. "'Hi tech'…" muttered the angel under his breath. He silently reviewed the procedure, and made a final decision; he rotated a large black knob labeled "Power" clockwise until it stopped and its indicator read "Full."

He struck the domed button. On the screen, the beam darted, and the two lights bloomed like novae.

2

Far below, yet very high above Earth, towering cloud castles drift, tinted gold and red by a lowering sun. A bird, or say perhaps a spirit, roaming thereabouts might be puzzled to hear now, of all things, music. But there it is: faint and far off, a lone violin, irresistibly attractive, which, as the observer draws nearer, resolves into Bach's Sonata I for Violin Solo, Presto. The invisible fiddler caresses each note, despite the brisk pace, and draws a sweet, birdlike tone from the high register, and a deep, reedy growl from the low.

Up, up, sunlight and shadow, colors now muted, now glorious, the observer mounts the cumulous ramparts, until finally the player comes into view. On the highest parapet, a slender, winged silhouette sways to the wild music—an angel—framed in the rays of the lowering sun.

Swinging out of the shadows, around to her illuminated side, the observer sees the angel who had been so terribly battered in the wreck that had taken the lives of John and Carrie Bradford—and had separated her from Kate.

She still appears to be a waif of twelve or thirteen years, but of a startling beauty now that her wounds are healed. Waves of thick white-blond hair frame her heart-shaped face and fall to her waist, swinging as she plays. Great, powerful wings—white feathers with long, iridescent blue crescents at their tips—make her body seem yet more slender and delicate. Her wings are asymmetrical; the right droops and its tip angles inward, crossing behind her knee, the break having healed imperfectly. A faint scent of jasmine surrounds her.

Though she has recovered from the terrible mauling, and plays with extraordinary energy, she is not truly well. Her beauty is wan and fragile, though a hint of her robust native state of health lies beneath her pallor.

Her eyes remain closed as she sways. Music radiates from her like warmth from the sun. And—utter incongruity—a weathered canvas knapsack hangs by a strap from her left shoulder.

Suddenly, like a tiny rocket shot from Earth, a hummingbird vaults up from the misty canyons and halts, hovering in front of the angel, his plumage blazing bronze and green. For a moment, he floats so still he seems painted on the sky, then he begins an aerial dance, a figure-eight pattern in time with the angel's music, his head and neck flashing rose as he swings and turns. At odd beats, according to an arcane musicology, the feathers of his crown mirror the sun in brilliant golden flashes.

He ends his dance, moves closer to the angel and in a long, vigorous chitter speaks in the song of his tribe, the Calypte Anna.

CB

The angel startled, great blue eyes flashed open, and her music halted mid-phrase. A smile bloomed, and she dipped her head to the tiny hovering creature.

"Well, there you are, my good bird!" she said, with the warmth that lives between old, old friends. Her voice was soft and slow, with a Virginian cadence, and low, for one apparently so young, and the least bit hoarse, just so to charm. She leaned toward the bird, eyes narrowed. "You look tired. Will you take a little rest?"

A quick motion of her wrist, and now the bow dangled from her fourth finger and her first became a perch. The bird settled there. For a moment he made a soft ticking sound.

The angel's smile faded. "Still nothing?" The bird shook his head in the negative. The angel sighed and her gaze went far away. The hummingbird flickered to her shoulder.

With a graceful motion she stowed the violin and bow in the knapsack, like an archer returning arrows to a quiver.

"*Churrr…*" said the bird, in the Annas' meditative murmur.

"Mm-hm…" Eyes still far away, she stroked the little bird's head with a fingertip.

She stared down, hard, into the hazy canyons, toward the darkling Earth. Then, resigned, she sat cross-legged on her vaporous parapet.

"Well, thanks anyway," she said, sighing, "for scouting down there…time and time again."

"*Chp…chp, chp.*"

"That's right…we'll never give up. I just know she'll hear me. And I *know* she'll come to the music. Some day."

The hummer's wings buzzed, he stretched and preened, recovering from his long travels. The angel's wings moved like a resting butterfly's: dip and rise—pause—dip and rise again. A fleeting frown marred her porcelain face.

"There were those couple of times…I'm sure it was her…and not so awfully far, either." Her voice rose and quickened a little. "I *know* I'd know her if I saw her. If only I didn't get so sick down there, I could just…"

The bird interrupted with an assertive, full-throated chitter.

She stopped, chastened. Her voice returned to its normal pitch, colored again with resignation. "I know… But if she'd just hear me, if I could just bring her right below us…well, then it'd only take a second. I could dive down there and…" Her gaze turned inward.

After a long, silent moment, she cupped her hands before her.

The space between her hands began to glow. Brighter, brighter—until a tiny sun floated there. Its blaze revealed the deep sadness written in the angel's face.

"I just *have* to get this to her..."

Her breath stopped for a moment, and her eyes narrowed before the sphere's brilliance. Then with a deep breath and a sigh, she parted her hands and the little sun vanished. She rubbed her eyes and yawned delicately.

"How can it be that I love someone I don't even know?"

How indeed? She had been roaming Earthly precincts for over a quarter century, as time is reckoned there, though she couldn't have accounted for it, having been stricken with a nearly total amnesia at some point before the event that had brought her to this plane high above Earth—barely in it and not of it at all. She had a vague sense of having wandered for a very long time, and she had equally obscure impressions of a few unconnected events and nameless personalities, images of which flickered through her mind for no cause she could assign—and of what significance she could only guess—but nothing more.

She was certain of only a very few things: that she possessed a precious Gift, that she had a solemn duty to deliver it to a particular young woman who lived in this part of the world, and that she might one day draw her near with music.

She was certain, too, that the nearer she drew to Earth in her quest, the more ill she became, and that if she approached the Earth too closely and remained too long, she would become ill unto death.

But most of all, though she couldn't have said just how she knew, other than by the weight with which the Gift burdened her soul, she was certain that not only the young woman she sought, but the lives of many others—perhaps generations yet unborn—depended on the success of her mission.

27

Eyes down, dejected, she didn't notice the faint glow blooming high in the sky directly above. The bird chittered again.

"Help? But we've been over that," she replied, disconsolate. "If we were going to get help, it would've been before now..." The light above suddenly intensified, penetrating her brown study. The angel turned her gaze upward. "Oh..."

The sky poured white-gold incandescence over the winged pair and the vaporous canyon walls reflected and amplified it. Entranced, the angel stood and spread her wings. The little bird rose from her shoulder and hovered beside her.

The world below disappeared, shined out of existence for the moment in the annihilating radiance. A thin, dazzling beam of white darted downward, and angel and hummingbird were engulfed in a blinding burst of celestial light.

A great beat of the angel's wings, and her vaporous perch exploded into a glowing fog as the two winged creatures soared vertically and vanished. The great light retreated, and the sun, so modest in comparison, again possessed the scene.

A white feather with a crescent of iridescent blue at its tip spiraled Earthward.

3

Were bird or roaming spirit to follow the feather down, down, into the clouds, and through them, descending into clear air, it would view the ocean, the coastline, the city of San Diego far below, and the sun a couple of diameters above the Pacific horizon. It would hear, too, the sound of an airplane's approach. A gleaming silver Taylorcraft, a small high-winged sport plane, zooms past in a shallow descent, tumbling the feather in its wake. The plane soon passes out of view and the feather resumes its lazy Earthward spiral. Directly below, on this perfect autumn day of 1940, lies San Diego's Ryan Field airport.

છ

The Taylorcraft floated down to caress the runway, and after a few minutes taxied to a stop on the ramp beside a Lockheed Electra, a silver twin-engine transport, "AirWest" in Art Deco letters on its side. In front of the Electra, near the fence that separated the ramp from the parking lot, sat a neat, metallic blue 1936 Ford convertible coupe, top down, Glenn Miller's "Tuxedo Junction" swinging from the radio. A small tag on the windshield read "Balboa Naval Hospital." Beside the car stood two women, both in their mid-twenties, one petite with a blonde bob, the other tall, with thick, sleek dark hair skimming her shoulders. The taller one leaned into the coupe and turned off the radio as the little plane's engine stuttered to a stop.

A trim, dark-haired man of medium height, about thirty, hopped from the plane's left door and approached the women with a cheerful grin and a confident stride. He wore khaki slacks and a light brown jacket over a tan open-collared shirt, and sunglasses—a military look, but without insignia, and nothing like a military bearing. He greeted the tall brunette with a smile and a breezy, "Hi, Kate," then seized the little blonde in a bear hug and exclaimed, "Dot, you've really got to try it!"

The man was a student pilot. He'd amassed all of two dozen hours of flight time in the dozen weeks since he'd begun, and his fledgling's enthusiasm itself tended at times to take flight.

Dot laughed. "I told you, Kate…it takes Ted a while to come down, even after he's landed."

Kate's attention, however, was on the plane. As she watched, another man alighted from the aircraft. He wore jeans and a well-worn leather jacket—a tall, lean, fair-haired and self-assured man—the kind of man women look at twice. He secured the plane's tie-down lines quickly, expertly, then turned to the others, removing his dark aviator glasses to reveal eyes of a striking dark blue as he approached. At first glance one might guess him to be about twenty-five, but upon a second look, taking in the aviator's crinkles at the corners of his eyes, perhaps thirty-five.

With discretion born of long practice, he took in the taller of the two women at a glance: the hair, so dark as to be nearly black, blue eyes, porcelain skin, the slender figure. But when his eyes met hers, his breath stopped.

She held his gaze, just more than an instant, but long enough. The tall pilot recovered his poise and smiled as he joined the others. He diverted himself long enough to offer Dot a grin and a familiar nod, but missed her reply as his attention turned back to her friend.

Ted broke the silence. "Kate, this is Sam McDonnell, flight

instructor. Sam, Kate Bradford. She works with Dot and me at the hospital."

"It's a pleasure," said Sam, his smile broadening, as he took Kate's outstretched hand.

"Hello, Sam." She hesitated. "Are you accepting new students?"

"Fat chance," Ted interjected, as he gestured toward the gleaming AirWest transport. "His freight business is getting so big, I have to beg him to keep me on."

"What a shame," said Kate as she withdrew her hand. "I'd love to learn to fly."

Sam's smile widened still more. "When would you like to start?"

Dot, an inveterate matchmaker, intervened. "Why don't you two discuss it at dinner with us…the Pacifica, about eight?"

Sam didn't waste a second. "That's fine. Kate, can I pick you up?" She hesitated again. *He seems decent enough…and Ted thinks well of him… And I have to learn…*

At that moment, a white, blue-tipped feather spiraled out of the sky and drifted to Kate's feet. Intrigued, she picked it up, examined it. The iridescent blue tip flashed in the sun. Distracted, Kate looked up, "All right."

She looked back at the feather and made as if to toss it away, then stopped. With a shadow of a frown, she put it in her purse.

☙

The scent of night-blooming jasmine surrounded Sam as he walked between the starry-blossomed hedges that lined the path to Kate's little Craftsman bungalow, its light blue siding appearing white in the moonlight. A profusion of plants and shrubbery embraced the house, including a couple of thickly-vined trellises. Roses, hummingbird bushes, trumpet vines and alyssum competed for his notice. More plants in an eclectic medley of

31

pots graced the deep porch. Sam admired the profusion of flora as he stepped up between the porch's square cobblestone pillars and knocked on the door. As he waited, he noticed a single chair at one end of the porch.

When Kate opened the door, for the second time that day she took his breath away. She wore a royal blue gown that was the soul of simplicity. Her hair was up—again, simple elegance. Her silver earrings, too, were understated.

"You look lovely," said Sam.

She smiled her thanks. "Come in! Just give me a moment," she said, as she went to fetch her wrap.

The living room mirrored Kate's taste in evening wear, nothing superfluous, no clutter, but it was saved from austerity by the drawings and paintings on the wall opposite the entry, by the well-filled, built-in bookshelves that flanked the door to the dining room on the left, and by the warm colors of the décor. To the right, a stone fireplace provided a cozy rustic touch. Sam noticed its immaculate interior. *Hmm...hardly used.*

He crossed the room for a closer look at the artwork on the wall. Though a wide seascape on canvas dominated, Sam was diverted by what at first glance looked like a framed and mounted menu but was in fact a program: *Concert by Fritz Kreisler, violinist...New York...1908...*followed by the program's pieces and, near the bottom, a scrawled autograph: *For Carrie...*

He turned to the seascape and admired the way the artist had captured the varying translucence and shifting colors of the waves as they broke. Lower and to the right was another water theme, the view from a riverbank to the opposite wooded shore a quarter-mile or so distant.

But the image that fully captured Sam's interest was a watercolor of a young girl: corn silk hair and cornflower eyes, a white dress, a Zen-like suggestion of pale foliage for a background but otherwise void of context. The girl's eyes were cast downward, her expression hauntingly sad—a study in tranquil grief, which was what so arrested Sam's attention. *Can't be more than thirteen, but…seems much older…she's suffered some terrible loss.*

There were two or three smaller pen-and-ink drawings, and though they were well-executed, Sam spared them only a glance, his gaze drawn back to the sad girl.

Each picture bore the initials "MKB," modestly small, in the lower right-hand corner.

"You've found your way to the gallery," said Kate, in a mock aristocratic inflection as she returned.

Sam replied in ironic kind. "Thank God you've come. I was afraid I had become lost."

She laughed, genuinely amused. And grateful—laughter helped hide her unease—the unease she always felt in such situations.

He gestured toward the wall. "You're quite a collector of 'MKB.'"

She laughed again. "I *am* MKB." He gave her a puzzled frown. "Mary Katherine," she explained.

He looked at her with a new respect. "You're very good."

"I'm glad you like them." She gave her pictures an offhand glance, then turned back to Sam. "Ready when you are."

He returned her smile, and, in keeping with her earlier jest, half bowed and gestured toward the door, where he took her wrap and settled it about her shoulders.

4

The Pacifica, with its outsized dance floor, its capacious stage often featuring the best of the big bands, its first-rate cuisine, crisp linens on its tables and the even crisper service of the staff, was a fine example of the ballrooms popular in the America of the 1930s and 40s.

But what the Pacifica's clientele valued most, even if they were not entirely mindful of it, was that the place provided a bright diversion from eleven grinding years of the Great Depression and more recently from the increasingly grim war news from Europe and Asia and the shadow that news cast over the rest of the world.

A clarinet soared over the throb of a swing band playing Artie Shaw's "Frenesi." A whirling mirror ball spangled the walls, tables and the crowded dance floor. The music and lights and ambiance worked their magic: animated conversations punctuated with laughter swelled and receded, faces radiated cheer.

Kate and Sam, Ted and Dot shared a table and after dinner drinks. They also shared similar states of mind, in that each one's attention was divided between appreciation of the music—the Tommy Shawn Orchestra was by consensus the finest of the local bands—and private preoccupations.

Sam's was, of course, Kate. Over the years he had seen a fair number of women casually, but those who knew him well had begun to suspect that he was becoming a confirmed bachelor.

The fact was he had nearly married some years before; his intended had accepted his proposal, then abruptly and without explanation left him. In time he mended, mostly, but he found there remained a few cracks in the foundation of his capacity to trust. Still, he was a man, and a generally confident, good-looking one whose career lent some dash to his image, so it was only natural that he asked women to go dancing, to see a movie, to join him for dinner—if little more. If a small voice occasionally whispered to him that he wasn't getting any younger, that he should think about settling down, he replied that he was far too busy with AirWest to consider it, and what kind of man would ask a woman to join him in what would certainly be a neglectful marriage?

But in the hours since he had met Kate, since the moment that her eyes had taken his breath, the voice had become louder, more insistent, and unsatisfied with his stock reply—in fact, insinuated that perhaps AirWest wasn't, or shouldn't be, the sole reason for his existence. Sam was enough of a realist to recognize that he was falling in love, so he set about adapting to his new condition and tried not to stare overtly at Kate, even as he slipped deeper in thrall to her with each stolen glance.

Dot's private thoughts were unambivalent. Had she lived in an earlier era, she would have been a professional matchmaker, for she truly had the gift, and tonight her mind was focused, like the spotlight that illuminated the soloists in the band, on the newest subjects of her favorite avocation: Kate and Sam and the subtle resonance between them. She searched her memory once again for something like the strange chemistry she had felt from the moment Ted had introduced them, but even though she had had a major hand in many challenging but ultimately successful matches, there was something unique in this potential pairing and it chafed her that she couldn't put her finger on it.

Not that she lacked background information. She knew Sam

only casually, but well enough to have long since identified him as exceedingly eligible. And as she and Kate were best friends, she was well aware of the latter's—reserve, to put it discreetly—regarding men. Not that that mattered; Dot loved a challenge. But what *was* it about these two?

Amusement was the main element of Ted's inner distraction. After eight years of marriage, he could almost narrate Dot's thoughts on occasions like this. She was like a pup at a root when she sniffed out the remotest possibility of pairing up a couple and the results were usually touching, and often hilarious. These episodes were like movies or novels come to life, and the look on Dot's face told him this would indeed be one to watch. Poor Sam—he has no idea, thought Ted. They were becoming friends, but were not yet so close that Ted might have grasped how gratefully Sam would welcome Dot's success.

Two distinct concerns diverted Kate from the Tommy Shawn Orchestra, one all too familiar, the other utterly unexampled. The first was the revolving complex of fear and resentment toward her lifelong inability to feel the least scrap of womanly emotion for a man, and the old inner defensive dialogue that played out, wearing deeper an already well-worn path, whenever she was thrown together with a man in what the casual observer—or Dot—would call "a date."

The other was the problem with her right hand, its novel and urgent need to compulsively draw white feathers with blue-crescented tips. True, there was the strange instance of such a feather falling out of the sky to her feet earlier, but why should that incite her hand to violent rebellion? What possible causal connection? Was the old neurosis beginning to infect other parts of her mind?

Kate was one of those who believed that everything had a rational explanation, and was also reliably calm under pressure, so she didn't betray a trace of her inner turmoil to her companions.

Whatever lay behind it, it gave her—even if she risked being thought eccentric, or perhaps even a bit rude—an escape from Sam's eyes, from his barely concealed ardor. So she let her hand have its way, to dash across a scrap of white paper it had retrieved from her purse, again seemingly without her volition. Another feather, white with a blue crescent at the tip.

Sam turned to Kate. "You haven't told me what makes a pediatric nurse want to fly airplanes." She was distracted; another feather was taking shape under her pen. After a moment, she finally looked at Sam.

"The war," she said, in a grim tone that contrasted with the Pacifica's bright atmosphere.

Dot interjected, "She has a terrific idea, Sam. Kate, tell him!"

Kate's gaze went far away, but at last she said, "I was in Spain. Guernica. I'd finished college, and my aunt and uncle had given me a trip to Europe. Some classmates and I were in France when we heard about the raid. We got there two days later." She paused, her gaze still distant.

They waited. She went on, "You think of...of things like earthquakes, fires. And then it...then I realized that...that... *people* had done this. Deliberately. With premeditation."

Suddenly she returned to the present. Her eyes swept those of her companions, and she continued. "We went to the hospital to volunteer. It was mostly in ruins, but we did what we could."

Again her gaze went far away. "The thing about modern war..." She paused. "...is the burns. You've never seen anything like it. And high explosives don't distinguish between combatants and children. You can't imagine...rows and rows of little..." Her eyes moistened. "...the burns."

Sam broke the heavy silence, "I'm sorry. But what does it have to do with your learning to fly?"

She said, with sudden urgency, "The world's catching fire… China, Spain, Poland, France and the Low Countries. Now, England…the Blitz. Cities are burning, and there'll be more. There'll be more children like Guernica's."

Dot interrupted. "Kate, tell him! Sam, she has a beautiful idea."

Kate drew a breath, then spoke carefully, "It's a…a clinic, sort of. For children…for kids that have been burned. But you see, what's new is that it's movable. The idea is to standardize everything…equipment, supplies… staff, even, all designed to fit on planes, like those big DC-3's. Then, like the automobile industry, make one, the prototype, then turn out bunches of them and fly them all over the world. And the world's going to need them."

"Sure, like a franchise," Sam said.

"Exactly! War moves fast now. We have to make aid move faster…"

"And if you could fly, you could almost be everywhere at once. Coordinating, pitching in when a unit needs help…"

"Yes!" Her eyes were alight, her usual reserve gone.

Sam considered. "When do you start?"

"Well… There are still some details…"

"Like…?"

She started to speak, but the fire had gone out of her. In the ensuing silence, Dot sized up the space between Kate and Sam while Ted watched Dot, wondering how she'd save the moment—as she always did.

"It's going to happen, Kate," said Dot, buying a moment, "I know it will."

The awkward moment was broken when the bandleader, Tommy, stopped by their table to greet his old friend Sam. After a brief tête-à-tête, Sam followed Tommy to the stage and sat at the piano. He played a languid introduction, then led the band into "When You Wish upon a Star," the haunting theme from the hit movie *Pinocchio* of that year. Unlike Cliff Edwards, who had lent his lambent tenor to the animated Jiminy Cricket, Sam sang in a smoky baritone. If the effect was strikingly different, it was no less beguiling, as the hush that settled over the room attested.

Captivated and surprised by this new side of Sam, Dot noted well that his gaze rested on Kate throughout. Kate, however, appeared not to notice; her hand was running away with her again. More feathers. Different sizes, different perspectives—all of them white with blue crescents at the tips.

But when Sam began the last verse—about a bolt from the blue, and fate seeing you through—the music finally penetrated her awareness. Her hand paused. She seemed to listen to something very distant, as much as to Sam. The last ascending, notes—the promise of dreams coming true—seemed to linger after the song was over.

As the room erupted in applause, Sam returned to the table.

"Why, Sam, that was lovely!" Dot exclaimed.

"When did you…" Ted interrupted, incredulous.

With a dismissive wave, Sam replied, "Mom got me started soon as I could reach the keyboard."

He paused, remembering. "Say, I forgot to mention…I'm doing a Christmas Eve show at the Fox. Can you come? You too, Kate."

"We'll be there if we aren't working," replied Ted.

Kate didn't respond, though, because Dot had taken her arm and was towing her out of the room.

☙

In the ladies' room, Kate fumbled in her purse for her lipstick as Dot fixed her in a level gaze, then asked, "Do you have any idea?" Kate sighed and gave a hint of a shrug.

"Kate, I know love at first sight. Trust me."

39

"I know you do. But you know me, too, and you know I can't."
Avoiding Dot's eyes, Kate leaned toward the mirror and drew
an arc of rose across her upper lip.

Dot rushed on, "I know. But for pity's sake, be practical even
if you can't be romantic! Think about the clinics! The kids...The
money's the only thing holding you up." She paused, weighing
her next words. "Besides...if things...oh, you know, went right,
you might...maybe you could, well, learn. Oh, you know!"

Kate only seemed to ignore her. *Dot has a huge heart, but she
just doesn't understand...*

Dot faltered, then rallied. "You know, Sam really doesn't have
to teach at all. He does it just for a few people...ones he likes."

"And...?"

Dot was divided. She was on the verge of saying words that
she felt she must say, but that Kate could rightly resent. On
the other hand, her matchmaker's blood was up, running at full
steam, and she was sure—absolutely certain—that Kate and Sam
belonged together. Then, too, she loved Kate's idea, admired her
for it and wanted almost as much as Kate did to see it come to
fruition, and that made her go on.

"OK. I've done some homework: AirWest's the second biggest air freight business in the western U.S., and will likely be
the biggest by next year. You're looking at a lot of money..." She
paused. "All that...and he's good-looking, too..." She stopped,
afraid she'd gone too far.

Kate remained silent, but reflected, *She wants so to help...but
can she really think I'm so mercenary? Has she forgotten...again...
what I am...am not, I mean...oh, God, I don't want to talk about it!*

Dot couldn't help herself—she bashed on, "...and, trust me,
he's nuts about you."

Kate snapped her lipstick case shut, then turned to Dot, her
eyes bleak. "I couldn't cheat him. I couldn't live a lie."

Sam watched Kate search for her keys in the dim porch light. She opened the door, and then turned to him, "Thank you so much, Sam. I had a wonderful time." Her smile was pleasant.

Sam moved toward her, and then checked himself. *Not yet...* "If you're serious about flying, meet me at the airfield Saturday morning at eight," he said.

Her smile brightened, even as she shushed the old voice inside. "All right."

Kate watched Sam drive off, then walked through the house to the back patio, to the murmur of the surf beyond the picket fence that guarded the edge of the cliff. She sank into a lounge chair, drew her wrap against the damp night chill and sighed, watching thick, moonlight-rimmed clouds rolling in fast from the ocean. For a moment, a single bright star appeared. She dwelled on it until the scudding clouds swallowed it.

5

Gerard watched the novae in the monitor dim, fade, and vanish, as the subtle atmospheric shift that had persisted throughout the operation likewise diffused. He rose from the console and found himself surrounded by inquiring faces.

He shrugged. "No idea. I've never seen the like."

Despite the elder's declaration of unenlightenment, the other angels' curiosity erupted in a babble of questions. Gerard shrugged again, withdrew within himself and pondered. Because he was a figure of deep respect there, the angelic babble became muted, that is, the younger angels tried not to disturb him as they busily discussed, speculated, theorized, theologized, philosophized, and otherwise abandoned themselves in examining the peculiar intersection of the transcendent golden shift with the appearance of the never-before-seen lights.

Suddenly, the cascading chime of the Aviary's doorbell sang out, and the angels grew quiet, the bells not having been heard in a long time.

The crowd parted as Gerard made his way to the tall, graven wooden doors, one of which he swung open to reveal the angel lately seen high above Earth performing her fiery violin solo in the towering, glowing clouds and later quietly lamenting her lost—someone. Her violin and bow poked out of her rough knapsack and her companion perched on her shoulder, mostly hidden in the folds of her cowl. She looked thoroughly baffled—and very tired and pale.

Gerard and the newcomer regarded one other in mystified silence. The young angel wore a look of mild apprehension until she saw the others crowding behind Gerard. Recognizing that she was among her own kind, she sighed and stood more at ease. The elder spoke first.

"Come in, do come in, Love! You can call me Gerard. And who might you be?" Before she could reply he went on, "But pardon me…we were expecting some kind of bird."

"Oh! Well…" She gave him a bright look—as if to say, 'you're in luck!'—then continued as she stepped in, "I'm Laurel." Tilting her head toward the hummer as he peeked out of his hiding place, she announced, "And this is Huey…I mean, his real name is…

"Heironymus!" cried Gerard, as he and the bird recognized one another. The hummer zipped from the younger angel's shoulder and put on a spectacular exhibition in front of the older one, shuttling back and forth, chittering and chirping. Finally he came to rest on Gerard's shoulder and churred contentedly as he rubbed his head against the elder's neck. Gerard offered his finger as a perch. The bird jumped aboard and the elder gazed at him, delighted, and full of the affection of old friends long parted then reunited.

"And where have you been all this time? We hadn't precisely given up on you, but…" He looked at Laurel with fresh bemusement. "Well…if we're known by the company we keep, you come highly recommended indeed! I expect we've a good deal to talk about, you and I…and some others. But for now…"

He bowed, ushering her into the great hall. "Know that you're welcome altogether, Love, and be assured that nothing would please everyone more than that you feel entirely at home."

He gestured to the banks of flowers. "Do feel free to help yourself, Hieronymus, if you're feeling at all peckish. I'm told the hollyhock is quite good just now." Huey chirped and zoomed off to taste the recommended nectar.

Gerard regarded Laurel more closely. *Is she unwell? However that may be, sure and she is very, very tired.* He noted, in the back of his mind, that among all the scents of the many blooms thereabout, the perfume of jasmine was now ever so slightly greater.

The other angels crowded around to greet Laurel, their voices a kind of music. When the introductions were over, Laurel took in the great hall. She tried to decide which of her many questions to ask, but Gerard spoke first.

"So then…would you happen to know what all this is about?"

With the slightest frown and a tilt of her head, she countered, "What is all *what* about?"

He regarded her another moment. "Perhaps I'm getting ahead of myself. Allow me to explain. A number of things have come together lately: first, a long…how shall I put it…Mystery, so to speak. For quite some time there have been hints…suggestions that there was some great purpose underway that would at some time require our help. Second, the shift we felt just before we brought you here…" She tilted her head again at this. He continued, "… and third, that you should come accompanied by Hieronymus, who was long a resident here until he was sent to Earth to keep an eye out for things like that first matter…and never was heard from again until now."

She took a moment to sort out Gerard's words. "Well, I don't know anything about any 'mysteries,' or 'shifts…' And as for Huey…he's just always been there." She smiled. "I'm so glad to know he's back home…but 'great purpose…'" She trailed off and seemed to withdraw into herself.

"Yes?" Gerard urged.

"We should talk about that," she replied, coming back to the moment.

He smiled, hoping, anticipating progress on the long-vexing question—the "Mystery," as it had become known. "I confess, if you are indeed a clue to our puzzle, I hadn't expected one of such a tender age to come into view."

She cocked an eye at him. "I'm almost a million," she observed.

He cocked an eye back at her. "A million what?"

Game, she stared back hard, but it didn't work. Her mock sternness cracked, and she conceded the point with a laugh, its chime mingling with the other bell tones that echoed through the great room. She recognized that she was beginning to like this dear fellow a great deal.

It was easy to become distracted in the 'Works, as they called it, and presently the great number of birds arrested Laurel's attention. She gazed up and all around. The birds looked back at her, their chirping a little tentative, as if they knew that things were now somehow different.

As she regarded them, something rose inside her, strong, ancient—older than she herself, yet an elemental part of her: the spirit of music. To her eyes, all before her became new, and yearned to be expressed in sound.

Laurel began to sing, a lithe modal melody, in a strange and lyrical language that Earth's most erudite linguist would be unable to identify. She concluded a single verse, then raised her right arm. The birds in some strange way came to attention— indeed, all present in the great room held their breath. Her eyes turned right, then left, then closed. She resumed her song, and with the subtlest motion, moved her right hand in small, slow, graceful arcs in time with her singing. The birds on her right began softly to trill and warble along with Laurel's song. After eight measures, a swift, graceful lateral motion, and the avian chorus on the right divided into two harmonizing parts. Another eight, then with her left hand she made a beckoning gesture. The birds to her left joined—and the great hall began to fill with a strange and magnificent music.

She ceased singing and the delicate direction of her hands gave way to broader gestures of her arms, then her entire body began to sway and the music swelled. The sound intensified even as it grew more refined, and the stones of the Aviary's ancient walls fairly glowed as they echoed this music so strange yet so fine.

Near the peak of it all, her gestures slowed as she coasted the tide of sound to a brief halt—the holding of a breath—and in a fluid motion drew her violin and bow from the knapsack. As the breath released and the tempo resumed, she cracked the bow's hair onto the strings in a descant over the original melody that soared above the ethereal birdsong, shimmering like a sun peeking now and then through broken clouds. More and more, a strange loveliness, and eventually—as the angelic avian symphony developed—grandeur.

The other angels looked on, first in astonishment, then in exaltation as the extraordinary newcomer wrought her transporting music.

Suddenly, Laurel's eyes opened as a peculiar discomfort intruded. *I should be thinking of...her.*

The mission—the great purpose—penetrated her musical ecstasy, drew her mind back to the puzzle of the forgotten time, and the time of wandering, and a sense of duty undone began to oppress her. Her playing's exuberance lessened as her mood darkened. *Everything's different...but nothing's changed. What is this place, and how did I get here, and what does it have to do with her? This is not where I'm to seek her.*

She ceased playing, and her arms slowly fell to her sides. The birds continued their glorious singing, the power that Laurel had imparted to them lingering a while, but gradually they grew still, and the space was soon filled with the murmuring of the angels.

The full effect of her long exile, the enervating influence of her long nearness to Earth, the fruitlessness of her unrelenting search, the world-rending event that had brought her here to the Aviary—a place both welcoming and oddly familiar yet still strange, and in no clear way helpful to her duty to deliver the Gift—all of these things began to tell. She returned the violin and bow to the knapsack and took a wobbly step toward Gerard. She couldn't recall ever having felt so tired.

"Gerard, where *am* I?" she asked.

The elder, however, under the music's sway, had drifted from the here and now to some distant elsewhere. Questions of his own began to crowd into his mind: *Who is this young soul? Why was I commanded to bring her? Is she indeed connected some way to the Mystery?* And a decision: *Time to get the others involved…*

Laurel's tug on his sleeve brought him halfway back, and she spoke again, "All I remember is…light. Beautiful, bright light." She closed her eyes. "It's like Heaven here, but…"

Though Gerard's bemusement didn't quite leave him, he laid a gentle hand on her shoulder and steered her toward the door. At last he replied, though a bit absently, "Oh, call it Heaven's lowlands." He faced her. "Aye, the heart of the place is indeed Heaven, and yet…it brushes up against the old Earth often enough."

The "high tech" equipment had captured Laurel's attention. She gestured. "What's all this?"

His gaze moved over the gear. He tried once again to reconcile the glass and hard angles and flashing lights with the old things. Without looking at her, he finally murmured, "Oh, just stuff."

"Hmm…" She slowly surveyed the angels, the gear, the birds, Gerard, all the rest of the Aviary.

At last returning to himself, Gerard headed for the door with resolve. "Come along, Love. We've some others to meet."

But before he had gone two paces, a swishing sound followed by a collective gasp and much fluttering of wings arrested him. He turned to see Laurel lying unconscious on the flagstone floor, angels rushing to her aid. He lifted her in his arms as if she weighed nothing, and hurried out the door.

j

Branch 92's clinic was modest, illness being so very rare there except in the occasional new arrival who had not quite shaken off Earthly things. Like the larger buildings, it was in the Mission style, though it had a proportionately greater area of windows to allow much light to enter, light being the universal healing agent in that realm.

Gerard stood close by Laurel's bed looking down at her pale, sleeping face, his own expression grave. Huey, perched on the piping of the pillow on which Laurel's head rested, likewise kept vigil. So absorbed was Gerard, he didn't notice the entrance of an ethereally beautiful angel. Her waist-length hair was snow white, her face ageless. On Earth, one might guess her to be about forty. Or, at a second glance, perhaps twenty. Then again, if she were to tell you she was sixty, you would believe her. The newcomer laid a hand on Gerard's arm, drawing him from his reverie.

Gerard's look of concern shifted from Laurel to Branch 92's chief healer. "So, what is it then, Aurora?"

"First things first," the physician replied, with a significant look. "She's Higher Order." Aurora sounded not quite so matter-of-fact as she had wished. Gerard nearly succeeded in concealing his surprise, but not entirely.

"Higher Order" meant that Laurel had not come to Branch 92 as had nearly all of its current residents, that is, by having been

48

incarnated on Earth, and then having, in the fullness of time, died. Aurora's tests had established that the angel, though she had arrived from Earthly precincts, had never been born there, had never lived life as a mortal. Yet she clearly had come here from that dark and dangerous world and bore the unmistakable traces—the scars—of human experience. In the final analysis, however, if she had not been born of a woman on Earth, and was of the pure angelic fabric, so to speak, she originated from On High and so her presence required the most careful consideration.

Aurora had in fact reflected a good deal without arriving at any conclusion, and so had looked forward to telling Gerard in the hope that he might be able to provide some insight into the Mystery.

Her hope proved in vain, though, because Gerard, after hearing the facts, had simply shaken his head, admitted he was as baffled as she, and asked what else she could tell him about the new arrival.

"It's mostly a matter of exhaustion," replied Aurora. "You know how the journey fatigues the birds. No different for an angel, especially one of her age. A little time off her feet will put her to rights."

Gerard held her eyes. "'Mostly'…?"

Aurora made an equivocating expression. "Well, in fact…she did test positive in one category."

Gerard's eyes questioned.

"It's rare," she continued. "I've never seen it first hand. I've only heard of it. Call it 'Earth Sickness.'"

"And what might that be, precisely?" Gerard asked, his concern deepening. "And what prognosis?"

Aurora considered her reply a moment. "To answer your last question first, she has nothing to fear as long as she remains here, or any similar place. As to the illness itself, little is known, it being so rare. But as to what we do know, it seems to afflict those of us who find themselves on or near Earth's surface without, shall we say, certain protections."

"I'm not sure I follow…"

"Well, we all have friends down there, of course, but they are there by design and so are protected from…" she paused.

Gerard nodded. "The Earthly toxins." He gestured for her to continue.

She hesitated again, as if avoiding a topic somehow distasteful. "Should an angel go there without sanction, those protections are absent, and so the illness finds an opportunity."

"Is it you're suggesting she was down there without permission?" He gestured to the sleeping angel and went on, incredulous. "Can one be a rebel and yet have a face like that?"

"There's a possibility, a slim one, that she was on assignment, and something went wrong. Some unanticipated event may have thrust her off the path and left her exposed."

Gerard thought a long while. Then he leaned over Laurel, laid his hand on hers and whispered, "Ah, Love…where have you been, and what's happened to you?"

6

Kate made her way through the hospital's labyrinth of corridors on her rounds. At her third stop, Dot was already attending, working over a tiny figure swathed in bandages. "So this is our new girl," Kate observed. Dot nodded as she continued working. Kate asked, "Why was she brought all this way?"

Dot looked up. "Her grandfather's a retired admiral here. He can't travel, he wouldn't hear of leaving her there…and he has the influence."

"What was she doing in London?"

"Her father, the admiral's son, was the naval attaché there. He went before the war, so he brought the family along. I understand he'd made arrangements to send them home when the Blitz began, even though no one expected they'd hit population centers. But then the first night of the London raids, their house took a direct hit." She lowered her voice, leaned toward Kate, "It's just her now."

Kate stepped closer. The girl was beautiful despite the scars visible as Dot refreshed the dressings. Damp waves of pale blonde hair lay on the pillow. Her eyes were pressed shut, her breathing quick and shallow. Kate shook her head. Then, with a tiny moan, the girl opened green eyes that wandered before fixing on Kate.

Kate's breath stopped for a moment. She smiled, captivated, her eyes moistening. Dot again paused in her work, and noticed

Kate's distraction. She leaned closer to the girl, gestured toward Kate, and said in a hushed voice, "Sally, this is Kate. She's going to help take care of you." She turned to her colleague. "Kate, this is Sally, the bravest girl in the world." Sally smiled faintly, her gaze still fixed on Kate. Then her eyes fluttered shut.

Kate remained transfixed—which didn't escape Dot's notice. When her work was finished Dot smoothed the covers, marked the chart. The nurses stepped into the corridor.

Kate was still visibly moved. "How did she last this long?

Dot considered, then shook her head. She regarded Kate a moment longer. "Be careful."

Kate, the least bit taken aback, replied, "I'll be fine." Dot held her gaze a moment longer, touched her arm, and left.

Kate returned to Sally's bedside. She watched the girl's uneasy sleep a long while. "I'll see you through this, Sally," she whispered. "I promise."

7

AirWest's office at Ryan Field was utilitarian, even Spartan—and smaller than might be expected, given the operation's size. Odors of fuel, paint, lubricants, and exhaust mingled and permeated the space. Frequently, the walls hummed with the deep music of radial engines.

Sam sat at his metal desk, poring over a thick ledger. He wore a work shirt and jeans, and a well-worn leather jacket with a fur collar hung on the back of his antique swivel chair. The door opened to admit a young man of about twenty-two, also in jeans, with a workmanlike sweater and a wool watch cap. "What's up, Greg?" asked Sam, without looking up.

"Been on the phone with Canady," Greg replied.

"What now?" Sam finally looked up. "As if I couldn't guess."

It was a familiar story, and Greg's look confirmed Sam's suspicion. "He wants more time. Two weeks."

"Not a chance. Last time it turned into two months." There was no heat in Sam's voice, just a steely finality. "He wants to borrow money, he can go to a banker."

"What do I tell him?"

"Tell him he owes storage on top of the freight. I'll never collect it, but it might light a fire under his worthless tail. He's due in full…now…but tell him I'll give him five days. Then I sell the cargo on the market."

"Got it."

"Lock up his stuff in Hangar Two. If he comes up with any cash in the meantime, give him what he can pay for. He gives you any bull, you let me know."

"Right, Boss." Greg turned to leave, but Sam's voice arrested him.

"Greg, when you start your own outfit, never do business with a drunk."

Greg grinned. "You bet, Boss!" He nodded, headed for the door. Halfway there, a knock sounded.

Sam raised his voice. "Come in!"

The door opened, and in stepped Kate. She wore slacks, a light leather jacket, short boots, hair in a pair of thick ponytails. Sam was on his feet in an instant. Greg pulled off his cap and stared.

"Well, look who's here! I had a feeling you were serious," said Sam. "Kate, Greg, my right hand man. Greg, this is Kate, our newest student."

Greg shook Kate's offered hand, as her smile weakened his knees. He recovered and made for the exit. As he passed behind Kate, he mouthed a silent whistle at Sam.

"Get on that other business then, Greg." Sam's voice was stern, but his eyes gleamed.

Greg snapped a half-mock salute, and then closed the door behind him. Sam turned to Kate, regarded her levelly for a second then began to grin.

"What?" she asked, smiling self-consciously. She gestured to her jacket. "Isn't this the kind of thing fliers wear?"

He nodded. "It's perfect," he said, his smile widening.

"Oh, good," she said, relieved.

Sam gestured toward the door. "Let's get started."

The Lowlands of Heaven

CB

Twin radial engines throbbed as an AirWest Electra rolled down the runway at Ryan Field. Shielding her eyes against the sun, Kate watched the massive aircraft float off the runway, still a magical thing to her, as Sam finished tying down the Taylorcraft. The two started for the office, but after a couple of steps Kate stopped and turned back to the little plane, with a delighted smile. "I never guessed! It's just…it's…it's so…"

"Isn't it?" Sam smiled too, but his eyes were on Kate. "You did well. I think you might have a knack for it."

She gave him a "no kidding?" kind of look as they turned again for the office.

"It's customary, you know, after your first flight, to have lunch with your instructor," Sam observed.

"It is, really?"

He tried a straight face and failed. "Nope. Just made it up. You will, though, won't you?"

She laughed, but her glow diminished a bit. Sam didn't let himself notice when she took a little too long to reply.

"All right," she said at last. "But I have to watch the time. I need to be at the hospital."

"I thought you were off today."

"I am, but…" She sighed, and said, "I'll tell you at lunch."

CB

They shared a table at the window of a little waterfront café, watching the ferry from Coronado glide toward the pier. As they waited for their orders to arrive, Kate doodled absent-mindedly on a napkin—again, the feather.

She finished the drawing, then finally looked up. "Her name's Sally. She just turned six, but she shouldn't even be alive."

"Will she pull through?" Sam asked.

"If I have anything to do with it." She shifted in her chair and the faintest shadow flickered over her face. Sam put his hand on hers, lightly. She tensed and gently withdrew her hand.

"Her whole family was wiped out. She had a twin sister…for some reason, I can't bear to think of that." Her eyes welled, and she struggled for a moment. "Sorry."

"Nurses have hearts, too."

She gazed at the bay. "Most do."

Their orders came, but they discovered that they weren't very hungry. The conversation flagged and a shade of melancholy settled over them. A Dorsey ballad played on the radio.

Sam finally broke the gloomy silence. "Tell me more about your idea…your mobile hospitals. What's stopping you?"

She hesitated. "The money. Until this year, there just wasn't any to be had. Now there's tons of it, but it's all going to things related to the armed forces."

Sam watched passengers board the ferry for the trip back to Coronado. After a moment he looked back to Kate. "You have it all down in writing, don't you?" She nodded. "Make it as complete as you can and bring it when you come for your next lesson."

She smiled. "I'll be sure to."

He returned her smile. "Don't keep Sally waiting."

He rose, dropped a couple of bills on the table, and offered his hand to Kate as she stood. Her touch was still tentative, but her smile was sincere.

"Next Saturday, same time?"

She shook off the last of the gloom. "You bet!"

8

Branch 92's university lay among vast parks of rolling emerald lawns, groves and ponds. Though its buildings and general character resembled those of Earth's great academies, its campus was far larger than any of those, thus Gerard, Aurora and Laurel had time for a leisurely talk as they made their way to keep an appointment with one of the faculty.

Gerard had explained to Laurel that this professor, Abel, was concerned with—in fact was nearly consumed by—the Mystery that had arisen so long ago and had proven so intractable. He had said further that Abel had been keenly interested when he heard of Laurel's arrival and had been almost beside himself when Gerard told him of her concert with the birds, suspecting a connection between that and the Mystery. Abel had insisted on meeting Laurel immediately, but Aurora had insisted, more successfully, that he wait until the newcomer was fully rested.

Laurel seemed a different creature from the one who had arrived here not so long ago. The shadows were nearly gone from under her eyes; her complexion was clear and pink and seemed to glow as if filtering sunlight from within. Her step was light, her carriage erect and graceful. The only visible evidence of her late ordeal was the asymmetry of her ill-healed wing.

"Now, Love," said Gerard to Laurel as they and Aurora strolled the campus, "About Abel. He's not a bad fellow, but you should know that he's a bit...how to put it...eccentric. He's had rather a difficult time, you see, and he's still…" He searched for a word.

Aurora provided it: "Adapting."

"Just so."

This oblique dialogue piqued Laurel's curiosity. "Adapting to what?"

"Well, it's a delicate matter," Gerard replied. "Finding himself here came as rather a shock. It still makes him uneasy…gives him a bit of a twitch, you might say."

Laurel frowned. "Shock? Why, for goodness' sake? I mean, what's to adapt to? It's so nearly perfect here."

Aurora took up the tale. "In his Earthly life Abel was an eminent scholar and as such, took himself and his beliefs quite seriously…among them the notion that the human mind can grasp All."

Laurel halted, and stared in mute astonishment.

Aurora continued, "But in another respect, he *had* no belief."

Laurel cast a quizzical look at Aurora, then glanced at Gerard, who answered with a flick of his eyes upward and then back to hers.

A beat, then she understood. Her hand shot to her mouth. "Oh!"

"All his life," Aurora continued, "he had equated death with annihilation."

"No!" Laurel interjected. "Poor soul!" She played out Abel's immediate post mortem experience in her mind—the confusion and the terror, then the healing Light, and the Creator's infinite mercy.

She smiled then, and a light grew within her and shone from her. Then she asked, "But why should he still be troubled? He must know he's loved."

"He's a complicated fellow," Aurora replied as they resumed walking. "For all his boastful atheism, he had a deathbed conversion…as so many do. But when he awakened, he was tormented, first by having been wrong...never mind what his being right would have meant...and then by his last-moment renunciation of his worldview. His confidence was shattered, and in his confusion he concluded that the worst of what he'd heard of the Creator was true, all the 'anger' and 'vengeance' and so on, and thereby condemned himself to 'purgatory,' or rather, his notion of it."

"Why so willful?" Laurel asked.

"The usual reason. Fear," Aurora said simply. "In Earthly life, the illusion of his intellectual certitude gave him a great deal of power over others. Having been proven wrong, and so fundamentally, he's desperate to avoid looking inside, afraid of what he might find. But the irony of course is that he will learn the Truth *only* by looking inside."

"Exactly so," Gerard interrupted, "He's simply traded the conceits of his atheism, and the wild notion that the limited can grasp the Limitless, for the arrogance of second guessing the Creator's love for His creation."

"In due course," Aurora continued, "Mercy, as it always does, took an interest and guided Abel to the university. It's believed that the continuity with his Earthly existence, laid over the Love he receives here, will reconcile him to Reality."

Their talk was cut short by their arrival at the Library, where they were to meet Abel. The building's front entrance, like that of the Aviary, presented a pair of great carven oak doors, one of which swung inward just as Gerard raised his hand to pull the bell cord.

A face, pale and narrow, eagerly peered around the door, and Gerard greeted it with a joshing, "Expecting someone, Abel?"

The pale one ignored the jibe. His eyes devoured Laurel, who, for her part, was oddly moved by his gaunt gracelessness, even as something about his presence seemed subtly to sap the well-being she'd begun to recover in Aurora's care. He stepped onto the threshold, continuing to study Laurel with a kind of raw intensity she'd not encountered before at Branch 92. The only sound for a second was the faint rasp of his breath. "An exotic!" he exclaimed so abruptly that Laurel startled. Then he muttered, mostly to himself, "Nothing I love more than a stranger," and made the brittle expression that for him served as a smile.

Gerard and Aurora, long accustomed to Abel's self-absorption and unaccountable affinities, let the slight pass.

Laurel tried to reply, "But you don't even *know* me!"

But before she could speak, Abel jostled past them with an abrupt, "This way."

⊗

Laurel and the elders rested on the shaded grass beside a pond while Abel paced before them. A few geese and ducks sailed aimlessly on the still water and muttered among themselves as the elder angels told the younger of the Mystery that had nettled Abel for so long.

The story had begun with the arrival at Branch 92 of a lark (this having been in the days before doves were employed) bearing a desperate message from a distressed, perhaps disordered, mind on Earth. What it had lacked in coherence it made up for in passion.

The angels whose task it was to process such things found they needed to invent new methods to sort it all out, but even after their best efforts, the result was fragmentary. Among the contents they managed to isolate were a notion of a child in deadly danger, some hazy idea of angelic intervention, a sacred Gift undelivered, and a couple of olfactory impressions: a faint whiff of the Adversary—which surprised no one, given the message's general tone—and, to the perplexity of all, what was with some effort identified as an essence of crushed dandelion.

Laurel's attention came to a sharp focus at the mention of a "sacred Gift" and she tried to interrupt Abel, but he give her no opening.

As to what to do about the strange message, no one could guess, or rather, many guessed, but none of their surmises, upon examination, suggested any action they might have seriously considered.

The inquiry had slowed, then stopped, and the peculiar event gradually faded from everyone's memory—everyone's but Abel's. The dogged scholar's disposition that had followed him from the grave asserted itself anew and he haunted the Library for what might have been ages, combing the stacks for anything, any clue that might have helped to demystify the enigma. His Earthly narcissism was evident here, too. After an especially exhausting session Abel had found himself wondering whether this strange and unexpected place awarded anything like a Nobel Prize.

No one in Heaven or Earth could have faulted his diligence, but as of Laurel's arrival all he'd been able to add were a couple of items, as vague as the original ones: that at some point, the angels of Branch 92 would have some unspecified further involvement in the matter, and that music somehow fit into the equation.

Abel finally wound down, looking paler than he had at the beginning of his account. "That business about music…that's where you come in," he concluded, thrusting a finger artlessly at Laurel. "I'm sure of it, after what Gerard told me about you and those birds."

Laurel ignored his rudeness. "I suppose that could be so, but you mentioned a Gift. Could it be this?"

She cupped her hands before her and half closed her eyes. In a moment the tiny sun glowed into being between her palms. The others gasped, and gathered around the better to see. Abel fell to his knees and grasped at the little star so forcefully that, had it been substantial, he might have knocked it from her hands. But not only was it ethereal, it was given to Laurel's care alone, and Abel jerked his offending fingers back with a yelp, blowing on them.

Laurel remained serene and detached throughout the manifestation, then gradually returned to the present as her hands drifted apart and the luminous sphere faded. She looked up, as if to say, "Well?"

Abel continued to blow on his singed fingers. Gerard and Aurora exchanged one of those long, deep looks that Laurel had noticed they sometimes did. They all were silent for a good while.

At last Gerard observed, "It seems certain that we have 'a sacred Gift,' which, since it's in Laurel's possession, implies 'angelic intervention'…"

Aurora continued, "And we have 'a musical element,' as Abel pointed out, and I can't imagine I'm only one who suspects that the time has come for us to be involved…whatever that might mean."

"Yes, but…" interjected Abel. He faltered, having nothing relevant to offer, but nonetheless feeling entitled to be involved in the discussion.

"But what about *her*?" cried Laurel. The Gift's manifestation had fully revived the spirit of her quest, from which her new circumstances had diverted her.

Gerard and Aurora resumed their silent communion and after a moment said, softly and simultaneously, "Thin place…" They both chuckled—it was a phenomenon long familiar to the pair, this sharing of thoughts.

Abel scowled, stung at encountering a term of which he was utterly ignorant.

Laurel asked, "Thin place? What's that?"

"We'll soon show you, Love," replied Gerard. "But we've studied enough for now, and besides, our presence…yours in particular…is requested at a certain event and we should be on our way."

❧

Bells pealed and sang, silver, bronze and gold tones soared through the bright sky, under slivers of the gold and silver moons, the wild, cascading sound the closest to madness that such a sane place as this could ever approach.

The angels gathered as always they did when the bells rang. The church, located at the center of Branch 92, was small compared to the university and the Aviary, but since the residents understood the entire region to be a House of God, there was little concern about the modest size of the building beside the campanile. Its main purpose was to provide a familiar comfort for the newly arrived faithful.

But when the community's general presence was desired—on high holidays, or to observe comings and goings of special significance—the change ringers gathered at the campanile and performed "The Exercise." On the rare occasions when all hands were needed to bend their efforts to some urgent matter, the first to arrive at the tower would ring the great bronze tenor bell, the one of deepest tone and farthest reach, by itself.

This gathering however was a double celebration, thus the merry cascading of the circle of bells. A new arrival and a homecoming were the reasons for the affair: Laurel, the newcomer, Hieronymus, the returning prodigal, though Laurel's nickname for him, "Huey," was gaining currency.

It was an altogether informal affair. Many had already made Laurel's acquaintance, and most had known Huey before his disappearance, so it was more a casual mingling than a formal observance. There was, however, more aerial activity than usual

63

for such gatherings, the avian element of the community eager to welcome their hummingbird brother home.

Laurel was simply, universally loved, so the hummer's reappearance was the more intriguing matter. Where had he been? Why had he remained away so long? Why did he return—and why with Laurel? The one thing generally known was why he had left: as anciently larks, and more recently doves, were employed to bring unformed prayers and such up from Earth, hummingbirds were the ideal scouts and a few were assigned to Earth at all times with instructions to report anything of interest. The receipt of the passionate and fragmentary message Abel had lately described to Laurel had compelled the Elders to send a request to Huey, who was then on station below, to report. But no report ever came, and he was not heard from again until he reappeared at the Aviary perched on Laurel's shoulder.

Aurora had sought the help of those specializing in avian idiopathies and together they put the hummer through as thorough a battery of tests as that to which Aurora had subjected Laurel. As best they could determine, he had at some time early during the blank period, met Laurel and bonded with her intensely—perhaps so much so that his assignment was crowded out of his awareness—and indeed his devotion to her was clear to all.

Additionally, he was found to suffer from a "sympathetic amnesia," also the result of the powerful bond the two had formed. Thus all were disappointed that so few questions could be cleared away, though this was more than made up for by the knowledge that both angel and hummingbird had had good company during their dark interlude.

One angel of the gathering asked Laurel what was next, now that she was out and around and looking so much better.

Her gaze became distant and her mind again reached for the

nameless girl she had sought for days, years, unnumbered. Aurora cast a glance at her. Laurel caught the look and felt restrained—remembering her new condition, this new place.

"Music, I suppose," she finally said, at a loss as to how to reply.

"And rest," Aurora interrupted. "Don't let her looks deceive you," she said to the others. "She's had a long, rough go down there. Her doctor prescribes an extended vacation."

Laurel rolled her eyes in mock exasperation to show what she thought of any enforced idleness, even as she acquiesced when Aurora drew her gently to her. Huey, who rested on her shoulder, yawned as if to show that he had a rather different opinion.

Gerard approached with Kaira and Benedict in tow. "Say there, Love…these two have been pestering me for a look at the way things were done before all the high tech nonsense came about, and they've finally cornered me. Care to come along?"

❧

Two young angels sat in a secluded hollow in the side of a hill overlooking the ocean, among short, gnarled juniper trees and ivy and jasmine, with a small, rippling pool in the middle of it, the momentary widening of a brook seeking the sea. Bees droned and a gentle sound of surf cast a calm spell over the place.

The younger of the two appeared to be about twelve, her fair skin contrasting with the deep auburn hair that brushed her shoulders. The other was a dark-haired, sturdy lad of fifteen or so. Their eyes met briefly, then they nodded slightly and each took the other's hands, not in an affectionate way, but rather, in a manner casually ceremonial. Their eyes closed, and their expressions, though serene, implied concentration. The sounds of the bees and the surf suffused the hollow.

Neither of the young angels heard the faint step of Gerard and his young companions approaching. Their minds were by then

65

utterly still but for the filaments that mingled and spiraled down, down, to Earth, seeking a bird who had absorbed the spirit of a human's concern—request, gratitude, or blessing upon another.

Soon, such a bird, a lark, came into view and the tendrils wrapped tighter and focused, fusing into a beam, invisible to all but the intended target, to whom it was radiantly, indescribably attractive. The bird instantly flew toward the glow high above. The silent pair felt the bird's attention lock to the beam, as a fisherman feels his line shiver and tauten when the bait is taken.

*Up…*they thought in unison, the first volitional ripple in the still surface of their minds since they had joined hands. Far below, the tip of the beam intercepted the bird's path and bloomed like a tiny nova, and in that instant the creature found herself in an altogether different sky, high above a somnolent hollow where two young angels held hands in silent communion, where bees murmured, and surf whispered.

The pair had been motionless for some while when a silver chain of sound dropped from above to herald the lark's arrival. The bird fluttered down to perch on a branch that overhung the space between the two. The young ones, hearing the rush of wings, released hands and smiled up at the lark, pleased to meet an old friend. The bird neatened up her bill on the branch like a chef sharpening a knife, preened for moment, then tucked her head under her wing and slept.

"Nicely done, Emelia, Victor," Gerard said as he led Laurel, Kaira, and Benedict nearer the hollow from the discreet observation point they'd taken up as the two had begun their hushed ritual.

Gerard introduced all around, then recounted how Victor and Emelia had together practiced the Old Way since the time the Mystery had arisen. Precisely since that time, in fact, because it was they who had called up the frantic lark who had nearly died of the message she carried—on the very first day of their practice.

"Would you like to join us?" Emelia asked. Indeed they would, and before too very long the circle of five had collected eight larks and a pair of doves as the elder sat by admiring. Three of the birds carried gratitude, and two—two!—good wishes, unencumbered. It was like the old days, Gerard thought.

By then, though, the buttery sun was lowering and, of the moons, only a thin silver ghost haunted the horizon. Gerard suggested that they'd done a good bit and so they set off for the Aviary, birds nestled on shoulders, to see that messages were timely delivered.

9

Tormented by her burns and chafed by her dressings, Sally tossed in the limbo between sleep and wakefulness. Sensing someone at her bedside, her eyes fluttered open, wandered a moment, then found Kate. She smiled and, painfully, reached. Kate took her hand.

"Hi, Darlin'! Dot said you wanted me."

Sally nodded. When she found her voice, it was a hoarse, tiny whisper. "I'm 'sposed to tell you something."

"Really, love? Who told you that?"

"Suzanne."

A faint chill rose in Kate's back. "But, honey, your sister's... not here."

Sally nodded. "I know. She's..." Her eyes wandered. Then her gaze returned to Kate and she smiled. "She's everywhere."

Another chill, more intense, so that Kate shivered. She forced a smile, then at a loss, shook her head.

The girl tried to speak, but faltered. At last, it came, with great effort, "Suzanne says...says I should tell you...it'll get better."

Kate closed her eyes, made herself breathe, and forced from her mind the fact that the dying often speak of seeing those who have gone before them.

"What will get better, love?"

Sally's eyes went far away again for a brief space, as if she were listening to a far-off voice. "The thing that makes you sad."

The girl had grown very pale. She yawned, and then seemed to sleep. Without opening her eyes, she sighed and spoke again, barely audible, "But…you got to stay put." Her breath deepened. Exhausted, she slept, truly slept, for the first time in days.

Here, so deep in Kate's mind that she barely perceived it, an idea germinated—that of a desperate, irrational hope, disguised in the form of a bargain. Had she seen it clearly enough to articulate it, she would have said, "If Sally recovers, I will become complete." Even as her desperate hope for two souls stirred, the sternly rational part of her intervened: *No. You mustn't…*

Kate stroked Sally's forehead and watched her sleep. "I'll stay put, darlin'…as long as you need me."

10

Gerard, Laurel, Aurora and Abel strolled over immaculate rolling lawns meandering among tranquil groves and scented gardens. Huey followed them, more or less. He darted about, sampling the many blooms, occasionally joining the other hummers' impromptu aerial ballet.

The angels stopped by a fountain, not much more than a heap of rocks bubbling sweet, cool water. A silver dipper hung on a convenient limb of the eucalyptus overarching the spring, an invitation to pause and refresh themselves before walking on.

They came to a small garden enclosing a circular reflecting pool. The pool rose about hip-high within a low stonework circle. The rim, a foot wide, was studded with uniformly shaped—oddly knurled—stones set at about two-foot intervals around the full circumference. Small boulders randomly scattered in the garden were in fact a sort of furniture, chairs, low tables, the odd chaise longue, all upholstered in thick moss. Gerard leaned against the pool while the others chose seats.

Laurel asked of Gerard, "You said something about a…what was it? A thin place?"

He tilted his head to the pool. "Right in front of you."

Laurel frowned, puzzled.

"A thin place is where different worlds come close together, perhaps even touch." He looked at the water. "Much can be seen from such places…at times."

Laurel went to the pool and peered into the water. As she leaned over yet further, her hand came to rest on one of the peculiar knurled stones, and a wavering flicker of light appeared, deep in the dark water. Laurel startled, then peered hard into the blackness. She bent still closer, inadvertently turning the stone a little as she did. Again the flicker, brighter now, and for a fraction of an instant, the young angel saw, or believed she saw—a face. Or rather, a dim, wavering array of shadows and light that suggested to her imagination the handsome face of a young woman, a woman with fair skin and hair so dark as to be nearly invisible in the black water. At the same time, an echo of a single syllable reverberated in her mind—but what was it? She leaned down yet more, as if straining to hear.

"*Kate*," a far, faint voice whispered deep inside her.

Shock and fascination—and something else, unnamed—straightened her. Her hand slipped off the stone. Light and shadows vanished, and again she looked into dark, placid water.

Her hand rose to her chest. "It was her…" she whispered. She grew agitated. "I saw her," she said, her voice rising, "I *know* it was her!" she cried. Exaltation chased the stunned expression from her face. Calming herself, she turned to the others. "Her name's *Kate*," she said, as if she had just discovered the deepest secret of Creation.

"Did you see that, Aurora?" exclaimed Gerard. "No one's ever gotten so much as a flicker on the first try! Or the first five, for that matter!"

Aurora joined them and peered into the darkling water, as the elders regarded Laurel with renewed curiosity and respect. "It takes most a long time to develop a rapport with the water," she said.

But Laurel didn't hear her. She couldn't have said how long she'd been on her quest to deliver the Gift; she knew only that deliver it she must, and as soon as she could—and now she was sure she knew the name and face of the one she sought. She stared hard into the blackness, demanded of it to reveal the secrets she so desperately needed. *Where different worlds come close…maybe even touch.*

Huey appeared as if responding to some clairaudient call. He hovered, droning, at her shoulder.

Then with a powerful beat of her wings, she was on the pool's rim. Another beat, and she hovered over the dark water. "Kate! I'm coming!"

A shriek and a wild flutter of feathers—Gerard had launched himself like an arrow, seized Laurel around her waist, and brought them both to the ground. Abel and Aurora scrambled to the pair and helped them to their feet.

"Well done, Gerard!" Aurora said.

Laurel's expression went from stunned to heartbroken, and she fought tears. It was too much. She had been sure she'd found at long last the way to complete her task, but it was not only that her hope was dashed—the fellow she was coming to regard rather as a beloved uncle…

How could *he?*

"But I…But she…I could've…" she cried.

"Hush, Love," whispered Aurora, drawing Laurel to her and guiding her to a mossy chaise. "Not that way. You can't do it that way."

Gerard turned a level but kindly look to Laurel. "You must never use the pool as a means of travel. You mustn't even think about it."

A tear spilled down Laurel's cheek.

Gerard extended a hand. "Come, step over here," he said, as he led her to the pool.

He put his hands on two adjacent knurled stones. "Watch now."

His hands caressed the stones. Ripples of light appeared in the water and rapidly resolved into an image—a terrible image of an angel, a youth, deathly pale, floating in a dark icy void, rimed with frost, his open eyes opaque and sightless. Laurel gasped.

Gerard gave one of the stones a slight twist. The awful apparition dissolved, to be replaced by a young female angel, submerged in a dark ocean, tangled in long, undulating seaweed fronds. Her mouth was slightly agape, her eyes, like the other's, were open, sightless. Fish darted close to her face. Laurel's hands flew to her mouth.

Gerard lifted his hands from the stones. The ghastly image faded, and the water again became calm and dark. His arm around Laurel's shoulders, Gerard led her back to her seat beside Aurora. "The pool…such times as it cooperates…is splendid for study, for viewing other places, or other times…the past…or even possible futures," said Gerard, "but it's deadly dangerous for personal transport. Those young ones attempted it, and…well…" He tilted his head toward the pool.

Laurel interrupted. "No one…not ever?"

Gerard looked away, remained silent a long moment.

"Oh, some have said one…two, perhaps, managed. A long, long time ago…perhaps things were different then. But mind you, that's all conjecture." He looked at her pointedly. "Certainly nothing on which you would want to gamble your existence."

"But how could such terrible things happen to them? Here, of all places?"

Another long silence ensued as Gerard regarded Laurel. "You must remember, this is not Heaven, but one of its lowlands…a place between Earth and Heaven. 'Virtue' and 'knowledge' here, though higher than their Earthly counterparts, are yet imperfect and incomplete. No one here is perfect, nor innocent. Perfection comes to each in his own time."

He studied her, then asked, "What do you know of free will?"

"It's the Creator's gift to us. His greatest gift...after His Love."

"True, but what some do not understand is that with it comes responsibility for the outcomes of our choices. Those young ones you glimpsed in the water...it's said that their journeys were motivated by idle curiosity, and not in the service of some greater good...so happy outcomes were hardly to have been expected."

She nodded, holding his gaze.

He tilted his head toward the pool. "Then you understand the danger?"

"Oh, yes," Laurel replied as she leaned against Aurora. Like a chill fog, fatigue had begun to creep over her. It seemed contagious; the vigor seeped out of the gathering as a whole.

Abel broke the stillness. "We, perhaps I can say 'I,' have been baffled by this matter for..." He made a helpless gesture. "I don't think you know how I've struggled with it." The others nodded, tired, yet patient. He continued, "There are the ordinary things you, Aurora, Gerard, deal with, but you have your traditions to tell you what to do. But I...I have to study, and hypothesize..." He managed to stop himself before he said, "...and apply my superior intellect."

Gerard's, Aurora's eyes met for an instant. Abel began to pace, his eyes smoldering.

What Laurel and the elders could not know was that one cause of Abel's agitation was resentment of Laurel's rapport with the pool's dark water. Throughout his acquaintance with it and its reputation as a place of forbidding and perhaps treacherous power, it had always been, to his own experience, a pool—and nothing more. Though he had stared until his eyes stung, though he had squeezed the knurled stones as if they might yield water, he stared ever and only at that implacable dark surface. And though he resented Laurel's effortless command of the pool, he was resourceful, cunning even, and as might be expected of his type, had begun to think of ways to turn the angel's advantage into his own.

Gerard and Aurora were accustomed to Abel's preoccupations. They recognized that he was still, to himself at any rate, a scholar, as he had been on Earth, and as such could tempt himself to focus narrowly at the expense of the larger view. They, in their wider outlook, knew better than he that he was on a path, as were all, and understood that a part of their duty was to be tolerant, within reason, of his tendencies, and helpful.

Aurora said, carefully, "Of course, Abel. Everyone knows how hard you work. What is it you're suggesting?"

"Isn't it obvious? The gift she carries? Her way with the water? The scouting bird that came here with her? She is *the* key to the Mystery!"

This took the elders by surprise, since the idea held little potential for Abel's own aggrandizement. They wondered if perhaps he was finally becoming free of himself.

Gerard gave the professor a long, level look, then said to Laurel, "Well then, why don't you give it another go? See what you can see?"

The young angel went to the pool, drew a deep breath and quieted herself inside. Then she laid her hands on two of the knurled stones as the others gathered and looked on silently.

Light, very faint, stirred deep within the blackness. Suddenly the image of the young, fair-skinned, dark-haired woman reappeared, very clear. Laurel blinked, the others murmured. The image had barely registered before it disappeared, replaced by a luminous scroll bearing a runic text.

The elders gasped as one. Laurel turned to them, quizzically, but before she could turn so far that she'd have to release the stones, Gerard commanded, "Stop!"

Laurel froze in place, and the elders leaned over the water, visibly tense.

"Unbelievable," Gerard muttered.

"What?" asked Laurel.

"This is very rare, this text," Aurora explained. "Clearly, you have an extraordinary rapport with the water. Ambriel is the only other one I've known who can bring it."

"And not often, at that," Gerard added.

Aurora continued, "Keep your mind very still and focused, Laurel. This is a great bit of luck for us…the runes yield far more information than the water normally provides. But this state is very fragile…it can vanish at the least disturbance."

"Or for no reason at all," Gerard added.

Laurel exhaled and made herself very still inside. She lightened her touch on the stones, with only the tips of her fingers touching them. The scroll began to turn.

Gerard began to read, interpreting aloud as the text rolled by. "The one you seek is an old soul…possibly a *great* soul. The indications are that she might accomplish much…were she complete."

In a hushed voice, Laurel interrupted. "'Complete'?"

Gerard held up his hand and continued reading. "She has a grave deficiency. She is without the thing…the spiritual element…that allows her to love. Not generally, mind you, for she loves, in quite the normal way, her family, her friends, those she serves in her work. She loves children with an especial devotion. What's referred to here is the bond between a man and a woman, *that which would allow her to love the one who is ordained to help her fulfill a grand destiny, the one who is meant for her, and for whom she is meant.*"

He paused as the text suddenly stopped rolling. The elders held their breath, expecting the scroll to vanish. Indeed the image began to go dim and hazy, but after a moment, clarity returned.

When the runes finally moved again, Gerard exhaled and continued, "There's apparently more to it…" He frowned, and muttered under his breath. "These texts can be maddeningly obscure…"

"But, why…how is she incomplete?" Laurel mused, as much to herself as aloud.

"The result of an accident," answered Gerard, picking up in another part of the text. He said to her, an aside, "The dreadful sort of thing that happens down there with appalling regularity."

He continued reading. "Just before Kate was to have been born, a railway train struck a young family's automobile. The father died at once, the mother, pregnant with their first child, died within the hour. The one you seek was born of her dead mother, barely alive herself."

Gerard paused a long while, reading, then resumed. "The violence of the event separated her from the vital element mentioned earlier." He paused again and tension filled the silence.

"What?" Laurel demanded. "What is she missing?"

Gerard turned to face Laurel. "You. Or rather, the Gift."

Laurel nodded, willing her breath not to quicken, afraid the text would vanish as Aurora had warned. *Yes…yes. I almost remember…*

The text continued to scroll. Aurora took over from Gerard. "The truth you've forgotten, Laurel, is this: you are a Messenger of Love. You are ordained to give Kate the Gift you hold in your heart, the spiritual element in which rests her ability to bond with her one true love…and so become whole."

Laurel breathed deeply. At last—at long last—answers. *My heart swells with gratitude…*

The text rolled on, Aurora translating. "You were intended to deliver the gift at the moment of Kate's birth, and so had formed a bond with her, rather as if you were twins."

She turned to Laurel. "Such things are not unheard of, but are very rare indeed. To bond with Kate, you needed to create a subtle body of your own, not so susceptible to injury as human flesh, but vulnerable nonetheless."

Aurora paused and gently touched Laurel's ill-healed wing, then continued reading. "In order for the gift to be given, Laurel and Kate must be in the same world. Kate, being human, is bound to Earth, so Earth is her one, her only world until her spirit is released by way of her death."

She paused while the others absorbed this, then continued, "Laurel's condition is different…and presents grave challenges. Though she retains something of the para-physical form she assumed for the purpose of bonding with Kate, Laurel's essential nature is ethereal, and therein lies the problem. She is not suited…not at all suited…to Earth's environment. It's too coarse, much too harsh for her. Consequently, she becomes ill in proportion to her nearness to Earth's surface."

"Music," Abel interrupted. "Is there anything about music?"

Laurel turned her mind in that direction, and the scroll stopped rolling. Suddenly, it flickered and the water went black.

"Well, that's likely all," Gerard said, resigned, but Laurel focused her mind with all her might, and the scroll flickered back into view, though a bit blurry and much dimmer. Gerard, anxious to glean the last grain of information from what he knew from experience would be the last seconds' opportunity, leaned closer to the water and read aloud, a note of desperation in his voice.

"Laurel is a Messenger of Love. And as music is Love's most fluent language, she possesses a prodigious talent. Because the gift she bears is Kate's greatest need, Kate will be attracted most powerfully to Laurel's music. Indeed, she will be attracted to Laurel herself, by the fundamental magnetism of their relationship." He heaved a breath, calmed himself.

Laurel meditated on this, then asked, "But, why don't I remember any of this?"

Aurora shook her head. "The record isn't helpful there. It could be due to the violence of the wreck, or the result of some later event. We simply don't know enough to say with certainty."

Gerard was straining to make out more details when the water abruptly went black and still. The elders knew from the water's peculiar dead look—more a feel—that the session was over. Laurel felt a pang of disappointment, but seeing the elders' resignation, heaved a sigh and surrendered. By silent consensus, Laurel, Aurora and Gerard stepped away from the pool, exhausted.

Abel, who had been pacing frenetically during the session, stopped and whirled to face Laurel. His cheeks burned as his eyes pinned her. "At last!" he exclaimed, loudly, startling the others with his outburst.

"Don't you see?" Abel exclaimed, no longer directly addressing anyone present. His breath quickened. "How long have I studied? How long have I struggled? How long have we hoped for change?" He began to tremble as he stabbed a finger at Laurel, who involuntarily drew back. Abel's voice broke as he shouted, "She's the one we've been waiting for!"

"Abel!" Aurora barked.

"Get a grip on yourself, man!" interjected Gerard. "We need facts, not hysteria."

"Yes. Please be rational," Aurora added.

Abel calmed, and the silence lengthened as exhaustion crept over them. Though Laurel spoke only half aloud, all heard her: "How am I going to get to her?"

11

Kate and Sam shared an outdoor table at the Mission Café, before them the boardwalk with its streams of passersby, the low concrete seawall, the beach beyond, and then the sparkling Pacific Ocean. Glenn Miller's "In the Mood" wafted to them from the radio inside.

Kate doodled on a paper napkin while Sam riffled through a thin stack of papers on the table. At last he straightened them, put them in a folder and looked up at Kate. She laid the pen down and held her breath.

Sam hesitated, then said, "All my instincts tell me to stay a thousand miles away from this."

Kate breathed out, her expectant glow dimmed. "Of course. I understand…"

Sam continued, "We're talking about doing business in war zones, after all. It's hard to even begin to calculate the risks involved."

She tried to mask her disappointment with a smile as she reached for the folder. Sam put his hand on it. "I'm not finished. The only way I'd consider supporting this is if we work together."

Her guard went up. Sam paused, then went on, "I wouldn't do it for just anyone, but I believe in this. And I believe in you."

She gave him a searching look. He reached for her hand—which eased out of his reach, as if of its own volition. Sam seemed, suddenly, somehow out of his depth, his habitual self-assurance evaporating. Kate's hand—again, seemingly with a will of its own—found the pen, and resumed drawing on the napkin, even as her unreadable eyes held his.

Sam took a breath, gamely went on, "I…I like to think… with your vision, and my experience…and well…well, just the rightness, the goodness of your idea…" His voice trailed off. He turned to gaze at the ocean while he regrouped. *For God's sake… it's as if I were thirteen years old…this isn't me…* After a moment, and a deep breath, he resumed, "I like to think that this thing might…bring us closer. I'd like for us to be closer."

Kate's eyes dropped, hiding the conflict inside her. *The lives that could be saved, the suffering that could be relieved…at the cost of living a lie. It's getting hard not to hate myself…*

She returned to the moment and tried to meet Sam's eyes. "It's…it's generous, very generous of you. But, 'closer'…well…" She shook her head, then stopped and closed her eyes. *I can't believe I'm saying this. He's laying my dream right in my hands. I must be insane.* She took a breath and resumed, "I must seem so horribly ungrateful to you, but you see…I can't. I mean, I can't *explain*…" She faltered, her distress deepening by the second. The silence became palpable, painful.

Sam started to speak, then stopped, managing to hide his hurt.

Kate found her voice at last and stuttered on, "I don't expect you to understand. I don't really understand myself. You see, something's missing…missing from me." She fought for control. The voice inside ran away with her again, *But I have to tell him…try to. It would all be a hideous fraud if I accepted under false pretenses. And it couldn't last anyway…not that way.* She rallied a little and hobbled on, "That doesn't make very much sense, does it? I'm sorry…I'm so sorry. Thank you. I'd better go."

She stood and practically fled the scene. Sam watched her

hurry down the boardwalk and disappear. He turned a desolate look at the folder containing Kate's business plan, then noticed her napkin—covered with sketches of blue-tipped feathers.

℅

Laurel's new house was small and simple, but as far as she was concerned, far beyond satisfactory. Like the sun, the moons, and nearly all other particulars of Branch 92's environment, it had been dreamed into being by the inhabitants, in this case, Gerard, Aurora, and the young ones, Emelia, Victor, Kaira, and Benedict.

The elders had entreated the old, reclusive fellow named Ambriel to contribute, and though he tried to beg off on grounds of modesty and general disengagement with current affairs, they finally persuaded him at least to choose the location. He had settled on a place a bit back from a cliff at the northern point of a little cove about four miles up the coast from the village.

Here Laurel could enjoy a panoramic view of the ocean to the north and west, with the additional interest of the cove and its south shore with its purple waterfalls of spring blossoms and, in the southern distance, the rise of the seaward peninsula that defined the great bay south of the village. Just off the cove's south point, a picturesque rock thrust about a dozen feet above the ocean, depending on the tide, and provided a gathering place for the ocean's birds. In the offing, to the right of the peninsula's rise, lay two islands, their silhouettes roughly mirroring one another, like bookends. Most days, they appeared as gray ghosts haunting the horizon, though when the humidity was high, they were lost to view entirely. On clear days though, they appeared so near and distinct as to seem nearly within arm's reach of Laurel's cliff.

By some standards, the house may have seemed a bit over-done. Angels' needs of course differ from those of humans, but the architects, even the elders Gerard and Aurora, had come to this sphere of existence through the fire of human life, had known worldly scarcity and the terror of dispossession, among the other terrors, and remembered them—if only in the deepest shadows of recall. The very ancient ones, and those of the Higher Orders, were not so encumbered, thus Laurel's deep gratitude was mingled with perplexity. What was she to do with this Heavenly real estate, this overabundance so lovingly bestowed?

The exterior was typical of local dwellings—light tan stucco with a red tile roof, large windows supplemented by many skylights. The four rooms were arranged in a U shape providing a central courtyard facing westward to the ocean.

The interior was spare, but elegant. The small, simple sleeping chamber contained a low bed, and a window-wall draped with diaphanous silk curtains provided a muted, misty light. Though angels typically don't require much in the way of sleep, the room was in this case needful because Laurel was still worn from her Earthly sojourn and Aurora's order of rest was still in force.

There was a living room, nearly as simple as the bedchamber, with a stone fireplace, and spare, modest yet comfortable furniture for intimate gatherings. The walls were plain but for a seascape in oils, and two smaller canvases asymmetrically framing the fireplace: a hummingbird at a trumpet vine, and a study of a petite blonde angel and a young, dark-haired woman of Earth, walking arm-in-arm in a garden.

The kitchen was small and modestly equipped, but, Laurel wondered again, how much use for cooking have creatures whose sustenance is subtlest light? Aurora solved the mystery when she pointed out that Laurel would find the kitchen useful for preparing teas and nectars for visitors.

The architects had provided an additional room, the "music room," they had thought of it, but as Laurel's only equipment was her old fiddle and bow, the room seemed superfluous, though of course she appreciated the thoughtfulness it represented.

The grounds were more sumptuous. A garden, intimately enclosed by a variety of trees and hedges, surrounded the house and was filled with the whisper of a small fountain. Along the north and south walls lay tidy rock gardens. The taller trees created a shading canopy that overarched the little estate.

Gulls hovered overhead, and flights of pelicans surfed the updrafts that climbed the cliff's face.

The designers had been as mindful of Heironymus and his tribe as they had of the angel when they chose the plants and trees that ringed the house, so it was no surprise when Laurel and Huey, accompanied by Gerard, Aurora and the younger ones, came to accept the gift, that someone had already taken up residence.

As they wended up the path to the house, Huey spied the white-tipped tail feathers of an attractive Anna darting and hovering over a row of honeysuckle. He left his orbit about Laurel in an instant, raced to hover momentarily before the female, then soared vertically to an altitude of about a hundred feet.

A brief motionless hover, then he tilted and plunged like a meteor. His flight path leveled so that he hurtled in front of the object of his affection just as he made a high, sweet, hollow tone like that of a bamboo flute, a sound not vocal, but rather made by his tail feathers, precisely spread, reed-like, at precisely the right instant, in the ancient ritual of the Calypte Anna. The note was louder than any he could make vocally, his capacity for speed so superior to the capacity of his tiny lungs. In the next instant he hovered above and in front of her and chittered triumphantly. Then he rose high again and repeated the performance a half-dozen times.

Throughout, the bird with the white-tipped tail, observing tradition, perched—regal, motionless, atop the honeysuckle like a princess on a reviewing stand—and with her the angels watched, enchanted, their heads swinging in unison as Hieronymus soared and dove and sang his love.

When he was certain of his intended's attention, he began the customary figure-eight shuttling dance before her, his crown and throat flashing shades of red from hot pink to deep, iridescent rose, with an occasional burst of white-gold. But as much as she had appeared to admire his majestic vertical flight, his heart-stopping dive, and his virtuoso tail-feather chirp, she either didn't care for the way he danced, or his luminescence—or, perhaps, wished to test his devotion—and so darted off and vanished into the dense twisting juniper at the rear of the garden. Huey pursued and likewise vanished. Avian exhibition concluded, the angels headed for the house.

Gerard grinned, then chuckled. "What?" asked Aurora, barely keeping the lid on a giggle, the other's mirth being contagious.

"Poor Hieronymus," he said, suppressing a laugh.

The others stopped and looked at him, all puzzlement.

Gerard continued, "'He chased her 'til she caught him,' the old saying goes. Little Samantha there had conceived a fancy for Hieronymus…pardon me, I forget that he's become 'Huey'…just before he disappeared to share Laurel's mysterious adventures below. It was no accident she was here today."

Voices ran together as the little group clamored to know what in the world the elder was talking about.

He relished their suspense for a space, then said, slyly, as if with conspiratorial knowledge, "She was lying in wait."

The others smiled and "ahh'd" as they came to understand.

"But, how did she know…?" Kaira began, but seeing the glint in Gerard's eye, finished for herself: "Oh…"

Everyone laughed.

Inside the house, Laurel discovered she was at a loss as to

how to properly welcome them, so, improvising, asked Gerard if he would offer a blessing. He gladly assented, and said:

"May it please You, bless this place, and those who dwell here, all who enter…and those who pass near." His thoughts turned to those below on Earth, so he continued, "And may all hearts remember You, and turn to You, and come to You, and so may the world be healed."

A moment's silence, then they murmured together, "Amen."

12

Laurel stood at the pool, alone, gazing into the dark water. The light was dimming, and tendrils of mist crept in from the ocean. The silver moon was halfway from zenith to the horizon, the gold almost directly overhead.

Though the revelations from their earlier time at the pool had spurred Abel to redouble his efforts to solve the Mystery, he had learned nothing new, at least nothing concerning the critical issue: the question of how Laurel and Kate might come together in one world. Not that Laurel had expected him to.

To her dismay, the legacies of their respective existences on Earth collided. Ordinarily, as a Higher Order being, she would have had no difficulty with him, but circumstances were not ordinary. The essence he exuded as a result of his clinging to his long-dead Earthly self was toxic to the quasi-physical body she retained from her Earthly sojourn. On one hand, she felt deep empathy for him, in that her fine sensitivity felt the torment and confusion that sprang from his lingering attachments. On the other hand, owing to the remnant of physicality her mission had required her to assume, and its sensitivity to Earthly poisons, she could not help but be repelled by him. The very things that flawed his nature and stirred her sympathy were at the same time toxic to her, and given the weakened state of her health, she could abide only limited exposure to them. Hence a further trouble: her need to discreetly keep a certain distance made her feel uncharitable, and this stung her heart.

Further, she harbored doubt about Abel's ability to plumb the Mystery. After all, she herself, Aurora, and Gerard had discovered more about it in a few minutes at the pool—due, apparently, to her affinity for the water—than Abel had since the arrival of the message that had started the whole business. Those observations—and intuition—told her that she'd do well to take an active hand, which is why she stood now at the pool, in the fading light, gazing at the black water as the ocean mist began to drift about her feet and the pool's foundation stones.

Laurel leaned closer. She took a breath, then gently touched the knurled stones on the rim. Nothing happened for a moment. She focused, recalling the image of the dark-haired young woman she had seen before in this same water.

A spark flashed in the depths. Laurel drew a sharp breath and her hands fluttered, rising slightly. She composed herself, and as she laid her hands back on the stones, whispered, "Kate..."

A thread of light, iridescent green shading to blue, wove through the darkness like some luminous water-serpent. As the angel stood transfixed, the thread expanded in a burst of light that filled the pool. When it subsided, a dim glow suffused the water, and Laurel made out, far in the depths, a wavering, glimmering rectangle.

She leaned closer, and gave one of the stones the barest twist. The rectangle zoomed closer. Another twist, the image enlarged again. *Ahh, I see...* Laurel manipulated both stones, refining her sense of their functions. She refocused her thoughts on Kate and suddenly the rectangle clarified, became a window. And there before her was Kate, asleep in her bed, as she was at that moment on Earth. As Laurel watched, lips parted and breath stilled, Kate stirred and turned toward her, framed in the wavering window. Her eyes flickered open for an instant though she remained asleep. The picture blurred, but Laurel restored it with a tap on one of the stones.

Far below, in Kate's bedroom, a thread of light like that which Laurel had seen in the water slewed across the mirror that hung above the dresser—and though Kate was oblivious to the light itself, the angelic influence that lay behind it jumped the gap and touched her soul.

She rolled toward the mirror, and the dark, restless dream of Sally that had vexed her sleep left her, replaced by a supernal calm as she hovered suspended in a field of golden light. She felt loved as never before.

As she basked in this well-being, the light began to compose itself into a face, seen as if through swaths of hurrying mists, and for a moment she thought, *Sally?* But no—this blond girl had blue eyes and was older—in some indefinable way, much, much older.

Above, Laurel caressed a stone and willed the image to remain focused. Gingerly, she removed her hands from the stones and cupped them before her. The little sun, the Gift, bloomed and she extended her hands toward the water.

Kate drew a long breath as her dream world grew warmer, brighter, and the girl in the mist seemed to smile ever so slightly. The delicious sense of well-being, of being loved, deepened, and a word whispered in her mind: *Promise.*

So high above, Laurel murmured, "I promise, I'll find a way to come to you…and then you'll be whole." She parted her hands and gazed at Kate's shimmering image as the Gift's light faded in the air before her. Kate's breathing slowed and deepened—the light of her dream faded along with that of the Gift, and she slipped into a deep slumber. Laurel pondered as she watched the still form in the luminous water.

"I have something for you now…a song of your very own.

A token for you to keep until we meet." She began to sing—a graceful melody in a bright mode, in her strange, lovely language. For a time, she wove a tapestry of poetry and melody, and then ended on a long, low, tender note.

The light in the water began to flicker. Laurel touched the stones—a tap, a turn—but it was no help; she was losing contact. She gazed a moment—sorrow, longing, and affection mingling as the water dimmed to blackness. *Good night, love…*

೮

"I'm worried," said Aurora. She and Gerard sat in the secluded hollow overlooking the ocean, by the rippling pool where Victor and Emelia had demonstrated the Old Way to Laurel, Kaira and Benedict.

As conditions on Earth—the approach of Christmas and the ever-widening war—generated more traffic at the Aviary, which in turn made ever greater demands on Gerard's attention, Aurora had become Laurel's first companion and confidant. The younger angel's tales of her pursuit of Kate by way of the pool had kept her captivated, but the lack of any real progress led her to ask Gerard to steal a little time from his work for them to meet and discuss the matter.

"Tell me, then," said Gerard as he leaned toward her.

"She's learning…becoming familiar with Kate and her ways…" Aurora interrupted herself, "She has an astonishing way with the pool…as you've seen, but still, as always, the water's…" She shrugged. And he nodded, in the silent way intimates have when they rehearse common knowledge. "It frustrates her when it doesn't cooperate." Neither Gerard nor Aurora had been surprised that the runic scroll, so rich, so tantalizing, had not reappeared.

"Anyway," she went on, "She's happy to learn more of Kate, but it must lead her straight back to the original problem, mustn't it?"

90

He nodded. "Not even a clue about getting them together?"

Aurora shook her head. "No. 'So near yet so far.' And there's this: I tested her again. I had to insist…she's hardly ever at home…always at the water, always searching." Aurora paused. "And she's still not well."

"No surprise. She's still in virtual contact with Earth," Gerard observed. "So, of course she's not healing as quickly as…"

"Exactly. But on the other hand, Laurel radiates the benignity of the Gift, and some of that apparently finds its way to Kate."

"To what effect? Can she tell?"

Aurora brightened. "I was coming to that. Laurel was startled to see that Kate has begun seeing a fellow. He's obscure, but she likes to hope that perhaps it…" She paused. "Well, she's not sure what. It just seems vaguely hopeful to her. But that's the extent of the good news, I'm afraid. Between the pool's stubbornness, and her slow recovery, she's getting discouraged. We're no closer to getting them together."

Gerard nodded absently. "What of Abel?"

Aurora considered. "He's thrashing. He was 'on the verge of a breakthrough' for a while, but he's been very quiet lately."

"No surprise."

"But I wanted to tell you something peculiar that my last tests revealed: Music acts as a curative on Laurel, so I'll prescribe that she devote some attention to it. It would have a healing effect in reducing her exposure to Earthly negatives and, not least, provide a diversion, which she badly needs. But if I know her…and I do… she'll nod and tell me it's a fine idea and then run right back to the pool. I know your work takes most of your attention now, but still, I thought you might find a moment to give her a nudge."

"Count on me. It's a fine idea." A thoughtful look crossed his face, and he continued, "All of this brings Ambriel to mind. Do you suppose he could be persuaded to…"

"Linger a while? Lovely idea! I'll go see him."

"Ask him if he wouldn't like to get his old 'cello out again…and I'll bet he could help set Abel to rights, too, sure enough." He paused, then asked, "By the way, when did you last play your viola?"

Ambriel, the most senior of the Branch 92 elders, had been in relative seclusion for some while, gathering his energy, focusing his consciousness in anticipation of his imminent ascension to a higher plane. He had been resident in Branch 92 out of memory, and it was known that he, like Abel, had been a scholar in his Earthly days, and had continued so in the True Life, adding there the study of the 'cello.

Ordinarily it would be unthinkable to interfere with such a revered and beloved soul at such a time, but Laurel's arrival and the renewed general interest in the Mystery made for extraordinary circumstances.

Aurora did visit Ambriel directly, and as she had expected, found him amenable.

଼

Laurel had been at the pool for time untold. The seemingly omniscient runic text that she had summoned during her first session, to her great disappointment, but as predicted by the elders, had since eluded her. Since then she had found herself limited to observing Kate, in time as Earth reckoned it, usually from the vantage point of glazed or reflective surfaces that happened to be near Kate. Though the angel could "follow" her object of interest in places where there were no such surfaces, the effect was less than satisfying. Absent a window or mirror near Kate, Laurel felt as though she were about to lose sight of her altogether—and sometimes did, the water abruptly going black as it had at the end of her first session.

But when a clear crystalline surface was available, Laurel

dared to hope that she was really seeing Kate as she was. One particular, and favorite, vantage point appeared with regularity, a skylight in a corridor of the hospital where Kate worked.

Just now, Kate was attending the little girl again. Her devotion to the child moved Laurel deeply, but that sentiment was more and more alloyed with a troubling undertone. *Dread?* Laurel forced her mind back to the matter at hand, the search for anything, any sign that might suggest a way for her to enter Kate's world and deliver the Gift.

Though the vagaries of the waters kept her knowledge of Kate and her life indistinct and fragmentary, still she could tell that Kate's attachment to the little girl had increased, and that her unease with the man Laurel had sensed but had not seen, and who seemed attached to Kate, had diminished. Again she wondered. The girl was connected with Kate's work as a healer, that much was clear. *But the man…how did he fit in? So frustrating…*

Laurel's attention had wandered, and the image in the water twisted as if caught in a whirlpool. Her mind snapped back to the water as her hands adjusted the stones in pursuit of clarity. She wouldn't have admitted it—was hardly aware of it—but the extended vigil was telling on her. Laurel was far from recovered from her dark sojourn on Earth, and her obsession with Kate and the pool were not helping her to heal.

13

Three thousand feet above the Pacific Ocean, just off Mission Beach, the Taylorcraft whirled down, down, spinning like a silvered maple seed, throwing glints of sunlight to complement the broad, glittering path the sun cast on the sea. In the cockpit, Kate, wide-eyed, watched the ocean's surface whirl, a sliver of the beach swinging at the edge of the picture filtered through the flicker of the windmilling propeller.

"…and…three…" she said, her voice tight, as the slice of beach swung to the right side of the windscreen for the third time. At once, she pressed the right rudder pedal to full deflection, centered the wheel, and pushed it forward to lower the nose even further, battling the instinctive urge to pull back.

The airplane ceased rotating, and Kate felt the wings bite the air as the craft regained flying speed. Only then did she ease back on the wheel. When the ocean dropped below the engine cowling, her right hand eased the throttle forward from idle to cruise power and the engine ceased popping and stuttering and resumed its accustomed growl. She let out her breath and her eyes returned to something like their normal size.

Sam, in the right-hand seat, said, "Not bad. I think you've got it."

Kate was an excellent pilot—a "natural," Sam had said—but she had struggled with spin recovery. The feeling that the plane was in a death spiral drove her to the edge of panic and the

94

correct action—pushing the wheel forward—had felt simply suicidal to her. Sam had taken this one weak spot as an affront to his ability as an instructor and pledged to get her through it. In the course of things, his instincts had been reliable; he knew when to push her and when to back off, letting her rebuild her confidence by practicing the maneuvers she had taken to naturally. This event, then, was a triumph for both of them.

"I've got it," Sam said as he took over the controls. He dipped the right wing toward Mission Beach and gestured. "There's the Café. If it were low tide you could practice your crosswind landing on the beach and we could grab some lunch."

"Then thank God it's not low tide," she replied, laughing. "I've had enough for today."

They settled into a companionable silence as they continued north parallel to the shoreline, big winter surf rolling up the beach below their right wing and the eight-hundred-foot-high swell of Soledad Mountain looming ahead. Sam eased back the throttle and they drifted lower. At 400 feet, he leveled off. Crystal Pier—its dense wooden pilings roughened and mussel-encrusted by more than a decade in salt water, its gleaming white rails and its dozen-and-a-half stripe-roofed, whitewashed cottages on the landward end of the deck—drifted toward them.

Kate watched the cream of the broken waves sweep in, glide to a halt and clarify, and then slide back under the next breaker's advance. The second of the winter's storms had peaked the day before and there was a good deal of power in the water; occasionally the remnant of a larger wave lapped against the base of the cliffs. Even from this vantage, the surf exerted the same hypnotic effect on her as when she watched it from her back yard. She thought of the millions of years it had gone on, this war between water and rock. Though the intimation of eternity made her feel very small, she nonetheless found comfort in it. That impression, the fatigue of the challenging lesson just ended, and the drone of the plane's engine combined to make her drowsy.

Suddenly, a fast-moving shadow ahead and to the left seized her attention. She cried out in delight as a great vee of pelicans flashed by in the opposite direction, fifty yards to the left at the same altitude. They passed far too quickly to tally.

She turned and flashed a delighted grin at Sam. "Did you see…?"

"Friends of mine," he deadpanned. "I asked them to come by and greet you."

She laughed and Sam's affection deepened in proportion to her joy. He found himself—again—daring to hope that Kate might yet come to love him. If she could express such strong and pure emotion over a flock of birds, well… *Patience.* They were already shoulder-to-shoulder in the cramped cockpit, but he yearned to reach and draw her still closer. *Be patient.*

He swung west of False Point then turned northward again as they left Pacific Beach for La Jolla. He dipped a wing and gestured. "Look at the change in the water. North of the point it gets a lot clearer." Kate looked ahead and behind. There was indeed a difference. Back toward Pacific Beach and Mission Beach, the ocean seaward of the breaking surf was a turbid green. North of the point it was pellucid blue.

The cliffs here rose to thirty or forty feet and the ground to the east was latticed with the mostly empty streets of what had been intended as a residential neighborhood. Perhaps two dozen houses sat on land that had been prepared for hundreds. Bankers and real estate speculators—intoxicated on the exuberance and easy money of the 1920s—had planned a thorough buildup of the many undeveloped areas around San Diego and indeed had made a good start. Then came the Crash of '29 and, after a falsely reassuring lull, the Great Depression. The easy money evaporated, development shuddered to a halt, and the streets below had lain barren for a decade, ghosts of the vanished confidence of the mad, florid '20s.

A minute later they were over the miniature island of Bird Rock, a rugged stone rampart twelve feet high and eighty long and about a hundred feet off the shore, all depending on the tide. At extreme lows, it ceased to be an island and became an outcropping. A great colony of black cormorants—hawk-billed ducks, Sam thought of them—gathered there, sharing their sanctuary with a half-dozen brown pelicans. Sam throttled back to lose a hundred feet of altitude and began a left-hand circle around the rock to allow Kate a closer look. A few birds looked up, and two of the pelicans lifted off and flapped seaward, but the flock remained for the most part indifferent to the loud, gleaming intruder. Kate knew Bird Rock from her solitary walks, but was surprised at how different it appeared from the air. She studied the tiny island, its planes and contours, the arch at its northern end, its colony of birds, the way the fat winter waves shattered against it and then poured in torrents back into the ocean—until Sam rolled level and crossed over the little cove just north of the rock.

Past the cove's north side were more of the eerie paved streets serving empty lots. Sam had noticed this area in the months since his business had begun to thrive. He glanced at Kate, who was watching another vee of pelicans ahead. He banked to the right and spotted the acute angle where one of the barren streets arced west to meet the cove's north end and then caromed off the cliff to continue north along the shoreline. Yes, on one of those lots, either side of the point, right on the cliffs—he'd build her a house. Build *them* a house. If his business continued successful. If the coming war didn't somehow kill him. Or kill her, for that matter, given her dream that he had determined to make come true. If the world kept revolving on its axis.

Kate disturbed his reverie. "Nice place to put a house," she observed. He followed her gaze and nodded. He completed a circle around the point, then resumed their northward course along the shore.

In less than a minute he dipped the right wing and announced, "Your house." They were indeed over Kate's bungalow. Sam pointed and began another circle to allow Kate a clear view of her home. Though they were only a couple of hundred feet up, it struck her that the house and yard looked awfully small considering the hours, the days of work she'd put into it. But as they circled she began to smile, liking the novelty.

Sam completed a second turn around the house then headed north again. He pointed out the crescent seawall of the Children's Pool and the elegant resort hotel, Casa de Manana, whose 1920s grandeur clashed with the present time's austerity. A little farther up, the shoreline turned briefly east to form La Jolla Cove, where the northwesterly winter swell slammed directly against the backing cliffs. To Kate it seemed as though the fountaining spray from the Cove nearly reached the plane's altitude.

East of the cove, where the shoreline turned north, a rock shelf—long and deep, high above the water, sheltered by its obliqueness to the northwest swell's onslaught—held what appeared to be all the pelicans in the world. Sam angled seaward for a space then reversed course so that the enormous rookery was on Kate's side. She gazed down, fascinated. She saw birds clustered in sociable groups, birds making impossible contortions as they preened, birds sleeping on their bellies with their great, improbable pouched beaks tucked under a wing. Now and then one or a pair floated off the rock on seven-foot wingspans to soar over the water, while others arrived, nearly stumbling upon landing, then doing the fussy, fluttering drill of folding their wings. Kate marveled at the contrast—how these waddling creatures, so homely and ungainly on the ground transformed into paragons of grace the instant they spread their wings and floated off over the waves.

A movement to seaward caught her eye. She exclaimed, "Look! They're surfing!" A dozen pelicans dove one after another from altitude down to less than a foot before the face of a twelve-foot breaker. In disciplined line-astern they rode the wave of air that the huge roller pushed ahead of itself. Occasionally a wing tip brushed the face of the wave. As the crest finally broke, throwing a great plume of spray, the birds pulled up, wings beating for altitude as they circled to have another go.

Sam watched too, and warmed again as he felt Kate's joy. She turned to him and grinned like a child. "I love to watch them do that," she said. "Don't you?"

Sam took a last look at the rookery as it disappeared behind them. He throttled up, trimmed the plane to climb and set a southerly course to retrace their tour of the coastline. "I love anything with wings," he replied at last.

Kate seemed not to hear, then said, half to herself, "We'll have to bring Sally here when she's better."

But Sam heard. "We'll fly her around the world, if you want."

When they reached five hundred feet he throttled back and re-trimmed. "You've got it," he said. "Fly us home." She took the controls, full of confidence, like the natural flyer Sam knew her to be.

◌

Venus floated above a fading salmon-tinted sunset as Sam turned onto Kate's front walk, and jasmine perfumed the cool evening air.

She was dressed casually in light slacks and a dark blue sweater, but Sam thought her lovelier than ever.

99

She may indeed have been more beautiful this evening, objectively, not just in Sam's eye, and the new warmth he perceived had a real basis. True, she did not love Sam in the ordinary sense, but her affection for him had grown apace despite her strange deficiency. Also true: Sally had been holding her own, no worse if no better, and the irrational idea she kept hidden from herself, the conviction that Sally's recovery would somehow bring about her own completion—her "bargain" with the universe—had nonetheless seduced her. She dared now to hope.

She took the flowers and bottle of wine Sam had brought and gestured toward the kitchen. As he followed her through the living room, Sam was surprised and delighted to see a couple of logs blazing in the fireplace that had always been clean and cold before. A swing ballad whispered from the phonograph, and the aroma of herbs and a touch of garlic drifted from the kitchen.

"Smells delicious! What is it?"

She didn't answer at once, but set the wine on the counter, took a corkscrew from a drawer and tossed it to Sam, then found a vase in a cupboard and busied herself with the bouquet.

"*Pollo al horno con almendras y piñones*," she finally replied in a lisping Castilian accent, still fiddling with the flowers. "Fancy way to say 'chicken casserole'," she laughed. "I learned how to make it in Spain."

She had learned well. Dinner was a success, though Sam finished well ahead of Kate. Still keyed up from the morning's flying lesson, she had a dozen questions and twice that many comments as she recalled their hour and more together in the air. To Sam's fond amusement, she had begun to use her hands like an aviator—palms down, fingertips representing the plane's nose as she illustrated maneuvers and attitudes that were becoming, if not quite yet second nature, at least familiar. Sam found himself reliving his own student pilot days as he answered her questions.

When Kate finally wound down, Sam poured the last of the wine and changed the subject.

"I've mentioned your idea to a couple of people." She tried to appear relaxed. He continued, "The man who gave me my start has friends at a couple of the big aircraft manufacturers. He thinks they might provide you with a couple of transports. Or at least one to get you started."

Kate nearly choked on her wine. "Provide? But…those must be enormously expensive!"

"They are. And we'll still need to raise cash for staff and supplies and operating costs, but if this works out the way we want it to, the planes—the biggest capital outlay—will more or less be lent to you."

She was stunned. "That's wonderful! But why would they…?" She shook her head.

"They have their reasons. Anyone who manufactures war material is already making millions…small potatoes to them… by selling indirectly to the Allies by way of the government. If… when…we get into the war, the manufacturers will switch to a total war footing and start raking in tens, or more likely, hundreds of millions."

"Yes, but what's that got to do with…?"

He went on, "These days, big companies are concerned with their public image. Telephones and planes and radio are making the world smaller every year. Opinions get lives of their own and travel fast, and the big operators know that down the road, they're inviting trouble if they get painted as bad guys." He paused. "Like, for instance, as war profiteers."

Kate reflected for a second as her lips formed a silent "Ah." Sam concluded, "But if they can claim, at least in part, to be humanitarians…"

She considered. After a moment she said, "I see. Should I

feel used…or as though I'm about to be?"

"No, not at all. Listen. Be practical. Every successful man in history's had a lot of help. And times being what they are, you'd be wise to take your help where you find it." He paused. Her look told him she wasn't buying, not entirely. "You're afraid you'd be compromised. I understand that, especially after what you saw in Spain."

Indeed, she was recalling the sights and smells of Guernica, and imagining the fleets of bombers that had brought death and ruin to the little Spanish town, bombers that had been built and sold by industrialists—foreigners, not the ones whose generosity Sam was arranging for her, but industrialists nonetheless—men who got rich by dealing in the deaths of children. "I never thought *I'd* feel like a…"

"No," Sam held up his hand. "Two things: one, even if the war doesn't get bigger, the world needs the work you want to do. Someone's going to do it eventually and it might as well be you, now. Two, if it comes to another world war, we'll be in a fight for our very existence as a nation. In that case, your work will be needed more than ever, and no one will quibble about profiteering or 'dirty money.'"

She pondered a while, then finally nodded, but Sam suspected she still wasn't entirely won over. He looked at her a moment while two ideas fought inside him: admiration for her integrity, and impatience with her want of pragmatism. He concluded, "Think of it like this: even if the money, the help, *were* tainted, your work will cleanse it."

When it was time for Sam to leave, Kate accompanied him to the porch. Though his feelings for her had grown steadily stronger, he was ever sensitive to her peculiar reserve and had held himself to a particular code of chivalry. For Kate's part, her defenses notwithstanding, she had warmed to Sam, and she thought with some sadness that were she like other women she would have fallen in love by now.

Perhaps it was inevitable then, the tiny spark that, this evening, leapt the still wide but narrowing gulf between them. As Sam turned to go, the care he had nurtured for Kate's strangeness fell away like scudding clouds revealing the sun, and he took her in his arms and kissed her. To the surprise of both, she did not recoil. The event had overtaken them so suddenly that it had stunned them both to stillness.

It wasn't a long kiss, but they held each other gently for a good while afterward. They didn't speak, and both were strangely relaxed, given the ritual of separation that circumstance had enforced upon them until this moment.

Sam came to himself first. He released her, slowly, and took a step back. He couldn't think of a single worthwhile thing to say, so he said, "Thank you for…for a lovely evening."

Kate seemed not to hear. Her expression was serene in the dim porch light. Finally she stirred and managed a quiet, "Ah…"

This will need a lot of sorting out.

Sam understood. He opened the door and gently guided her through it. He said, "Goodnight, Kate," and left after he heard the bolt click into place.

Later, Kate sat in the chaise on the patio, a throw wrapped about her against the nighttime chill. The ocean had hardly any swell and small waves whispered on the cobblestoned beach at the foot of the cliff. She watched the clouds roll through the moonlight, as they revealed stars and hid them in turn. Her mind insisted on moving in a circle. She reviewed past episodes with boys and men, mostly dreary and sad—occasions to dislike men in general and herself in particular—then relived Sam's kiss. Round and round for how long she didn't know. Finally she made herself think of Sally and the safe ground she had somehow convinced herself that Sally represented. Her mind at peace, finally, she rose and went inside.

Just before she slept, she remembered, obscurely, her bargain.

14

The lowering sun silhouetted Laurel as she stood over the pool, and her hands touched the knurled stones with sensitivity and strength, much as a violinist's hands touch the strings and bow. Her eyes riveted to the water, she was all intensity, and occasionally the corner of her mouth flickered, the ghost of a smile. At other times she frowned, and coaxed the stones as the capricious waters threatened to obstruct her vigil, or to go dark altogether.

Now she observed Kate, Dot and some others decorating the children's burn ward for Christmas. Laurel began absent mindedly to hum the song that had been her gift to Kate. Kate, too, began to hum parts of the tune as she stood on a stepladder, positioning an end of a tinsel string on a wall, moving it according to Dot's directions.

The water, inconsistent as ever, today transmitted sounds with a burbling distortion, but Laurel managed to make out scraps of conversation.

"Raggedy Ann…for Sally…" Kate seemed to say to Dot with a look of happy anticipation. Laurel leaned closer and squinted at Dot's expression. It didn't seem to match Kate's mood.

"…maybe…not wait…Christmas…" Dot seemed to reply.

At that, a chill coursed through Laurel's breast, as her spirit vibrated in sympathy with Kate's. A bolt of dread flashed through her mind, and was as quickly blocked by a willful numbness. It was as though Kate had wrapped a gauze around the emotion. It wasn't the first time Laurel had empathetically experienced Kate's mind and emotions, and she reflected on how their spirits had grown ever more attuned.

"Don't be silly, Dot…" came through clearly. The rest was garbled. Again, the light in the water began to flicker and break up. Again she touched the stones, pursuing Kate's image.

Music swelled faintly in the distance—not that the angel heard it—a lone fiddle, the slow air, "Bovaglie's Plaid," mainly—seasoned with embellishments and excursions of the fiddler's fancy.

The music grew louder, but Laurel's spell didn't break until a deep thrumming rushed upon her. She looked up to see Huey hovering before her, his crown-feathers shining her the gold of the low sun. He chirped a greeting then darted away, back toward Gerard, who was mounting the slope to the stone pool, still playing the grave, graceful melody.

"Well, there you are, Love!" he said, as he drew the tune's last low, sweet tone, and as if the pool were the last place anyone would expect to find her.

"I didn't know you played!" she exclaimed, her solitary study forgotten.

"I'd nearly forgotten that *you* do. We haven't heard a note from you since you arrived, now, have we?" He raised an eyebrow. "You…who have such gifts…" Huey hovered beside him.

Independence—and guilt, because she had ignored her physician's prescription of music—fought to control what Gerard would see in her eyes. Finally she said, accusingly, only half in mock, "Aurora put you up to this, didn't she?" and darting a glance at Huey, who she now saw had made common cause with Gerard, "And you, too, you little beggar!"

"Not a bit of it! Came of our own free will, we did!" Gerard protested, with mock indignation to match hers. It wasn't strictly a lie, despite the truth in Laurel's words. In a different tone, he continued, "And I've been missing you," and that was unalloyed truth.

Her heart swelled at that, though she pretended otherwise. "Then why did you bring my violin?" she challenged, looking at the knapsack slung over Gerard's shoulder.

Gently as the breeze from the sea, he replied, "Because Aurora's right."

Laurel stepped from the pool and slumped onto one of the mossy benches, and her head dropped in fatigue. "I suppose so…"

When she looked up, Gerard was holding the knapsack out to her. Tenderly, he said, "Time for your medicine, Love."

She accepted it, and drew the violin and bow. Her eyelids flickered, and for an instant her heart turned, and she tasted the poignant flavor of some other time and place, lived, but beyond memory, and, for a briefer instant, thought she might almost recall the one who had made this gift to her.

The flavor and the teasing memory faded, but the allure of the old violin remained and captured her, and she held it fondly before her. Anew, it charmed her: the ancient, sooty scratches in the fine-grained spruce top, the flamed maple of the ribs, Guarneri del Gesu-like, no two sections at the same angle. The long, graceful, Stradivarian corners with the perfectly curving bee stings of the purfling, the not-quite-symmetrical sound holes—again, del Gesu. And the back—a single piece of deeply flamed maple, the rippling pattern ascending from right to left at a startling angle. She plucked the strings, tuned, and stood.

The years of exile, the banishment between worlds, the weight of her mandate, with no way to fulfill it in sight—the illness she bore in its service—all focused now in the part of her soul that was music, and she wielded the bow like a sword. Something very like the mad beginning of Paganini's A-minor caprice blazed forth in the lowering light, and none who were near would ever quite forget it.

After a while, after some of the birds had fled, after her music had veered into a place that made even steadfast Gerard uneasy, the elder stood and reached his hand toward Laurel's shoulder. But before he touched her, the music stopped like a scissored thread, and the angel wilted—head down, fiddle and bow dangling from limp hands.

As she returned to herself, Gerard muttered, "Ah, poor thing," then aloud to her, "Sure and you needed to get that out, but here, if you will, Love, give me a bit of help with this..." He played the jaunty first four bars of "The Girl I Left Behind Me," then paused and gave her an expectant look.

She was defeated. With a half grin she played the accompaniment in double stops. Gerard joined in with the melody and the two soon became lost in the paradisaic place where musicians go when the chemistry is just right. The birds began to return to the trees around the pool.

In the event, Gerard got more help than he'd asked for. Never more than an average player, he was astonished to hear himself embellishing the melody in ways he had only been able to imagine but which he was sure were beyond his skills. Then he felt it: his arms and shoulders and his upper body tingled with what was at once like an electric current and at the same time like the sun's warmth. How he knew it radiated from Laurel he couldn't have said, but knew it he did.

Nor did Gerard alone benefit. As Aurora had told him, music was indeed a tonic to Laurel, and soon the obsession that had been dominant for so long retreated to a relatively minor position in her mind. Tension flowed out of her, and she began to heal.

When they were played out, Gerard insisted that Laurel come away from the pool, perhaps join him for a sip of tea or nectar, or just walk. As they strolled, he mentioned that there were any number of musicians at Branch 92 who would no doubt love to form a group, perhaps more than one. He went on a while about how surprised she'd be at the amount of talent here, but that it lacked focus. Aurora played viola; he himself, the fiddle, of course; old Ambriel, the 'cello. And there were many others, all the various strings and brass and woodwinds were represented. And singers—why, practically *everyone* sang!

It was just that no one seemed to possess the—the whatever it took to sort it all out and put it in order. In fact, he himself had personally heard it discussed, more than once, what a sad matter it was that they couldn't seem to pull themselves together enough to form an orchestra or a chorus.

Yes, there was much sighing over the matter, there was. He shot her a covert sideways glance. Ah, if only there were someone competent to organize and lead them, the poor things…

Her eyes flickered as lost remembrance seemed, again, nearly to penetrate the darkness that lay over her sojourn on Earth and rise to her awareness. Her eyes narrowed, she tilted her head and, without the least bit of guile, said, "You were Irish down there, weren't you?"

CB

The sound of two fiddles rang from the rafters of the little church next to the Aviary. Gerard, to Laurel's delight, had demonstrated the old hornpipe, "Nelson's Victory." She'd gotten the melody at one hearing of course, but was now absorbed in trying out different accompaniments while Gerard played the tune. A few angels had drifted in and sat smiling and tapping to the merry rhythm.

So engaged were both players and audience, none noticed as Aurora and another entered and took seats behind the listeners. The companion was slender and of medium height, with white

109

shoulder-length hair. Like Aurora, his age was indeterminate, but something in his manner, a preternatural calm, a depth in his eyes, suggested great age. He carried a large portfolio in one hand and a 'cello, itself ancient, in the other. Aurora carried her viola. The two were quickly caught, like the others, in the bright web of sound Laurel and Gerard wove.

When the fiddlers ended the hornpipe and enthusiastic applause filled the church, the newcomers joined the musicians. Before Gerard could introduce the 'cellist, the old angel surprised everyone by making a splendid, courtly bow to Laurel.

Taken aback, the object of his deference managed an ingenuous smile. Gerard said, "Ambriel, I was about to introduce…"

The 'cellist interrupted, "Her spirit fills this place so entirely, it's as if I already know her." To Laurel, he said, "As you may know, I'm soon to…ascend. What a privilege it is to meet one of the Higher Order, if prematurely."

She considered a reply, but then simply took his hands in hers and inclined her head toward him in a gesture filled with grace and humility.

She indicated Ambriel's portfolio. "What do you have there?"

"A couple of Haydn's quartets." An eyebrow rose as his gaze took in the players. "Agreeable?"

Agreeable indeed. As they moved through Quartet #14, E-flat Major, more listeners wandered in and were immediately enraptured—all but one.

Around the beginning of the third movement, Abel stepped in, staying back by the door. He had never been moved by, had never seen the point of, music. A trivial pursuit for mediocre minds, he felt. And so it still struck him now—or, no. What was it about *this* music? He tried to hide from it, but couldn't avoid the fact that the solemn grace, the gravitas of the sound that swept over him seemed nearly to…to… *No! Only unserious minds allowed themselves to be distracted by this kind of nonsense. The measure of a first-rate mind is the extent of its influence over others.* His reason attacked the thought as soon as it was complete. *These musicians…or the composer…must be first-rate, then, given their influence over this lot…and over… No!*

His inner turmoil began to show outwardly during the silence after the third movement. Then the fourth began, and he reeled as the upper and lower voices took turns running a sort of merry chase that he just couldn't quite grasp. *Humiliation!* He couldn't tell which unsettled him more, his lack of understanding of the music or the waves of emotion—joy, gratitude—that poured from the audience like the sun's rays.

Then the music was finished and the crowd rose together and voiced their appreciation. Morbidly fascinated, Abel stepped up on the rearmost pew to see the quartet as they took their bows.

This child, this Laurel. She holds them in her hand, yet not one of them fears her. The thought lay on him. *Not as I managed my students…the sheep…and my "peers," in life.*

Though he had in himself the seed of shame for the comparison, before it could become thought, envy, like a snake, struck, and he hated her.

At that moment, Laurel's eyes caught his. A cold thrill swept through his breast, as if he'd been caught, *in flagrante*, in some shameful act. The warmth of her smile made it so much the worse, and he ran for the door.

15

Sam stood on the tarmac as the Taylorcraft's motor revved and it began to roll down the runway. Its nose drifted a little left but quickly corrected; the tail rose as it gathered speed and Sam, in spite of himself, held his breath. Then the plane was free of the ground and rising nicely. When it cleared the end of the runway, it banked left thirty degrees. Sam smiled as he raised a hand to shield his eyes from the low winter sun. He pivoted to keep the plane in sight as it turned left again, now onto the traffic pattern's downwind leg, on the opposite heading from which it had taken off. Its wings were level and it held a steady 500 feet of altitude.

He frowned. "Throttle back, now…" he muttered, then smiled as the engine's note lowered. When the plane was even with the runway's threshold, it banked again, throttled back a little more, and began a graceful descending curve.

The Taylorcraft continued its descent, a little bank here, a bit of rudder there, but all in all, a nearly perfect approach. Still, Sam held his breath as the plane crossed the threshold and leveled its wings. He exhaled as the wheels eased onto the runway without a hint of a bounce. He pumped a "thumbs-up" gesture toward the plane then jabbed a finger parallel to the runway, signaling the pilot to go around again. The motor roared and in a few seconds the plane was again airborne.

It circled the pattern twice more, the second time a little

wobbly on the final turn, but the third effort was as good as the first. After the final landing the plane turned off the runway and taxied to the tie-down area where Sam stood.

When Kate stepped out of the plane, she was all but vibrating, and she barely touched the ground as she ran to Sam. She tried twice to speak, and ended up just grinning and shaking her head.

Sam laughed. "All I can say is, Jackie Cochran better watch out!"

Kate, too, knew she had performed her first solo flight very well and nearly burst with pride and excitement. Sam spread his arms. She almost leapt into them before her old habits halted her and dimmed her smile. But then she shoved all that aside and threw her arms around him. For a moment she was free of the old fears and inhibitions. Sam smiled, eyes closed, face to the sun. Then, without thinking, he lifted her and whirled her in a circle. She caught her breath—and gave the old things another shove and laughed out loud.

They released one another and he regarded her a long moment. At last he said, "Tie the old bird down and we'll get some lunch."

At their accustomed haunt, the Mission Café, Kate was too excited to eat. She relived her fifteen-minute flight for the better part of an hour, and her exhilaration was contagious; Sam was so caught up by it that he too neglected his hamburger and fries.

By the time Kate finally wound down, the food was cold. The Depression had made a great virtue of economy; to waste was bad form. She looked at her plate, guilty.

Sam read her thoughts. "Don't worry, I have an idea." He called to the waiter for a bag for the leftovers. "Come on," he said to Kate. "Let's go meet some of the world's finest aviators."

They swung over the low concrete seawall that separated the boardwalk from the beach and, the tide being out, walked to the hard-packed sand closer to the surf. Low, solid-looking clouds on the horizon made the ocean seem a wide, wide river with mountains on the far shore.

A few gulls stood here and there in singles and small groups. All of the local varieties were in sight: big white Herring Gulls, similar looking but smaller Ring-billed, Western and California Gulls, and Sam's favorite, Heermann's Gulls, distinctive with their black legs and feet, crimson bills, and contrasting plumage of dove-gray backs and breasts, darker gray wings, and snowy white heads.

Sam took a french fry from the bag and tossed it toward them in a high trajectory. The three nearest birds lunged for it, yapping and squawking, before it hit the sand. While the largest grappled with his rival nearest in size, the smallest darted in, snatched the fry, and took wing for the ocean.

Then, to Kate's delight, in seconds, what seemed like every gull within a quarter mile had arrived and clustered around them with as much fervor as a revival meeting. A big Herring Gull threw his head back and trumpeted his shrill, barking "I'm the boss" cry, making Kate think of a madman's laugh, but none of the other birds seemed in the least impressed.

Sam offered the bag to Kate. She dropped a couple of fries before her. The ensuing stampede startled her, and she hopped back a step. The gulls set up a squawking din, eyes fixed on the bag in her hands. She tossed them a couple more fries and a couple of small riots broke out. Many were Heermann's Gulls and Kate laughed at their duck-like voices. While the white gulls mewed and squawked and keened, the gray, red-billed birds made an indignant, nasal "Aow! Aow!" When Kate tossed them another fry, the gulls erupted in a chorus of quacks as they fought for it, their webbed feet pattering on the damp sand.

"They sound like Donald Duck in a really bad mood," Sam remarked. Kate's laugh rang over the surf and bird racket.

"Let's make 'em work for it," he said, raising his voice above the clamor. He took a fry from the bag and held it arm's length at eye level. "Come on, we're flyers, too! Show us your stuff!"

More and more gulls arrived on the wing, and one of them swooped down to hover a foot away from the proffered snack. He lunged, backed off, drifted closer again. Sam stretched the fry toward him. The bird finally darted and snatched the bait from Sam's fingers. He held up another. Kate followed suit, holding hers high overhead. One plunged from above to slam into another that was about to grab Kate's offering, driving him onto her shoulder and making her stagger.

Sam laughed, "Bet you never thought of bird feeding as a full contact sport!" She laughed with him as she tossed the fry high in the air, and grinned as an especially determined bird dashed through the gaggle to intercept it.

When the fries were gone, Kate tore a large piece from a hamburger bun and tossed it as high as she could. A large white gull caught it and dashed away. While french fries were worth enough to cause isolated skirmishes, half of a bun was a rich prize and a general chase was on. "Watch 'em now," said Sam.

The bird in possession twisted and turned in maneuvers that blended extremes of grace and violence—a spectacle Kate couldn't recall seeing before—but the pursuers were just as skilled and resolute. The speed and sureness with which they rolled and turned, soared and dove—whether it was it play or combat they didn't know, but it riveted Kate and Sam.

"If the T-Craft could roll like that, it'd snap our necks," Sam said, all admiration.

At last one of the pursuers body-checked the gull with the prize; he lost most of it, and the others scrambled for the fragment that fell to the beach, and fought or played on foot until the scraps were gone.

By now the two had gone a good way down the beach and by

silent accord turned back toward the café, giving the insatiable birds the last scraps of their meal along the way. The murmur of the ocean lulled Kate as she finally unwound from the excitement of the day.

When they neared the Mission Café, she stopped and looked up at two pelicans soaring in close formation, nearly motionless in the perpetual ocean wind. As she wondered, marveled, meditated, the pair simultaneously dipped their left wing tips, reversed course and hurtled southward, sailing before the wind. She realized, as she lost them to the distance, that she felt a kinship with them.

"Wouldn't it be lovely to do that," she dreamed aloud. Sam watched the vanishing birds a moment, then put his arm around her shoulders.

"You have. You did today."

∞

In the Pacifica's private room that Sam had reserved, Dot walked around the cake on the table next to the wall, looking for just the right place for the small model plane she held in her hand. The icing banner, "CONGRATULATIONS!" with its subtext, "Kate's first solo, December 1940," was bigger and bolder than she'd anticipated when she had ordered it, and left scant room for the plane.

The room was half full of people, most of them Kate's colleagues from the hospital who weren't scheduled to work, but also a handful of AirWest personnel: Greg, Sam's assistant; Howard, the only one of the pilots who happened to be off duty; and Phil and Tim, two of the mechanics. It was still early and more guests were expected.

Dot stopped and stood scowling at the cake with its cheerful script. She set the plane down, lifted the Brownie camera that hung by a strap from her shoulder and snapped a few shots of the cake. Suddenly she brightened and breezed from the room.

In a couple of minutes she was back with a busboy who carried a ladder, a hammer, and a spool of string. The boy put a nail into a ceiling beam and held one end of the string, the other of which Dot tied around the airplane. She had the boy adjust the string for different altitudes above the cake, and finally told him to tie it off after settling on eye level.

When she stepped back to admire her work, a light patter of applause startled her. The AirWest boys had watched the whole operation, and approved. Howard grinned. "That's better...not in the goo, but in the air, where she belongs."

Dot smiled back and swung the model toward him. He caught it and flicked it back to her and returned to his colleagues.

Sam wasn't sure whether Kate really was the best student pilot he'd ever taught or if he had convinced himself of it because he was in love with her; he was certain, though, that she would have the finest First Solo Celebration anyone out of Ryan Field had ever seen, and smiled inside in anticipation as he turned into the Pacifica's parking lot with Kate at his side. He had told her that the evening out was in honor of her first solo flight, but had somehow neglected to mention that there was to be a party, so she was surprised and delighted when the gathering cheered her arrival.

The lively dinner, the communal warmth, the easy familiarity that had grown between Kate and Sam in the past weeks, the champagne toasts—all these combined to make Kate comfortable sitting so near to Sam or dancing with his arm about her waist, to liberate her from her habitual tension, and to give the world a glimpse of a Kate who might have been had her parents left for a midday outing a second earlier or a minute later some twenty-six years before.

And while the men took the occasion at face value, as being in honor of Kate's accomplishment, the women, influenced by Dot's remarks on her role as matchmaker, reached a different conclusion. And so Kate and Sam publicly became a couple, though of course the truth wasn't quite that.

No one minded Dot's gentle boasting. No one, perhaps, except Kate, who happened to overhear a veiled speculation about the announcement of a particular date. She caught Dot's eye and motioned for her to follow.

In the ladies room, Kate asked, "Aren't you getting ahead of yourself? He hasn't asked, you know."

Ebullient, and perhaps a bit tipsy, Dot replied, "That's only 'cause you're such stick-in-the-mud. Sam's smart enough to play it cool."

"I know how things look, but you shouldn't assume… Dot, you know me better than anyone, but…well, things haven't changed, not…not…"

Dot looked skeptical.

Kate hobbled on, "The thing that's missing… Well…it's…" She stopped, met Dot's eyes, looked away. "It's still missing."

Dot's skepticism turned to impatience. She leaned against the vanity and pinned Kate in her gaze. "'Still missing.'"

"It's…it's hard to explain. But…I made kind of a bargain. It… ah…it has to do with Sally…"

"What in the world *are* you talking about?"

Kate suddenly became self-conscious. She drew a breath and continued. "I know it sounds silly…ok, ridiculous…but I sort of made a deal with…I don't know…the universe, I guess, that if…I mean, *when*…Sally gets better, I'll find that…that *thing*. I mean, I'll wake up and be whole. And then it'll all be different with Sam and me."

Another thought crept into her mind. She began to see how

easy, how painless it was to delude herself under the cover of private thoughts, and then, when the delusion was put into words, if only to a close friend—still, though, brought into daylight—how shocking it was to wake up so far down the garden path.

Dot was now completely sober, and very grave. "No, it doesn't sound ridiculous. It's sounds *mad*. Don't you…"

She had been about to remind Kate of the facts of Sally's condition, and the infection that should have been under control by now if it was ever going be, but held back as she saw fear and humiliation creeping into her friend's face, and decided that she needed compassion more than the harsh light of truth.

Kate looked down, shook her head and muttered, "I know, I know…"

Dot sighed and took Kate's hands. "No, you don't. And neither do I. Nobody knows." She recalled a few unaccountable recoveries she'd witnessed. "You could be right, after all. Let's just say you are." She drew Kate toward the door. "Come on. It's your party."

The rest of the evening was cheerful and lively, with champagne and music and dancing—Sam had engaged Tommy Shawn's band. Dot kept busy with her camera. The boys made a game of the model plane dangling on its string over the remnants of the cake, whirling it in ever greater, faster arcs and spirals. It got a little wild—when Kate stepped in and gave it a great toss, the string broke, but Sam happened to be in the right place to catch it. Amid the laughter, Dot grabbed the model from Sam and re-tied it to the string so that the game could continue.

Kate clung, in her way, to Sam, for another notion had crept into that place just below her everyday awareness: if her bargain with the universe—fate, whatever—regarding Sally's recovery had been not compromised, but seen in an unaccustomed light for the briefest moment, the rationalizing part of her mind from which it had sprung brewed a logic-twisting defense that turned the whole sad proposition on its head and whispered that if she were very nearly in love, then Sally must be very nearly well! *Ah...yes.*

They danced. Kate never knew well the fast, fashionable dances, though when she misstepped with a guest, she didn't do so too badly, and when she was with Sam, he guided her well.

Toward the end of the evening, when Tommy and the band tended toward ballads, she gave every dance to Sam, and responded so well to his lead that those who watched imagined that they had practiced together. When they played "When You Wish Upon A Star," she abandoned herself and laid her head on his shoulder and they glided with singular grace, in a separate world.

And so she kept the truth at a comfortable distance by dancing, and by having more champagne than she otherwise would have, and by dreaming, and by staying very close to Sam.

16

Abel stood deep in the stacks of Branch 92's library. He had searched from Philosophy to Physics, from Theology—both Middle Order and Higher Order—to Sociology, and nowhere had he found a clue to Laurel's mission, or rather, had he been honest with himself, he found no clue as to how he might turn the interest of her presence here to some advantage, to turn the spotlight on himself, as he had done for so much of his Earthly career.

He had never adjusted to life at Branch 92. Here, suffocating kindness and maddening tolerance came at him from every direction, without cease. In no face did he see any sign of ill will, discontent, or anxiety, let alone fear. The general absence of fear was what most frightened him about this place, for he had built a personal empire on it during his Earthly lifetime. With no one to fear him, it seemed at times as if he didn't exist at all.

He didn't really think quite so plainly as this; as much as he loved the spotlight, he was careful not to shine one inside, on his deeper desires and motivations—that is, the wretched remnant of his incarnation upon which he hung his name was careful about where it looked. His real self *yearned* to look inside, but of course, the husk of Abel that clung desperately to Earthly things kept that self gagged and hanging by chains in the dungeon. But regarding his cherished relationship with fear, in his dialogues with himself, he acknowledged only a need to be respected—*No crime in that!*—avoiding the fact that in Earthly life he had willfully mistaken fear for respect and that he had cultivated every means of inspiring it that he could.

On this occasion Abel was wrong in yet another regard: in assuming he was alone. Another soul approached—one who lately had devoted much reflection to the erstwhile professor's predicament.

"Well, there you are, Abel!" He jumped at the sound of his name and turned to find Ambriel smiling at him. "Sorry, didn't mean to startle you." The elder radiated good will. "How's the research coming along?"

The way these creatures look at one! Uncommanded, Abel's eyes cast about for an escape, but he quickly mastered himself and forced a casual tone. "Quite well, thank you. In fact I was just on my way to my quarters to organize my..."

Ambriel's look of good-natured skepticism silenced him. He felt cornered and his mind lost traction—words and fragments of thoughts began to tumble over one another. The elder's startling him so, then his looking right through him as if he were made of glass, the general off-balance feeling that was more or less his ordinary condition all crashed together to make him blurt out the first uncalculated words he'd uttered in quite some time.

"What *is* it about her?" He immediately regretted the unguarded words.

Ambriel's look changed again, to one Abel couldn't read. After a long pause, he replied, "What is it about *you*?"

Abel sputtered before recovering his voice. "Well, I...what do you mean? *I'm* not an object of interest here..."

"No?"

Abel's mind tried to flee in several different directions at once, but he remained rooted to the spot. "I don't, I don't..." He managed to silence himself.

"Let me help," Ambriel said, with infinite sympathy. "All of your agonies arise from a single error. You cling to Earth…to who you were on Earth. You are no longer that."

Abel stared.

"Break the shell. Break the infinitesimal shell in which you've imprisoned your magnificent spirit."

Abel stood trembling, consumed with inner turmoil. Finally, though not at all sure he really wanted to know, he asked, "How? How can I do that?"

Ambriel paused only a moment. "Go and see Laurel."

ଓ

Late afternoon light, lambent through the fog that crept in from the ocean, washed the garden that surrounded the pool. Laurel's hands rested on the knurled stones as she gazed at Kate's image in the water.

"So near, yet so far" had become the theme of Laurel's existence. Her daily visits to Kate had at first energized her and nourished her hope, the sight of Kate, her virtual presence, exhilarating. The "meetings" at the skylight in the corridor had become regular occurrences. Laurel felt almost as though she could reach into the water and touch Kate, but the insistent question of how to enter her world, without a clue as to the answer, had begun to oppress her.

She sensed someone climbing the slope behind her. She closed her eyes and felt the shadow of Branch 92's one troubled soul.

"Hello, Abel," she said without turning.

He halted. He had recovered somewhat from his encounter with Ambriel—*What was he coming to, that some ancient, mild-as-milk fellow could unnerve him so?*—and had decided on reflection, to the extent his scrambled thoughts could be so termed, that perhaps it would make sense to go and see Laurel.

He had avoided her since the quartet rehearsal. Even his well-developed powers of self-deception couldn't fully obscure his resentment of her, her effortless command of universal respect, and her progress, albeit limited, in gleaning details of the Mystery. Too, the sprout of conscience that had germinated with his last-breath conversion made it difficult for him to look her in the eye. But—ever the pragmatist—since he'd exhausted the resources at the Library, and since Laurel was making some progress at the pool, perhaps he'd do well to steel himself, have a peek over her shoulder, and see what he could see.

Only to be undone by two words: Hello, Abel.

That she knew him before seeing him and before he spoke was even more demoralizing than the ease with which Ambriel had shown Abel that he did not know himself. Laurel stepped away from the pool and turned to him. *That damned smile!*

"You don't look well," she observed. "Are you all right?"

He stood dumbly as she moved closer, then began to go on about overwork and that frankly he wasn't making much progress. Before he'd said many words, Laurel drifted away, her eyes unfocused over Abel's shoulder.

She let him ramble a little longer, before cutting him off in mid-sentence. "We're starting a chorale. First rehearsal is this evening. We'll see you there."

Both Laurel and Abel were weathering storms, though of different kinds. As Laurel became more and more discouraged by her lack of progress, her palliative was to embrace Aurora's prescription and immerse herself more deeply in music, hence her establishment of the chorale group. But the elders were becoming concerned: Aurora wondered whether her prescription was having harmful side effects, and worried that Laurel's distraction diverted too much of her energy from the pursuit of her mission.

Gerard shared Aurora's concern to an extent, but judged that because Laurel's devotion was so intense, and her problem so unyielding, the diversion likely did more good than harm. For her own part, Laurel at times accused herself of dereliction, but always traveled the same circle back to the recognition that she could hover at the pool without result only so long, and so succumbed more and more to music's call.

Abel's turmoil was more immediate: He feared he was losing his mind. Or, looked at another way, his identity. Ever since Laurel's arrival, his habitual "off balance" feeling had threatened to burst into full-on vertigo. Three events had pushed him near to the edge: the eruption of his resentment toward Laurel that had made him flee the quartet rehearsal had horrified him, resentment being, to him, a vice of inferior minds; his encounter with Ambriel in the library had led to the sensation that the borders between himself and that not himself were dissolving, that he was diminishing, that he might at any moment dwindle to nothingness; and finally, the offhand way Laurel commanded him just now had sprung a trapdoor under the remains of his confidence.

A part of him recognized at last his helplessness, while another smaller part, that containing the tatters of his old identity, barred the door against the interlopers that threatened to reveal...*what*, exactly?

❦

Abel was the last to arrive at the church for the first rehearsal of the chorale. The singers were in their places, and Laurel, at the podium, eyed him, guessed his vocal range and waved him to a place between Benedict and Victor in the tenors. From the music Ambriel had brought from the Library, Laurel had chosen Bach's Cantata 140, Sleepers Awake. She waited for the choir's attention, then with a motion of her hand, commenced the piece.

Abel, despite his inner conflict, wasn't entirely at sea. He had learned to read music as a boy, and the knack quickly returned. What chafed him, though, was that he was not here of his own choice. Laurel had *commanded* him to come, and he was still trying to come to terms with his helplessness before her.

Something else, however, was happening inside him. The power and the richness of the voices around him gradually displaced his shame and confusion and the sense of his own weakness that had oppressed him, and in a while, though he didn't measure the time, he began to feel contented for the first time since he had left his flesh to the dust.

All to the good, but then—the tenor solo. Laurel had cued him, pointed to him a measure ahead, and despite a twinge of panic, something deep inside him accepted the challenge, and at the same time he felt the galvanic current flowing from her, filling his head and chest—the same that the quartet had grown fondly to depend upon.

And he had seen her lips move, when she had pointed to him; her eyes penetrated the soul he had so long denied: *Simply be*, she had said to him, silently.

No one was more surprised than he when the unexpected glory of his voice began to fill the church. And as he sang, all that remained of his former self turned inward, gradually contracting into the smallest grain of space, and when it became as small as it could conceivably be, it compressed yet further, very nearly to annihilation, and then ignited like a birthing star, and Abel began to recall, as he sang, who he truly was. He swept the singers along with him in his re-creation; indeed they now were within him, and he within them. He simply was, and at last lived.

17

Sally moaned as Dot gently pulled a bandage from one of her terribly burned legs. She grabbed, trembling, for Dot's hand, and clutched it. The nurse left the injury for the moment to swab the girl's forehead. Long experienced, thoroughly professional, Dot kept her face carefully composed. *She shouldn't be here…shouldn't have survived London, shouldn't have survived the trip, shouldn't have lived a day after arriving here.*

She gently freed herself from Sally's frail grip, and returned to the task. *How long can it go on?*

Kate entered the room and joined Dot wordlessly, and soon the nurses finished the grim procedure. Kate studied the gaunt little face while Dot updated the record. *Come on, Sally, you can make it. You* have *to make it.* But a voice deep inside—a thought behind her thoughts—intruded. *Don't be a fool…* She thrust the voice away; she had gotten good at that.

Dot stepped toward the door, paused, and turned grave eyes to Kate. She searched her face a moment, put a hand on Kate's arm, then left.

Kate watched Sally a little longer. She swabbed her forehead and turned to go. A tiny, rasping whisper arrested her. "Thank you…"

Kate whirled. Sally's eyes were half-open and she smiled faintly.

"What, darling, what is it?" Kate asked.

"…for staying…with me."

"Well, of course, honey, I promised you…"

"I love you… Kate…" The girl drew a ragged breath, then let it out in a shivering sigh. She lay very still.

"Sally… *Sally!*" Kate gathered her up.

Sally's eyes opened, barely, one more time. A faint smile, a faint whisper. "Suzanne…"

She melted in Kate's arms. A sigh, then the dreadful stillness. Kate confirmed that Sally was gone. She sat, cradling the small form, rocking her, in silent tears. After a while, she laid Sally on her bed, covered her, and walked from the room.

18

Low, heavy clouds obscured the sunset as Sam turned onto Kate's front walk, and the jasmine's perfume was dispersed in the damp, fitful wind that blew from the ocean.

He became concerned when she didn't answer after his third knock, but at last the door opened. Once again he took himself to task for not fully grasping what Sally had meant to Kate. A corner of his mind reflected on how insidious love's selfishness is, how quickly it can undermine the old growths of generosity and consideration.

She looked haggard and her slow smile was a pitiful ghost of the joy she had come to express more and more freely in the weeks before Sally's passing.

She stepped back and made a vague gesture inviting him inside. Passing through the living room he glanced at the fireplace, dead and cold and forgotten, not even a decent part of a log to start a new fire—just ashes. Silence accompanied the chill. Ordinarily, she had music playing on the phonograph when Sam arrived, a big band, or one of her Kreisler records, but this evening, nothing.

He followed her into the kitchen, where she turned a bemused look to him. "I hope you're not too hungry. I..." she trailed off and gestured to some half-finished preparations. She stared at the odds and ends of utensils and foods—potatoes, makings of a salad, herbs, filets Sam had ordered delivered there earlier—and finally shrugged. He shook his head slightly and stepped toward her. He moved to gather her in his arms but she slipped away to the sink and picked up a half-peeled potato. She gazed out at the wind-whipped foliage of the side yard as Sam stared at her back, hesitant. Her hand fished up the peeler from the bottom of the sink. He finally laid a hand on her shoulder, but she gave no hint that she was aware of it.

He moved beside her, and her face in profile seemed graven in stone. It reminded him of the old admiral's face. Indeed, Sam had thought of Kate and the admiral, the uniformed man in the wheelchair, the man of a different era, as being cut from the same cloth—or granite—at Sally's funeral. Both faces had remained utterly rigid, greeting visitors, lingering over the small white casket with its alabaster doll asleep in shirred satin, though at the graveside, Kate's eyes had remained dry while tears coursed down the old seaman's weathered cheeks as he watched the last of his bloodline lowered into the earth.

At the time, he wondered at her strength, admired it among the other things, fine and great, he had come to admire in her, but now Sam wished she would weep—show *something*.

Kate jerked back to life and began hacking at the potato. It was as if her grief was so dislocating that she could not move or think in the normal gradations. She was either utterly still or agitated. Sam gave her shoulder a gentle squeeze, then, at a loss, busied himself with routine kitchen tasks. For a long time the only sound was that of the wind shuddering under the eaves and moaning around the corners of the house.

Before they sat down to dinner, Sam put on a record—Kreisler, a violin sonata, neither grave nor bright—to relieve the atmosphere that hung in the house like a suffocating vapor. Few words were spoken, little was eaten, and eventually they rose and cleared the table. Sam fetched some wood from the stack outside and built a fire while Kate moved things around in the kitchen.

Later, as they watched the fire, Kate said, "I wish I could…" Her voice startled Sam. It had been silence, and more silence—she hadn't said two dozen words the entire evening. The music had stopped, and neither had put on another record.

"Wish you could what?"

"Believe…" She paused, "…the things he said. The Reverend. About it being like a ship going over the horizon…" She turned an odd look on him. It puzzled him, then he understood that she was silently inquiring whether he believed.

He stared a long moment into the firelight. He nodded. "Yes." He turned to her again. "What *do* you believe?"

She held his eyes a while, but then her gaze drifted away. At last she said, "They took us to church, my aunt and uncle. Aunt Grace took it seriously, but Uncle Roy," she paused, "I think Uncle Roy just went through the motions to please Grace and because he thought it was good for us—my cousins and me, I mean—to give us the ethical foundation." She was silent for a space. "But…as to believing…I mean literally…" She shook her head. After a moment, she continued, "I felt closer to Uncle Roy when he talked about 'progress,' and 'science,' than I did to Aunt Grace with her 'trust the Lord,' and 'it's in God's hands,' and that sort of thing. It just never seemed *real*, do you know what I mean?" Sam nodded as she went on. "I was good in science at school, and the more I learned about how the world works, physically, the more the church stories… Oh, I don't know, it all just kind of faded into the background. But I never really rebelled, or anything. The last two or three years of school, I was like Uncle Roy. I just showed up on Sundays to please Aunt Grace."

Sam got up to tend the fire. Kate asked, "How about you?" He poked at the logs, then returned to sit with her.

"My folks weren't church goers. But more than once I heard

Dad say, 'You can pay respect to your Creator while you're plowin' the back forty just as well as you can sittin' in a fancy building in town…maybe better.'" The firelight played on his face. "Made sense to me."

"But what are you supposed to make of an idea like, 'your Creator'?"

He gazed at the fire a while "Oh, we can't know, exactly. Not the way we can know things in, say, a mathematical sense." He shrugged. "That's why they call it 'faith,' after all."

His confidence mystified her, mingled as it was with what struck her as avowed ignorance. "And that satisfies you?" she asked, her skepticism apparent. "It's enough?"

He considered, then said, "The existence of everything…the world… 'the universe'…is proof enough for me. Some say the idea of an infinite, discarnate intelligence is unbelievable. But I say the idea that we…and all this," he spread his arms wide, "arose out of *nothing* is what's unbelievable. Something created it. Something underlies it all. I can't grasp who or what, but there has to be a source. 'Creator,' 'God'…I'm not particular about what people call it, but I never doubted that it exists."

She regarded him silently, this unexpected side of him. Echoes of Guernica—and Sally—whispered at the edges of her mind. "Whatever they call it, it has a vicious mean streak, doesn't it?"

He was silent for a long while. Finally, he said, "Maybe it's us."

She was incredulous. She began to speak but Sam cut her off.

"We were created with free will. That's what's meant by 'created in His image,' you know."

She gave that a moment's thought, but the physics and mathematics she had been taught crowded around the notion and shouted it down, so she replied, "I believe that everything runs according to settled physical laws."

"I respect the laws of physics," he replied. "I take them very

seriously every time I fly an airplane. But they only go so far."
He paused. "In describing reality, I mean."

She shook her head, exasperated.

Sam considered. *This is a minefield…should I even try?* At last,
he decided. He owed it to her—to them.

"Some say, because of the suffering in the world, that God
either doesn't exist or is inhumanly cruel. I say they haven't
thought things through. I believe God gives us choices. And if
He hadn't, we might as well not exist."

She stared, clearly unmoved.

"A human life has meaning only in relationship to God, who
is the source of meaning. A life unaware of God…or in denial of
Him…is transient, unanchored in eternity, and so, meaningless…
at least from its own perspective. But God created us with the
ability to learn and—more important—the capacity to choose."
He paused. "If we didn't have free will, if everything we did was
predetermined, either by your almighty laws of physics, or by
some puppet-master of a god, we wouldn't be human, would
we? Our 'existence' wouldn't be worthy of the term. It would be
no better than not existing at all. Worse, really.

"Three things: first, we know that we don't much value things
that are simply given to us, but we value highly the things we
earn by hard effort. Second, the greatest good is to know God,
because not knowing Him is to be less than whole…and to know
Him is to approach completeness."

The words "less than whole," and "completeness," struck deeply,
stirring a familiar sadness in her. And something else. *Hope?*

Sam continued, "Because God is aware of the first thing, he
gave us the wherewithal to realize he exists and the ability to
approach Him, if we make the effort. We all have the potential to choose for Him or not. If we didn't have the ability to
choose…free will…we'd be automatons, and our existence would

be meaningless. Finally, the Good isn't apparent to the human mind except in contrast to evil. And it's the pain we experience when we choose to deny God that teaches us to choose again, correctly. You could say that suffering...what we see as the evil... is the fire that tempers our souls."

"It won't do," she said, a bit more vehemently than she had intended. "What if you die before you 'choose correctly,' as you put it? Then all your 'tempering' is for nothing...it's just suffering, nothing more. Death finally makes it all meaningless."

Sam smiled. "I'm getting to that."

These questions had been settled long ago as far as she was concerned, but now she was beginning to feel disoriented. And this new side of Sam! He had always been so pragmatic—and here he was, not only going on about God and eternity and good and evil—but unsettling her with it. She had always easily outmaneuvered Aunt Grace's church friends, but none of them had had anything like Sam's view of things. She felt herself being backed into a corner, and so she played her ace.

"Nothing you've said makes any sense whatever of children being blown to bits or burned alive! Those kids in Guernica didn't *choose* what happened to them!" She didn't notice that her breath had quickened, though Sam did.

This went to the heart of the matter, Sam reflected. *Minefield...* How could he make her see what he knew?

At last he spoke. "Try to think of a really terrible day you had when you were a kid."

She uttered a muffled mock-scream. "You keep going off in different directions! Stop it!"

He held up his hands, supplicating. "Stay with me. You'll see what I mean, I promise. Now...a bad day, a long time ago."

She reached back. The third grade. A question about geography—one of Uncle Roy's specialties, about which he had taught her well. She had known her answer was right, and had insisted, but the teacher, wrong—and insecure—had humiliated her before the class. She recalled the sting of the teacher's ignorant sanctimony and the other childrens' jeers.

Her memory unlocked, and a tale of a bedeviled day tumbled from her. The wrongful public humiliation, the fight with her best friend over nothing, the lost lunchbox, the relentless thwarting of everything she attempted, the sense that the world itself was a malign being dedicated to her torment, ending in the sudden encounter with the strange, nervous new boy, the violent shove and her stumble resulting in an ugly gash in her scalp and a lot of blood on her favorite dress. The kind of day that could only have been redeemed by curling up beside Uncle Roy—but he had been out of town on business. Though Aunt Grace had done her best to comfort her, she would never be Uncle Roy. Kate wound down and stopped.

Sam asked, "How much does it hurt now, today?"

She shook her head. "It doesn't. But then, it was just one day out of twenty-six years…"

"Exactly."

"Exactly what?" she asked.

"What everyone knows: time heals." He held her gaze a moment. "Now…what if you had unlimited time?"

She shook her head helplessly. "What can you *possibly* mean by that?"

"Suppose that a human lifetime is just one day in the life of the soul."

Kate stared at him bleakly, as if he'd confided in all seriousness a belief in the Easter Bunny. Sam ignored the implication of her look.

"Just suppose."

His certitude and the trust he had earned from her had kept

her listening longer than she'd ever done before in such discussions, but by now her confidence in him was beginning to fray.

Finally she heaved a breath and shook her head. "I can't begin to imagine. Life is a chemical process, and none of your choices or comparisons or metaphors can give it meaning because death is the end of it all."

He replied, blithely, Kate thought, "You're saying that death is annihilation. It isn't, though."

She leaned toward him. "There's no proof of that. And I should know. I've worked with dying people for…" Her voice trailed off and her eyes went far away. A vivid memory had intruded, that of Sally's dying moment, when she had smiled and whispered, "Suzanne…" the name of her dead sister. Kate stammered, "I…I mean, there's no *scientific* proof."

"There's no scientific proof that we *don't* survive," Sam replied, sounding more assured than Kate. "Neither side can prove its assertion. The only honest positions are to confess ignorance or to profess faith."

The flames crackled as she reflected on all this. In fact, she had seen more than a few instances of dying patients seeming to recognize presences or perceive dimensions invisible to others, but her scientific turn of mind had led her to conclude that these were nothing more than hallucinations characteristic of dying organisms.

"All right, I confess I'm ignorant. Or at least that I can't prove there's nothing after all this. But why are you so sure of yourself? Where do you get this 'faith'? Aunt Grace's church certainly didn't do it for me."

A long silence, then he shrugged and said, "Like I said, I just always believed…all this didn't just spring out of nothing. The farm…the seasons. I never stopped wondering at life and all its forms and its cycles. Then, when I learned to fly…" He stopped.

Some vivid moments of his student days appeared before him, and he smiled slightly. "The feel of it…the way your hands, your senses, all become…" he paused, "your own *wings*. The way the earth and sky…the weather…and lakes and the ocean look from the air. When I saw all that, I *knew* there was a God. I can't prove it, but I don't have to. I don't demand that anyone else believe as I do." He paused again, then looked into her eyes. "But it would be the finest thing in the world to be able to just…say a word, or touch someone…and have them know what I know."

All this was simultaneously familiar yet strange to her. As a girl, she had heard similar assertions from the devout of her aunt's church, but the depth of Sam's feeling, his conviction, were new to her. Still, she pressed again.

"But where does 'survival' fit in? I understand your wonder and your love of nature, but…"

He cut her off. "I have…an advantage." He hesitated, asked himself, again, if he really wanted to go down this road.

"Advantage?"

The sudden intensity of his look startled her. "I'm going to trust you. You're only the second person I've told this to."

She had almost become accustomed to feeling off balance through this talk, so she said, "Go ahead. Your secret's safe with me."

"I crashed."

"What?"

"I wrecked an airplane. Killed myself…sort of."

She was stunned. "What!" *Crashed? Sam? Killed…?*

"I was a kid…just fifteen. Didn't have thirty hours in the air. Just about enough to start thinking I was pretty good. In fact, I was so good I didn't need to remember to check the fuel level before I took off."

Kate's fingertips touched her lips in a gesture half-horrified, half-amused.

Sam continued, "It was a beautiful day for flying, if a little windy. I was about five hundred feet up when the motor quit. But that didn't bother me too much. Lower Michigan's pretty flat…lots of places to land. I picked old Joachim's farm…I knew the place…knew the field behind his barn was nice and smooth, though I'd have to land crosswind. What I didn't know was that the wind had gotten gusty. I was set up pretty well for the crosswind approach…upwind wing low…when a big gust came along. I corrected for it…got the wing down some more, little more opposite rudder to compensate…and then I was into the lee of that great big damn barn. All of a sudden, there *wasn't* any wind. It was like a rug yanked out from under me…and no more than a dozen feet between me and the ground. The left wing dropped like a stone…the tip dug in and the old crate cartwheeled. Remember those old Curtiss Jennies…all wood and fabric? Thing came apart all around me."

Kate's eyes were enormous.

Sam went on, "But the thing is…" He paused. "The funny thing is…I wasn't really there, exactly."

She tilted her head.

"Just as the wing tip hit the ground…now, I know how crazy this sounds…but just before it all went to hell, I was *outside*. I was watching it from about ten feet above. I saw the plane cartwheel, saw myself banging around the cockpit and then getting thrown clear just before the pieces came to rest. Turned out I whacked my head a good one."

She was incredulous, but managed to deadpan, "You're saying you were…in two places at once."

"Depends on what you mean by 'you,' I guess. My body was in the wreck. But what you think of as 'I' was floating up above it all."

Kate wondered vaguely why her credibility hadn't yet snapped.

"After a bit…and that's a funny thing, too…time was…well,

there kind of *wasn't* any time. But anyway, after a bit, so to speak, I did seem to be in two places…the place I described, floating above Joachim's farm, and at the same time moving down some sort of enormous passageway. It was like a dream…you know how things that just can't be seem perfectly normal when you dream? Well, I was in the world, sort of, where it looked like I was killed in a plane crash, and yet I was simultaneously moving up through this giant funnel." He extended his arms up and sideways while his eyes remained locked on hers.

"And that's when things started to get *really* strange. Pretty soon all the business on earth faded away and I started moving really, really *fast*. The funnel, or tunnel, had gotten dark inside, except for…it seemed like millions…of very fine iridescent filaments of every color you can think of drifting on the surface of the walls. I remember thinking that they were so thin, you couldn't have seen them with physical eyes…that they were visible only to a psychic, or spiritual, vision. After a while the passageway seemed to get wider and lighter and I slowed down. Pretty soon it was like I was in the inside of a cloud…no sense of up or down…or anything to get oriented to…and it was very bright. I was so astonished at all this that I really hadn't been thinking, you know, rationally, about any of it, the crash, the tunnel or dream or whatever it was. But then, after I'd stopped moving, or so it seemed, I saw my uncle coming toward me."

"What…why him?"

"That's what I wondered…since he'd been killed at Belleau Wood in 1918." Kate drew a sharp breath. A knife thrust at her heart as memory stirred: Sally's last word, "Suzanne…" But she needed to hear more, and deflected the knife's point.

Sam continued. "He was in his doughboy uniform, like in the picture grandma kept, and he was grinning like he didn't have a care in the world. His old collie, Jake, was there too. Funny thing about Jake…Jim claimed he'd taught him to count. Jim would say 'Jake! Three!' and the dog would paw the ground three times…or 'five' or anything up to about ten, I guess.

"Anyway, I was too stunned to say anything. When he got up to me, he put his hands on my shoulders and gave me a little shake and said, 'If God had meant for man to fly, don't you think He'd'a given him wings?' Then he laughed like it was the funniest thing in the world and steered me toward…well, I'll get to that. We just moved along…could have been seconds, could have been hours. Or years. He didn't say anything more. I was too carried off by it all to talk or even think. I just soaked up the good cheer that rolled off him, and the sense of well-being that seemed to come from every direction."

Sam gazed into the fire. Then, with a half-smile, he said, "Wasn't until later that it occurred to me I might've resented Uncle Jim's making fun of my screwing up and killing myself.

"Anyway, I noticed that it had been getting brighter. Uncle Jim stopped just as I began to be aware of the source of the light. He gestured in that direction…I knew he meant I should go toward the light, and then he…I don't know…faded away, I guess. So I was floating in this light-flooded space, and even though time had, in some way, stopped, right in front of me the light was getting even brighter, until it was as if I was looking right into the noonday sun, only it didn't hurt. At some point it…condensed, you could say…into a disk. A brilliant disk of white light with currents of gold drifting and swirling within it."

He paused and gave Kate a look so long and searching it made her uneasy.

"Now, this is gonna sound crazy," he continued, "which is why I haven't talked about it. But the light was…aware, conscious. And it…well, it *communicated*."

Kate was nearly incredulous. Had anyone but Sam said this,

she would've dismissed him as insane or a liar. But...

Sam stumbled on, "This light *knew* me...it...now, understand, time *there* isn't like it is here. I have to tell you these things one after another, but then, or there, it all came at once. I can't describe it. You'll just have to make what sense of it you can.

"The first thing was the most complete sense of well-being you can imagine. I was home...I mean, you don't know what the word 'home' means until you've experienced it this way. And I was loved. I knew...just knew...even if the worst you can imagine here in this world happened to me, I'd eventually be home here, and all of life's pain would fade...or rather, shrink to a vanishing point...compared with this Eternity. Then, suddenly, a million pictures blew through my mind like a gale. The light was somehow putting these impressions in my head. There were scenes...memories of my life...the good, the bad, and how it all affected other people. The space between people...somehow... disappeared."

He stopped, shook his head. "I... I can't do it justice. And then the light showed me things...I don't know, impressions... about how everything works and why everything is. But it said... that's not right...nothing was 'said,' it all just poured into me... it made me understand that I wouldn't remember these 'secrets' when I went back. That was when some of the joy went out of the whole thing: I didn't want to go back. But I knew I couldn't stay, that there were things I had to do here. Then everything brightened even more and filled me with the thought...the knowledge... that I couldn't even begin to understand how much I was loved."

His eyes went far away again.

"...Couldn't even begin..." he murmured.

He turned back to her. "And then I was staring up at old Joachim's granddaughter."

He interrupted himself, "Oh...about 'how much I was

loved'…It never occurred to me that it meant me alone. That applies to *everyone*. It's just that not everyone's lucky enough to get knocked on the head hard enough to find out." He laughed at his irony.

"So there was this little girl with big green eyes gazing down with the most serious look in the world. Her dad and granddad were there, too, but they were smiling and wiping blood off my face. Took me a while to figure out that they'd moved me… they were afraid the wreck would catch fire…they didn't know there wasn't any gas to burn." Sam chuckled, remembering. "Old granddad Joachim said, 'Thought you were a goner, Sam!'"

"How badly were you hurt?" Kate asked.

He pointed to the scar high on his forehead. "Just this. Shook the Joachims up, though. They told me later I wasn't breathing when they first got to me, but when they picked me up I jerked and sucked in a big breath."

Something moved on the periphery of Kate's mind, something that made her wary, but she waved it off, and returned to Sam's story. Again she felt an urge to dismiss it—but on what grounds? She knew Sam was honest, even to a fault. And anyone could see that he was of sound mind and that he was convinced of the reality of his experience.

"What do you think…" she asked, "what do you think it means? What do you think the light was?"

Sam considered before he replied, "I thought it was God… naturally enough, I suppose…but later…"

He seemed to drift away again. Then he said, "I never read much of the Bible, but you know, parts of it are all around us, woven into the culture." He paused, then went on, more certainly, "The line that kept coming to me again and again was, 'I am the light of the world.' Over time…couldn't tell you how, or when…I came to the conclusion that the Light was Christ."

"So…you became a Christian?"

Again, he reflected. "Yes. No…what I mean, I suppose, is that a lot of people who call themselves Christians would deny that I am one. I never joined a church…" He paused again. "I got even more like Dad…the farm, the sky, and then the ocean when I came out here…" He repeated the all-embracing gesture he'd made earlier. "All Creation is my church. But yes, if the light I saw is Christ, then I must be a Christian. But whatever I am, there's nothing I believe more than that the Light revealed Truth to me that day…and made me certain of immortality."

Kate held his gaze a while, then turned to the fire. *How lovely it would be to believe. But…* She shook her head slightly as she cast her thoughts back over the path along which her view of the world had grown.

"But…what *about* science? Evolution? That pretty much finished religion for most people I knew in college. Aside from you, I don't know anybody who *really*…"

She halted, and Sam stepped into the gap. "I never did buy the 'Darwin makes God obsolete' argument. As far as I can see, science only reveals a bit about how God goes about His business. It lifts the hood a crack and lets us peek at the motor. I mean, you can't be stuck on the idea that God's an old man with a long white beard, floating in space, pulling strings, throwing lightning, eager to punish you, if you…you know. No, we can barely begin to understand Him. You can look toward Him, point to Him… and if you're truly devoted, or gifted for a moment as I was, perhaps touch Him briefly…and *feel* for an instant the peace, the mercy, the love. But *fully grasp Him?* No, not from here. Not in this life." He paused.

"Remember Jake, my uncle's dog?" Kate nodded. "Assuming he really could count to ten, even so, if he'd lived to be a hundred, you couldn't have taught him calculus." She frowned. "A dog doesn't have the capacity to know calculus. And a human being simply doesn't have the capacity to fully know God. So He gives us Christ…Himself in a form human minds can, to some extent, recognize. So that we can…begin…to relate to Him.

"What people don't realize is that if you aren't flesh, but rather, a soul…which you are, and if that soul is eternal…immortal… which it is, and if God loves you, which He does, then ultimately, nothing truly unbearable can happen to you."

Stillness then, for a while—as Sam again relived his epiphany and again wished he could fully share it, and as Kate struggled with the opposing currents that whirled inside her.

The thing at the edge of her mind tugged again and spurred her wariness, and made her afraid. Something Sam had said…

Little girl…green eyes. It all came flooding back. Sam's story had distracted her from her sorrow, had conduced to the respite that grief mercifully grants from time to time. But now it fell upon her again in all its oppressive blackness.

Kate aged even as Sam watched her. She gasped a deep breath, and her tears suddenly welled and spilled. He gathered her to himself as she finally wept for Sally. She sobbed as if she would never stop, as if the sun would never rise again.

19

On Earth, the hard times dragged relentlessly on, the horrors of war burgeoned, and the fear of war grew in the minds of those not yet involved. Then, too, Christmas drew near. In consequence, ever greater waves of the subtle, unformed mental currents that might have become prayers rose toward Heaven's lowlands, and thus, as popular as Branch 92's new musical activities were, the ever greater numbers of birds arriving required that they be suspended. Nearly everyone was working overtime, so Laurel found herself back at the pool in the familiar—and frustrating—pursuit of clues. Not surprisingly, without the diversion of music, she slipped back into a nearly obsessive preoccupation with Kate and the restless, and still fruitless, search for a way to deliver the Gift. Now the only diversions from her vigil were those rare occasions when Victor and Emilia, or sometimes Benedict and Kaira managed to persuade her to slip away and join them in exercises of the Old Way.

Lately, at times, the water itself seemed bent on foiling her. Only after endless delicate adjustment of the stones would it yield up a clear image, and then only fleetingly. Laurel had managed to summon only fragmentary pictures of Kate at work and with "the Man," as Laurel thought of him. She could never tune his image finely enough to see his features, or hear clearly when Kate spoke his name, but she could sense his warmth and his devotion to Kate, which made her feel both guilty and driven,

145

that her inability to complete her mission created a barrier between the two below.

Other things she had felt and inferred in recent sessions also troubled her deeply. She lately sensed a multi-layered grief that seemed to combine both present loss and the fear of anticipated loss. Now it occurred to her that though she had observed Kate at the hospital, she hadn't seen the little girl in several sessions, and the implications chilled her. Then, too, there was the peculiar event a little while ago, when she had snapped awake from a deep sleep to a crushing sense of loss and misery that she knew could only have been connected to Kate.

Laurel touched the stones and the water momentarily revealed an image of Kate in the hospital lunchroom, staring vacantly—at what Laurel couldn't tell. So intent was she on the wavering image, she didn't notice Ambriel's approach.

He was about to speak when the gentle rolling thunder of a great flock of doves rushing toward the overburdened Aviary, a living overcast, distracted both of them. They watched until the birds receded in the distance and a hush fell over the garden around the pool.

"Anything?" he asked.

She shook her head, then raised an eyebrow to turn the question around.

He shook his head. "Nothing worth mentioning, Love. The others really were quite thorough in the times before you arrived. I've reviewed everything they put down, and have undertaken a good bit of my own research, but…" He shrugged. "I'm sorry."

They turned toward the sound of another flock some distance off, and watched its shadow flicker over distant hillsides.

"Christmas is coming," Ambriel continued, "And of course that always means a rise in the traffic Gerard and his crew must deal with, even in times of diminishing faith like these.

"And there's the war. Many blazes have already broken out and it bids fair to involve most of the Earth, sooner rather than later. More and more of those below know it's only a matter of time before they're drawn into the it, so they grow apprehensive and quite rightly ask for protection as the storm gathers."

Another flock, with another muffled roar, passed overhead as if to emphasize Ambriel's words.

"As to your problem," the elder continued somberly, "that just *right* thing we want…evades me." Laurel nodded, listless.

"And what's the occasion for all this hilarity?" Gerard's voice surprised them.

"What are you doing away from the 'Works?" asked Laurel. "Ambriel was just telling me you've been busier than ever."

"Missed you, Love. And besides, everyone needs a break now and then." He looked back and forth at the two. "No progress, then, I take it?"

The two shook their heads in unison.

At last Laurel broke the silence. "Ambriel mentioned the war down there. I'd forgotten."

Since Ambriel's mention of the coming World War, her eyes had blinked rapidly a couple of times as they always did when a ghost of her lost days tried to bubble up to conscious memory.

War. She shivered, and a strange mixture of emotions began to enfold her like evening mist from the ocean: though specific memory remained out of view, an infinitely deep sadness, fear in lesser proportion, and an indescribable yearning. *Why must it be so? Why can it not be otherwise? War…*

Seeking to escape this suffocating sensation, she looked again to the pool. She touched the stones—and a hurricane of sound and images exploded in the water.

A city burned as warplanes droned overhead. Bombs burst, randomly punctuating the rhythmic banging of anti-aircraft cannon. Gerard and Ambriel were galvanized, instantly drawn to the pool by the horrendous cacophony.

The horror deepened—flames roared as they engulfed entire city blocks. The image shifted, people ran through streets, showered by the flaming debris of tall buildings. Another shift—a small child sat, wailing, before the wreckage of a house. For an instant, Kate's face appeared, intense in flickering light, then vanished. A momentary darkness returned to the water.

Laurel gasped, her hands trembling on the stones. Then light returned, softer this time. The sound of a string quartet wafted up, accompanying the image of a wedding. A dark-haired woman and a tall, fair man stood at the altar. Yet again, the light whirled, the image shifted. A huge, sleek airplane surged by, very close. Through the flickering of the image, fragments of bold letters on the plane's side appeared: "House"…"Inter…" Abruptly, the light and sound turned harsh again. Images flashed in fast succession. A conflagration—a massive firestorm. A fresh, unmarked grave, picked out among many. Faster and faster the images whirled as the sounds merged into a merciless, cacophonous roar. Laurel recoiled from the stone as if it had burned her, leaving it wobbling in its cradle amid total chaos of light and sound.

Ambriel grabbed the stone, stopped its teetering. Instantly, stillness and silence returned. The elder turned to Gerard, eyes wide.

"Did you see? She touched several different times there. At least two *possible* futures…as nearly as I could make out." Gerard nodded, tense. Laurel, still half-stunned by the spectacle, looked back and forth between the two.

She turned to the pool, laid her hands resolutely on the knurled stones, and forced herself not to flee as the wartime scenes returned, even more terrible than before, in a vivid, ever shifting catalogue of horror.

The apocalyptic wail of an air raid siren assaulted their ears. A great fleet of bombers flowed like storm clouds through the night sky, casting its thunder on the blazing city below. The whistle of falling bombs blended into overlapping discordant shrieks as they accelerated into the inferno, and smudges of flak bursts bloomed like hellish black flowers, hurling steel hail through the formation. A shell made a direct hit on one of the raiders. Its midsection ignited in a great sheet of flame, and burning men fell as the plane broke into a shower of blazing fragments.

The scene shifted to a makeshift operating room where a team of doctors and nurses labored. Sounds of the battle outside continued, muffled, and blended with the moans of the wounded. One of the nurses looked up from her work. Laurel gasped, recognizing Kate. Then, a rippling string of explosions—ever louder, ever closer—until in an instant the room, the team, all vanished in a tremendous detonation.

Laurel screamed and leapt back from the pool as the horrific image faded. "It was Kate! I saw her! I saw her die! Oh…oh…"

Ambriel's eyes remained fixed on the water. "I know that city. It's London. And I'm sure we just saw some of what they call 'The Blitz' down there."

"And I thought we were peering into Hell itself," remarked Gerard. "Beggin' your pardon, Love."

"For all their blindness," continued Ambriel, "they've a sure eye for finding ever better ways of destroying one other."

"But—what does it *mean?*" Laurel demanded, trembling.

Ambriel looked out over the water, into space, for some time. *I cannot lie to her. But must I tell all? Would I sin to omit telling her that though this is only a* possible *future, Kate's appearance in it makes it a virtually certain one, should she start upon its path? But would Laurel guess anyway? Likely she would. Is there any way I can* not *tell her? No.*

"It means, Love…" he faltered. "It means that if Kate should go to London, she will die."

"Then I've got to go to her! I've *got* to!"

Aurora hurried up to the group, speaking urgently even before she reached them. "I'm sorry to interrupt, but, Gerard, they're asking for you at the Aviary. And Ambriel, Abel wants you at the library…" She stopped, struck by the somber atmosphere. "What is it? What's happened?"

After a moment Gerard answered. "Nothing…yet."

Laurel stood beside the pool, staring into the darkness there.

20

Kate and Sam picked at their plates in the Mission Café. Despite the midday sun that bathed the room through the window wall facing the ocean, and the upbeat music on the radio, gloom hung over them.

Sam broke the silence. "We both know you can do better…"

Kate seemed not to hear, but at last she replied, nodding listlessly, "I know."

In a cross-country navigation exercise, they had flown a triangular course northwest over the water to Santa Catalina Island, then east to Palm Springs, and finally south, back to San Diego. She had done well enough on the first leg, but then anyone would have—Santa Catalina was in view from the time they took off, so it was merely a matter of drilling a hole through the sky toward a bump on the horizon.

The second leg started to come apart soon after they made landfall near Dana Point. Kate couldn't actually see the second waypoint, as she could the first and so had to rely on dead reckoning. She drifted off course and strayed from the correct altitude.

Sam intervened more and more, offering gentle reminders. He was easier on her since Sally's death; she had become so fragile, he knew he had to abandon the crisp style with which he had brought her along earlier.

On the final leg back to Ryan Field, they stopped fooling themselves. Sam flew them home, though he passed control to her as they entered the pattern, which resulted in a sorry end to the dreary exercise. Consistent with the poor altitude judgment she'd displayed the whole day, she flared out four feet too high and dropped the Taylorcraft onto the runway like a set of car keys hitting a kitchen counter. They were silent on the drive to the Mission Café for their customary post-lesson lunch.

Sam faced a dilemma. Both his temperament and his love for her made him considerate of Kate's frail emotional state. On the other hand, he had a responsibility to see to it that his students were safe pilots. Painful as it was to admit, Kate's flying since Sally's passing could not be described as safe, but he simply couldn't find the words for what had to be said without wounding her.

Another part of his mind wondered at the depth of Kate's grief, so deep, it was as if she had lost her own child. What he couldn't know, of course, was the secret dimension of her heartbreak, the irrational "bargain" she had made with fate and that she had gradually—recklessly—come to believe in. She therefore grieved not only for Sally, and indeed she suffered as if the girl had been her own, but also for her shattered hopes of becoming whole, and of learning what love is, and so becoming worthy of Sam's devotion.

Duty at last got the better of Sam, and he began to speak, but Kate cut him off, lifting her hand in a gesture of preemptive surrender.

"I know what you're going to say. I shouldn't be flying…not after the last couple of lessons." An uneasy silence hung between them. Sam started to reply, but again she cut him off, slowly shaking her head. "No, don't. I know how disappointed you are. I know you had high hopes for me. It's just…it's just…"

For a moment it seemed that she might weep, but she controlled herself. He put his hand on hers, but it was like stone, as in the early days, before Sally, before Kate's fond delusion had grown. Sam, relieved of having to say the thing he'd dreaded saying, now needed to speak, but found himself at a loss for words.

Again, Kate filled the silence. "I'm thinking about making some changes…"

Something twisted in his belly. "What kind of changes?" he managed, though he was sure he didn't really want to know.

"Oh…I don't know. Maybe just a vacation."

"Sure, that makes sense, some time away from the…the old…" He waved, vaguely. "Then you can make a fresh start, when…" He faltered. She had that awful statue-like look again that he remembered from the graveside service.

Kate looked at her watch. "Well, I should go."

Sam could think of no real reason that she should, but he had formed the habit of handling her delicately, so he rose with her.

When he dropped her at her car at the airfield, he said, "Come by the usual time and we'll talk…" Again he faltered. "We'll work it out." Still distracted, she only nodded, got into her car and left with only a hushed, "Goodbye."

❧

Kate thought of her bungalow on the beach at La Jolla as a hand-painted miniature; small, adequate, but elegant in an understated way. The five rooms, all on the small side, were saved from being cramped by the open floor plan—and by Kate's loving touch and good taste. A good-sized, fenced-in back yard bordered the low cliff and overlooked the beach with a magnificent view of the Pacific Ocean.

In the time following Sally's death, the back yard was Kate's sanctuary. Wrapped in a quilt against the cold December wind, very still, her eyes hidden behind dark glasses that reflected the sea and the lowering sun, she huddled in a chaise-longue on the patio. She remained motionless when a hummingbird chased off an interloper. She didn't move when a pair of seagulls wheeled, keening, in a half circle low over the yard then dropped behind the lip of the cliff, nor did she appear to notice the click of the latch on the gate that opened to the walkway beside the house, nor the footsteps across the patio. She moved only when Dot sat on the edge of the other chaise, when she turned to touch the outstretched hand. Then she resumed watching the sun ease toward the water. Dot turned toward the ocean, too. They might as well have been a pair of statues, but for Dot's occasional discreet glance at her friend.

At last, Kate spoke. "I don't know what's wrong with me, Dot. I've seen children die before."

Dot leaned toward Kate and spoke. "There was a kid on my ward once, back in Vermont. He and his little pals sneaked into a building site…boys, you know. A lot of bricks fell. We all knew he wouldn't make it. But I fell in love anyway. He was ten." Kate seemed absent again. Dot continued, "The point is, you survive. I got busy. I didn't give myself time to cry."

Kate turned to Dot, removed her sunglasses, her eyes red-rimmed. "I thought I was finally becoming whole. She made me feel almost complete…after a whole life with an empty space inside." She put her glasses back on and turned again to the setting sun. The ghost of her sad, crazy bargain haunted her. "I…I thought I might start to see Sam…differently…the way a whole woman might…" A tear slipped from beneath the dark glasses. She took a moment to control herself. "…a complete woman."

Dot straightened up and sat on the edge of the chaise. "Ted's been talking with Sam. If you don't already know…if I can put it bluntly…you don't have money problems anymore. Your project is fully funded, if you want it to be."

"It would be so unfair to him. And so dishonest of me." She

paused, sick of the words that had returned, merciless, to inhabit her mind like an occupying army—deathly sick of them but powerless to refute them, helpless before them. "There are strings, you know. Sam's up for helping 'someone very close,' his own words…and fair enough. But that rules me out. I'm just not made to be 'very close' to anyone…not that way. But you know that."

She wondered aloud, half to herself, "How am I going to tell him?"

Dot leaned forward and her voice took on a slight edge. "It's time you got realistic, Kate. You have to do this, you know you do, never mind God knows how many kids that *need* you to do it…and will need it soon. And Sam needs you, too." She moved closer. "Marry him. You'll learn to love him."

21

Immeasurably far away, yet oddly near, another shared in Kate's and Dot's conversation. Laurel leaned over the pool, hands on the knurled stones, eyes following the shifting images, Huey perched on her shoulder. A turn of a stone, and the two nurses suddenly came into focus, accompanied by a papery, hollow-sounding facsimile of their voices. "…you'll learn to love him." Laurel leaned closer. The image dissolved into a blur of colors, the sound to a garbled murmur. Another tweak—the sound and image returned. "…I couldn't deceive him…"

Laurel's eyes narrowed. *Deceive whom? What do you mean?* She fine-tuned the stone.

"…leaving. I'm quitting the hospital…the house…" Again, the fickle water threatened to disappoint her. Again, she caressed the stone.

"…over for me here…his hopeless love…my wretched lack of…whatever it is. And Sally…"

Laurel's shoulders drew up. *I don't like the sound of this…*

"…I'm packing it in. I'm going to London."

Laurel's eyes widened in horror. "No. *NO!*"

With a quivering hand the angel clutched the stone as the Earth image went in and out of focus. "…the Blitz…where Sally was…a memorial to her…"

A beat of her wings, and Laurel stood on the pool's rim, quaking. "Not London! Kate! Not *LONDON!*"

Her attention turned inward—to a vivid picture of a young angel, submerged, motionless, tangled in undulating seaweed. Another, frozen in a dimensionless void, glazed eyes staring to infinity. She wilted for an instant, but then made herself straighten. She inclined her head, looked to the sky as if she might find there some help, an answer. For a long moment, she stood, a statue. *I must go to her.*

Then, a great beat of her wings—but as she rose, her foot struck the knurled stone and toppled it off the rim. A kaleidoscope of images exploded in the water, obliterating the last view of Kate, just as Laurel plunged in a great fountaining splash. Huey followed instantly.

൦ൠ

A short distance away, Aurora, Ambriel and Gerard hurried toward the village. Aurora glanced over her shoulder, back toward the pool. "I shouldn't have left her," she fretted.

"You have your duties, too, like the rest of us," said Gerard.

"True, but all the same..." She sighed.

The sound of a distant splash interrupted her. They froze. The first to recover, Gerard bolted back toward the pool, the others in trail. They arrived, breathless, to find the water still roiling.

"*No!*" Aurora recoiled, stricken.

A blue-tipped feather rocked on the dark, restless water.

Part 2

A Journey

22

On a chill December morning an ocean of fog rolled above the Golden Gate, the strait where San Francisco Bay and the Pacific Ocean collide in cold, perpetual violence. On the vaporous sea floated an angular orange island—the summit of the south tower of the great suspension bridge that spanned the strait.

So widespread was the fog that no man or woman directly witnessed the brilliant white beam that knifed downward from the zenith to the tower's top, striking there a blinding light, a facsimile of the sun, that blazed for an instant between the tower's twin spires.

A bird, or, say perhaps a spirit, roaming hereabouts might have been puzzled, after the burst of golden light subsided, to see what for all the world appeared to be a white chrysalis resting atop the south tower of the Golden Gate Bridge, and more puzzled still to see a hummingbird lift from the cocoon to circle the tower once, soar vertically to a hundred feet above the vaporous sea, then drop like a meteor and level out within a foot of the damp white chrysalis with the high, hollow, bamboo flute tail feather note that the males of his tribe sound when they are especially concerned to assert themselves.

The chrysalis stirred. A closer examination would reveal a sleeping angel, light golden hair and white, blue-tipped feathers wetly clinging to her body as she lay in a fetal position on the hard, cold steel. The hummingbird fanned her face with his

161

wings until she eased upright, opened her eyes, and yawned. Her full wakefulness needed some time, but then she stood and gave a mighty shiver, casting in all directions a burst of droplets that bloomed in a great rainbow all around her before the rising sun.

As she gently beat her wings dry, she surveyed her surroundings, the clear sky above, the sea of fog that lay at her feet and the few terrestrial features that the fog did not conceal: the tip of the bridge's north tower, drifting in and out of rolling reefs of mist, the peak of Angel Island to the northeast, and the low, dark rippling silhouette of the hills to the east. Then, just for a moment, the vapor parted to the south, revealing San Francisco's north shore. The hummingbird floated beside her, creating in the moist air his own bits of shimmering rainbow that shifted with his odd pivots and turns and complemented the play of sunlight on his iridescent feathers.

Laurel stroked the hovering hummer's head and said, "She's down there somewhere, Huey."

Wings dry, she prepared to dive, then halted, her nose twitching. After a long teasing prelude, an enormous sneeze wracked her, as Earth's coarse nature exerted its influence on her subtle frame. In a moment she recovered, then spread her wings and dove from the tower to plunge, followed closely by her companion, into the sea of vapor.

But of course, Kate wasn't anywhere near them. When Laurel had inadvertently kicked the stone from the pool's rim, the water's focus was, as Gerard might have said, "knocked into a cocked hat," the random result being that she missed her intended destination by about five hundred miles.

The instant of Laurel's return to Earth, the moment of the great brilliant burst of golden light at the top of the tower, went largely unobserved because of thick fog and the early hour, most of the area's residents being asleep.

The visible light, however, was only the least of the event, as other, greater, energies were at work. These were subtle, but owing to the nature of their source, profound of result.

From the tower's peak, a pure point of energy expanded toward infinity at a speed greater than that of light—the Earthly understanding of physical laws being irrelevant to the power that underlay the event—in a pulse that enveloped the local area and everyone and everything within it in an instant.

Among the results: The edges of a fault in the Earth's crust, miles beneath the strait, the pressures between them having built for ten thousand years, softened and merged and subsided, and an imminent cataclysm far greater than the one that had occurred here thirty-four years earlier was averted.

In Marin, as the pulse swept through him, a businessman tore in half a railway ticket and destroyed the letter that was his passionate response to the invitation from the woman in New York, and decided it would be better—altogether better—to remain at home with his wife and young children.

At the moment Laurel materialized upon the tower, almost directly below her, a young woman clutching the bridge's rail quivered as the pulse struck her. Then as the woman stared down at the wild, cold water, her expression moved from despair to perplexity to something like wonder. She recoiled from the brink, stood still a moment, then retrieved a folded leaf of paper along with the rock she'd placed on it beside the bridge's walkway. She drew a deep breath and tried to grasp why her many troubles, the torments of the last weeks and days and hours—unbearable, she had concluded—seemed suddenly, somehow, bearable. At the same time she became aware of a vague sense of gratitude budding within. She turned and began to walk toward home. After a dozen paces, she hurled the rock over the rail and tore the paper into small pieces, letting them flutter away.

Among the multitude of other such effects, one more bears telling: On Lombard Street in San Francisco, a tall, pale man in a long dark coat followed two teenage boys at a discreet distance, observing them, in and out of the drifting fog, as they ambled, smoked hand-rolled cigarettes, furtively tried the locks on a shop and a couple of car doors, and intimidated an elderly pedestrian. The man smiled as the larger of the two boys suddenly, for no apparent reason, seized the smaller in a hammerlock and knocked him against an alley wall until he whined for mercy.

The pale man was reflecting fondly on the logic of natural selection when the pulse of Laurel's arrival reached him. It struck him first in the pit of his stomach; his gorge rose—hot, sour acid burned his throat and filled the back of his mouth. It cost him more than a little effort to keep from vomiting. He spat, and steam rose from the pavement—one might have thought from the cold of the morning, but for the sulphurous tint of the vapor.

In the next instant he felt the pulse's greater effect—an inchoate sense of peril, of dread, of a menacing brightness in his mind that he must isolate lest it leap to his soul and annihilate the darkness there that was his essence. He so commanded himself, then swallowed hard and turned quickly one way then another, like a dog who detects an intruder, until his gaze inclined and settled, the fog notwithstanding, on a sure line toward the invisible summit of the Golden Gate Bridge's south tower. He forgot the rough boys and walked on, absorbed and grim.

❦

While Laurel and Huey glided Earthward through the dense vapor, a thirteen-year-old boy meandered down a sidewalk just off Lombard Street. He was handsome, if a bit gangly, and tall for his age, or would have been had he not slouched. He was slender, a condition common in the Great Depression, and his hair was too long, even for those meager times. But what caught the eye was his improvised attire, that of a knight of the Middle Ages. His costume was of common stuff but ingeniously made, notably the sword, a two-handed Scottish claymore, wooden, scaled down to fit a boy, but modeled to look quite like the real thing—and the helmet, not the discarded cooking pot popular among boys as fanciful but less resourceful, but rather a good if not perfect reproduction of a 14th century piece, painstakingly wrought of hammered and crimped pieces of cast-off tin. He carried the helmet under his arm, and the sword, in authentic fashion, in a sling over his back, so that the long hilt rose over his shoulder. The cloak that flowed over his shoulders completed the impression of a spectre from medieval times.

Strange that in the mid-twentieth century a boy might imagine himself a knight? Perhaps, but in 1940 both children and adults still read books and knew history and cherished the best of the past. And a few, those blessed with much imagination, chose to live there.

Suddenly the boy halted—seized perhaps by the memory of a heroic moment in some legend he'd lived in the hours he had spent in the public library—clapped the helmet on, drew the sword in a great overhead sweep and began the ballet of the swordfight with an imaginary enemy. At age twelve, when he had made the sword, with hours of study and careful craft, it had fit him like the weapon of William Wallace. But a year had changed the proportions of things; the boy had grown an inch or two and could handle the sword with one hand, as if it were a rapier. He advanced through the numbers—thrust, then retreat—the standard drill—ending in a flourishing parry, then forward again—*Attack!* The more engaged he became, the straighter he stood.

The strange, invigorating charge that had passed through him earlier had awakened his heroic imagination. At the end of his second offensive advance, however—just at *Thrust!*—which brought him to Lombard Street, a high-pitched shriek froze him in place.

"Froggie, lookit!" The smaller of the pair of teenage thugs, like a dog on point, thrust a finger at the would-be knight. The two were a half block away.

A nasty grin grew out of the dullness of the bigger boy's heavy, ill-favored face as he began a slow advance. "I see him, Dink. If it ain't my old pal, Wacky Jack…" Dink slunk in trail behind him.

Jack's heroic posture sagged back into its habitual slouch.

The tip of his sword wobbled feebly up and down, then sank as he backed away from the thugs. Memories of past humiliations assaulted him, try as he might to push them away.

This encounter recaptured the attention of the tall, pale man, who had been trailing along behind the rough boys as he pondered the import of the strange and unpleasant sensation that had surged through him a little while earlier.

The bigger boy, Froggie, made a false lunge toward Jack, and stopped, grinning. Jack stood his ground, trembling only a little. The claymore wavered.

"Sir Nance-a-lot!" Dink shrilled, half-hidden behind Froggie.

Jack made a tentative thrust toward the hoodlums, then caught a glimpse of the pale man's eyes as he approached behind them—and was undone. He turned and ran, the two thugs charging in pursuit.

He didn't get far—a truck lurched out of an alley and stopped, close enough to the nearest wall and to another truck parked on the street to hem him in. Trapped, he whirled and held his sword before him, more as a shield than a weapon. He tried to defy his tormentors, but managed only a wordless croak. He tried again, a quaver belying brave words. "Away with ye! Stand aside, I say!" The thugs eased closer.

"Whoa, that's some pretty tough talk, Nancy. Dink, you feelin' scared yet?"

Dink, still half behind Froggie, eyes bulging, head and shoulders bobbing up and down in excitement, replied with an idiot's giggle.

ભ

At this moment Laurel glided out of the low overcast, Huey in trail. They descended into the alley behind the idling truck that had trapped Jack.

Panting, the angel leaned against the dingy bricks. The smells of the city were noxious to her, and she coughed. And, too, she was cold—she shivered and drew her robe closer about her against San Francisco's damp December chill. The hummingbird hovered protectively before her, attuned to her distress.

"This is going to be harder than I thought, Huey," she said, still breathing hard. "Feeling kind of woozy already." She fought off a sneeze.

After a moment's rest she stepped, hummer alongside, to the sidewalk on the other side of the truck from Jack—and immediately tripped and nearly fell over a metal cover that two workmen had removed from a utility compartment in the sidewalk. The two grimy workers looked up and found themselves face-to-face with an ethereal, wide-eyed, winged apparition accompanied by a droning, hovering, glittering hummingbird. Everyone stared for a frozen moment, Laurel and Huey traded quick glances, then the angel gave the workmen an ingénue's smile and backed into the alley and out of their sight. Huey zipped after her.

"I din't see nothin'. Not a blessed thing," said one of the workmen. The other rolled his eyes toward a tap house just down the street. They rose and walked the few yards to the saloon.

In the alley, Laurel slumped against the wall. "Well, that

167

was…awkward." Her eyes flickered; something stirred deep in her memory. "Ah, yes…I can hide the wings." She arched her back, tentatively, grimaced and drew a sharp breath. Then her wings began to furl and compress. She gasped as her eyes filled with tears, but continued the painful operation. Soon, her wings were reduced to a flat bundle easily concealed in her robe. Huey likewise grasped the need for discretion and found his own concealment within Laurel's cowl.

03

On the sidewalk, Jack was backed up hard against the truck as Frog and Dink stepped slowly closer, all grinning menace. Jack's head whipped this way and that, only to confirm that there was no escape route. He waved the claymore unconvincingly at the bullies. "Rogues! Ye'll end on the gallows, else by the sword!"

The thugs howled with laughter. "Jeez, Dink, dig the wacky lingo!"

Meanwhile, the tall, pale man had crossed the street, covertly watching the showdown with growing interest. He fixed his gaze on Froggie, then slightly raised his right hand. The hand closed into a fist.

The atmosphere surrounding the boys' confrontation suddenly changed, as if the air had cooled by a few degrees. The cruel banter ceased, and a silence heavy with menace descended on the scene. Froggie slipped a hand into the pocket that contained a long switchblade. He stepped closer, his eyes growing deader and colder, until his foul breath washed over Jack's perspiring face.

The silence lengthened, then the thug spoke in a flat, quiet voice. "I'm sending ya back to Camelot, Nancy. In a box." His hand, filled with the ugly knife, began to emerge from his pocket. The pale man clenched his fist harder.

Suddenly, with a roar, the truck heaved out of the alley and onto the street, its noise breaking the dark spell and drawing everyone's attention. Dink was the first to recover. "Froggie! Lookit!" he shouted, as he thrust his finger at Laurel, now fully exposed, slumped against the wall on the far side of the alley, her breath still fast and labored from the painful exertion of hiding her wings.

The hoodlums gaped. Froggie forgot his knife, forgot Jack, forgot his murderous intent, and advanced on Laurel, who for all appearances was no longer an angel, but a very pretty twelve- or thirteen-year-old girl dressed in a strangely elegant fashion given the time and place. Her eyes widened as Froggie approached, his ugly face cracking into an uglier grin, revealing badly neglected teeth. He put on what he believed to be a suave manner. "Hiya, sister! New in town, ain't'cha!"

On the principle of honor among thieves, Dink staked his claim, "'Member, Froggie…I saw her first!" for which he was paid with a hard backhand to the side of his head. He staggered, almost fell, and looked up at Froggie, dog-like and baffled, but doltishly unresentful.

The bigger boy was almost upon Laurel. Her eyes widened yet more, and belatedly she looked left and right for an escape. Froggie rested a hand on the wall beside her, barring her way to the mouth of the alley. Dink, still rubbing his head, moved to her other side, like the pack animal he was. Huey zoomed out of his hiding place in Laurel's cowl, and made a close pass at Froggie, wings droning menacingly. He barely noticed, so thoroughly was he absorbed with Laurel.

With his free hand, Froggie fingered the fine material of Laurel's robe. "Nice stuff! Rich kid, huh?" She grimaced, recoiled, and suppressed the gag that Froggie's breath induced. "Lemme tell ya somethin', sweetheart, there's a lotta creeps in this town. Yer gonna need a man to watch over ya, see?"

His hand dropped to her waist, and his face leered mere inches from hers. She choked on his noxious breath.

ↄ౩

Five hundred miles to the south, Kate was cleaning out a closet. On a sudden impulse, she found a box of art supplies and rummaged in it for a drawing pad and pencil.

She began to sketch a feather, but stopped, dissatisfied. She discarded the page and started over, this time with the outline of a face, delicate and heart-shaped, framed in long, wavy hair which fell to the waist of the slender figure she sketched. Kate paused, frowned, and added—wings. *What in the world am I doing?* She stared, lips slightly parted, then tore the page out and started over again. When she again drew the wings, one drooped, as if broken.

ↄ౩

In San Francisco, Laurel's situation grew more dire. Froggie leaned to close the gap between himself and the angel. Laurel's eyes, in a desperate hunt for some possible escape, touched Jack's, who had crept closer to the ugly scene. By then, the thug was so close to Laurel as to cast a shadow over her face. He leaned yet closer, puckering his loathsome lips.

A voice rang through the alley, "Unhand her, villain!" The voice broke—the first two words girlishly high, "villain" in an authoritative bass.

Froggie spun—

CRACK!

—and dropped like a sack of cement. Stunned, he groped a hand to the side of his head. Blood oozed between his fingers.

Jack stood over him, gripping his sword in both hands. The wooden blade was cracked, skewed to one side. Laurel and Dink

170

stared at him. Jack's eyes again met Laurel's, and his submission was complete. For a moment, all was utterly still.

Then Jack went a little mad. As Froggie wobbled on hands and knees, the knight kicked him in the rear, hard. The punk's face slammed the filthy pavement. Jack kicked him again, harder. He threw the broken sword aside, grabbed Froggie by the belt and collar, yanked him to his feet, horsed him around face-to-face and with a solid right, broke his nose. But it wasn't over—Jack turned the offender round again and delivered a series of kicks, driving him from the alley. Froggie recovered only enough to look over his shoulder at Jack in utter astonishment, and then began a shambling, bloody retreat down Lombard Street.

Jack picked up the broken sword, brandished it at the devastated hoodlum's back, and yelled, "Banishment or death! For death shall surely be thy lot if ever again ye show thy vile face in these, my lands!"

He lowered the sword and stared after Froggie. After a moment, he turned back to the alley, where Laurel and Dink remained frozen, staring at him. Then at once Jack and Laurel turned to pin Dink in their gazes. The trembling little hoodlum's head twitched back and forth between the two, as a puddle surrounding one of his shoes grew larger by the second. Then, when Huey dropped out of the sky with an explosive *Chirp!* to hover droning and glaring about an inch from Dink's face, he was undone. He shrieked and darted between Laurel and Jack, out of the alley and down Lombard Street.

In the tavern a couple of doors down, the two workmen who had been rattled at seeing an angel in the alley shared a pitcher at a table by the big plate glass front window. Their heads pivoted as Froggie galloped by—bleeding, stumbling and blubbering. The two exchanged a glance. Then Dink flew past, howling as if pursued by the devil himself, but as it was, chased by a wildly chittering hummingbird. One of the pair refreshed their glasses and remarked, "I din't see nothin' neither."

In the alley, Jack and Laurel stood face-to-face for a long, strange moment. Then Jack dropped to one knee, took Laurel's hand in both of his and kissed it. She stared, astonished. For the first time in many minutes, her head cleared enough to permit a complete, if not very helpful thought: *I've fallen into a madhouse.*

She searched for words, but Jack spoke first. "Sir John of Lombard, M'Lady, servant. Or, if it please thee, Jack."

Madhouse. She started to reply, but a sudden need to sneeze overtook her. She fought it for a moment—and lost. Ah-*CHOO!*

Jack leapt to his feet. "Lady! Thou art unwell!"

She dismissed his concern with a wave. But she was wan, and shadows lay beneath her eyes. Jack removed his cloak and draped it over her shoulders.

She smiled and drew the cloak about her. "Thank you. I'm fine, really. But how *can* I ever thank you…um…Sir Jack? You were magnificent! Absolutely fearless!"

Gravely, he regarded her, then sank to one knee again, his head bowed, as Laurel tried to make sense of recent events. After a long meditative moment, he looked up to her. "No, Lady, 'tis I who owe thanks to thee. Thou hast given me a gift greater than life itself." She frowned and tilted her head, baffled. "Courage, Lady! Thou gavest me courage. But for thy presence, the game should have ended differently." He bowed his head, briefly, then looked up again, a hint of shame suffusing his face. "This I know… from experience most bitter."

With something like exasperation, Laurel tugged him to his feet. They faced one another, he worshipful, she with amused tenderness. She took his hand and he let himself be led, slouching, toward the alley's end. She looked over her shoulder. "By the way, you can call me Laurel."

Jack made a courtly bow. "A noble name for a heavenly being!" He paused, frowning, then his eyes widened. "Heavenly indeed! No lady, thou…rather, an angel!" He pulled free of her hand and struck a heroic pose. "What but an angel's grace couldst put wretched fear to flight? By my Faith, words are worthless to express my gratitude!"

Having no idea how to respond to this, Laurel just raised her eyebrows and made a tight-lipped smile as Jack babbled, then walked on. Jack slouched along behind her as she left the alley.

Across the street and half a block down, the tall, pale man's dark good humor had vanished, the chilling smile gone, replaced by the grim slash that was his mouth in repose. He took Laurel's measure with great care before he turned and walked away.

Laurel looked left and right as she came to the sidewalk, then turned to Jack. "You don't owe me any thanks…*you* rescued *me*, after all." He started to kneel and bow again, but she grabbed his hands and kept him on his feet. "Listen to me. I have to find my…um…sister Kate, and there's no time to lose. She's in trouble and she's somewhere here in San Diego."

For the first time, Jack's worshipful demeanor flagged. He frowned and observed, "But…thou art in San Francisco."

She hardly heard this. Her eyes were closed as she slowly turned a complete circle, hoping to sense Kate's spiritual signature and thus the direction to her.

Suddenly, her eyes flew open and she gasped. She found herself facing a billboard above the street, an advertisement for a first-aid cream, which, in the giant picture, was applied to a child's knee by a smiling model who, but for her hairstyle, might have been Kate. "That's her!" Laurel exclaimed. "That's *her!* Do you know her? Do you know where she is? Oh, I've *got* to find her!"

Perhaps by coincidence, the billboard lay south by southeast from her, exactly on a line toward San Diego.

173

Jack pivoted to follow Laurel's pointing—now trembling—finger and studied the image. His frown deepened as he shook his head. "Nay. That one I know not, Love."

The color drained from his face, only to rush back in a violent blush. He fell again to his knees. So absorbed was she in the Kate look-alike on the billboard that it was a moment before Laurel noticed Jack's latest prostration.

"Fie! Fie on me, to take such liberty!" he cried. "Canst thou forgive me?" His face was an inch from the pavement. "Though I do not pretend to deserve thy mercy."

Laurel frowned, baffled. "What in the world are you talking about? 'Liberty'?"

"I called thee…I spake as if to an equal. My shame is…"

Suddenly she understood, and laughed. "Oh! You mean, 'Love'? That's all right…they call me that."

He looked up. "Who doth?"

"Everyone. It's because…well, they just do. You might as well, too."

Jack flew into another paroxysm of self-abasement. "Oh, that I were worthy!"

"Oh, *stop*!" She pulled him to his feet. "Don't you have any idea how brave you are? Don't you have any idea how strong you are? Don't you…"

"…Fain wouldst I believe it so!"

"…have any idea how *ridiculous* you sound?! It's what, 19… uh…? Anyway, who *talks* like that now? Why do *you?*"

Jack's passion abated. "Um, 1940, actually."

"Oh. Well, anyway…" She turned back toward the billboard.

Jack removed his helmet, looked at her in a different way, and when he finally spoke, dropped the knightly argot. "It's that…it's because…I don't belong here. Not here…not now. I was born too late. So I read. And I dream. I make my own world."

"This is the only world you have, for the moment," she replied. Then she turned from the billboard and regarded him, eyes narrowing. "You just need to learn to like yourself, that's all."

He looked down again. "There's nothing to like."

She closed her eyes as if listening to a far-off voice. Then in a quick motion, she cupped his face in her hands and looked him hard in the eye. "Before the day's over…well, you'll see."

She released him, and then smiled blithely, as if the moment's drama had never happened. Again she started to turn toward the billboard, then halted. "By the way, this kingdom of yours, 'Lombard'…did you make that up, too?"

"Well, yes and no." Jack pointed to a sign on the nearby corner: Lombard Street.

Laurel laughed, touched his arm. Then she became serious. "I can't thank you enough for defending me. And for your company, which is so much finer than you think. But I just have to find Kate. Can you help me get to San Diego? There's not a minute to lose."

He considered. "There's the train. You could catch the Coast Daylight to Los Angeles, then it's just a short run to San Diego."

She brightened. "Perfect! What do I have to do?"

He shrugged. "Buy a ticket and jump aboard."

She tilted her head quizzically.

Jack continued, "That punk called you 'rich kid,' and you do kind of have that look about you. Say, if you have money…real money, I mean…you could fly down there, like a movie star! How are you fixed?"

"Fixed?"

"Yeah, you know…Fixed. Do you have money?"

"Well, I have my robe, and…ah…Ah-*CHOO!*"

"Bless you. Are your folks really rich?"

"…and my sandals. And…" She gestured, palms up. "That's all."

"I guess not, then," said Jack. He sat on the curb and pondered. "Darn. Well, I wish I could buy your ticket for you, but… Anyway, let's head for the railway. I'll think of something on the way."

They walked east on Lombard. By the time they arrived at the cable car stop at Hyde Street, Laurel was pale and a little short of breath. Shadows marred the porcelain skin beneath her eyes. Jack guided her to a bench. They sat, and after a moment she leaned against him.

After a short wait, the cable car arrived with a rumble of steel wheels and a clanging bell. Mike, the burly conductor, hailed the young knight, "Well, if it ain't Sir Jack! Hop on, son, you and your girl." He reached to help Laurel up, appraising her as he did. "Say, you never let on Guinevere was *that* cute!"

Jack took the kidding in stride, but, ever a slave to his mania for precise historical detail, replied, "You're thinking of King Arthur's queen, Mike. This is Laurel."

Mike warmed to the two and made a bit of a show. "Ah, well. A princess, then." He doffed his cap, made a courtly bow. In the same spirit, Laurel dipped a curtsey, but wobbled a bit on the way back up. Mike eyed her closely as he guided her to a seat. Jack offered Mike some coins, but the conductor winked and waved him off. Jack smiled his gratitude.

Mike turned serious. "Girl looks a little peaked, son. Good of you to give her your cloak, but she needs something more." He snapped his fingers. "Hang on. One o' them swabbies left something." He hurried to the other end of the car and returned with a sailor's pea coat. "There y'are, Love," he said as he draped it over Laurel's shoulders. "A mite big, but it'll keep the chill off."

She snuggled into the oversized coat, yawned, and drowsed. In a few seconds she was asleep, leaning against Jack. The clang of the cable car's bell as it got underway didn't disturb her in the least. After Mike concluded his business of collecting fares and answering questions, he took another long look at the sleeping angel, then raised his eyebrows at Jack. The boy replied with a shrug and a shake of his head.

When the car reached the Union Street stop, Laurel's eyes popped open to "…*ding dong verily the sky…is riv'n with angel sing-ing!*" as a band of street musicians performed a brisk rendition of the ancient carol. In a second she was on her feet and at the car's rail, just in time to join in the last of the sinuous "Gloria" and the emphatic "*Hosanna in excelsis!*" She leaned out toward the musicians. In the instrumental interlude she breathed deeply, as if she had been too long under water. She absorbed the healing music, and the grip of Earth's unwholesome influence eased. She took another deep breath and her pallor diminished.

For the band's part, their attention was irresistibly drawn to the waif in the oversize blue pea coat, gliding into the moment on the cable car, and a mutual affinity immediately sprang up. Before the car eased to a halt, Laurel hopped off to join the players, who welcomed her with their eyes as they played, as if they'd been acquainted all their lives.

She joined them, her voice bold, bright and clear, on the next verse: "*E'en so here below, below…*"

The little band, fairly competent to begin with, suddenly, uncannily, improved by an order of magnitude. Between lines, Laurel breathed, deeply.

"…*and,* ee-*oh* ee-*oh* ee-*o-o-oh…!*" Symbiosis: her color steadily improved as the group sounded ever more glorious.

The modest crowd around them began to swell. And to sing. "*Gloria…!*" the long, dizzying, ecstatic melisma of the ancient carol's chorus.

Jack, still aboard the cable car, observed all this with puzzlement. *What's gotten into her? What's going on?*

Mike was aware of the odd goings on, too. He tapped the

boy's shoulder, then his watch. "We gotta be on our way, Jack. Is she coming?"

Jack dithered for a second, then made up his mind. "We'll get the next one, Mike. Thanks." With that he jumped off and worked his way through the burgeoning crowd toward Laurel. By unanimous unspoken assent, she had become the group's leader. As such, she turned to face them and began conducting as she earlier had conducted the avian chorus at Branch 92. A magnificent tide of music flooded the neighborhood.

She was absorbed, lost in musical ecstasy, when a hand seized her arm. Jack turned her to face him. Laurel's eyes turned to him, but she didn't see him. "What are you doing?" he demanded. She returned to the here and now with a look of bewilderment. Jack released her arm and reminded her, "You said your sister was in some kind of trouble."

Her hands flew to her mouth, and mortified tears started. "Oh! I…I…" She floundered, then tried again. "Sometimes, when there's music…that's just *all* there is…"

"Well, come on then." He had been as captivated, as mesmerized as anyone there, and by the time Jack took her hand and led her to the cable car stop, another car was arriving. The group stopped singing and playing to bid Laurel farewell. None of the singers objected—by the same invisible spirit that united them for a few moments in Heavenly music, they understood that she must leave.

They resumed singing as Jack and Laurel boarded the car. The farther the car carried the angel from them, the more commonplace they sounded.

23

Gerard sat on a low stool, hunched over the pool, hand draped over one of the knurled stones. For hours, since Laurel's plunge into these very waters, he had searched for some sign of her. Knowing her motivation, he had mainly searched Earthly precincts, though a nagging fear plagued him, that some other, unthought-of influence might have cast her off to—well, to where indeed? The thought chilled him. Images drifted through the water, none of any apparent significance or with any unifying theme.

Aurora joined him. He looked up and nodded a silent greeting. "You look dreadful," she observed.

Gerard responded with a brief, humorless grin. "Not the merest trace of her." His head sagged in fatigue. "Ah, there's such… such worry and trouble…and hell down there. It's got the ether all in a swirl and a churn so that you can't make head nor tail nor night nor day of any of it." He looked up at her again. "Maybe you'd have better luck. Will you try?"

"Of course."

Gerard rose, stiff from his long vigil, and Aurora took his place. She bowed her head in meditation for a few moments.

Let the love of all who love her guide me now.

She touched the stone, and immediately an image, very dim, of Kate appeared. The picture dissolved into fragments of the London wartime scenes witnessed earlier. Just as quickly, those images faded, to be replaced by the scene of a wedding all bathed in golden light. A string quartet played, as Kate and Sam, radiating joy, stood at the altar.

Again the pool's surface broke into a kaleidoscopic whirl of apparently random images: children attended by a medical staff. Many buildings—interiors and exteriors—each larger and finer. Gerard and Aurora knew that they were seeing events in accelerated time. Fragments of words flew by, some attached to the buildings, others appearing in contexts impossible to make out. "House…" "Inter…" "Sal…"

Mingled with all of these images were portraits of Kate, older in each succeeding image. Her hair silvered, her eyes grew ever more serene. Her beauty deepened.

The water now glowed with a soft, golden light. Images of a multitude of children of all parts of the world filled the pool, most bearing scars from burns, but all now healthy and cheerful. Oddly, though they seemed to appear as a group, their styles of clothing were of different places and times, spanning several decades of the 20th century.

The smiling children vanished, replaced by a clear, steady image of a female television news reporter of the late 20th century, standing on an airport tarmac with Kate and Sam, still handsome and elegant in their 80's. In the background was a jumbo jet, "SALLY'S HOUSE INTERNATIONAL" emblazoned in huge letters on its side.

The shift of images caught the reporter in mid-sentence: "…Nobel Peace Prize for what many describe as one of history's greatest private humanitarian efforts. Operating for over a half-century, Sally's House has helped thousands of war's youngest victims all over the world. Specializing in burn…"

Aurora released the stone; the image faded. She and Gerard stared at one another in wonder.

Jack and Laurel strolled down Market Street in comfortable silence. Laurel had no trouble keeping up, for the time being. The music of the street performance had re-energized her and, for a time, ameliorated the Earth sickness They had gone quite some way when Jack said, "I haven't come up with a single thing… about getting money for your ticket, I mean." He glanced at her, his look an apology. She remained silent as they walked on. "But there *is* a way you can catch a train to San Diego." He stopped, turned to her. "It wouldn't be very comfortable. And it could be a little dangerous."

Laurel was unfazed. "That's all right!"

Jack smiled, admiring her. "I like you more all the time. Anyway, you could hop a freight…with two conditions. One, girls can't hop freights, so we'd have to make you look like a boy; two, you can't go unless you go with Tony."

"Who's Tony?"

"A professional hobo…and a friend of mine. He'll keep you safe. But if we can't find him, you're not going."

She gave him a narrow-eyed look. "Hm."

☙

Ambriel, Aurora and Gerard bent over the pool. Ambriel held the stone, controlling the flow of the runic text, which, to their surprise and gratitude, had reappeared. He struggled to control the capricious text, finally straightening to look at the others, grave. "Everything points to two…and only two…possible futures." He paused. Gerard and Aurora, impatient, gestured for him to continue. "Kate *must* marry this Sam fellow."

Aurora asked, "And what's he to do with it all?"

"He's part of the plan for which the Gift is meant to prepare Kate. Sam is *the one* with whom she can fulfill her destiny: to build the great institution that will save uncounted children."

"And if they don't marry?" Gerard asked.

"Then events flow into the other future. She'll go to London." Ambriel's expression became graver still. "And die there."

ᔕ

Sam sat at his desk going over AirWest's books. What he saw pleased him—and provided some small relief from his preoccupation with Kate. Though the country was in better shape than it had been five years earlier, no one but the government happy-talkers denied that it was still in the grip of the Great Depression. Though the federal government's massive and unprecedented intervention in the economy had put some people to work, now, seven years after the terrible year of 1933, unemployment was still over fourteen percent.

Sam closed the ledger and leaned back. He was deeply grateful for his good fortune. Despite the decade-long economic debacle, AirWest had managed to stay afloat—barely—for the first year, and had grown steadily from then on. Sam understood that he benefited from the leading edge of what would bring the *real* recovery, the war effort. He thought of Kate's scruples about accepting help from war contractors, but, he reflected, he was a pragmatist. He didn't see any virtue in standing in a bread line or swinging a pick on a public works project, even if he could get such work, when he could do well doing what he loved. Someone was going to make the money anyway, and if he funneled much of his fortune into Kate's project, then so much the better.

A knock on the door roused Sam from his reverie, and Greg stepped in.

"Hi, Boss!" Greg, good aide that he was, was attuned to his chief's emotions, and for the last while had been aggressively cheerful on the theory that the mood of a workplace amounted to the sum of positive and negative attitudes. He dropped a sheaf of papers on the desk in front of Sam. "Howard just checked in…en route, on time."

Sam nodded. "Good."

Before Greg could bring up the next line on the agenda, another knock on the door sounded. They traded glances, both knowing it was about the regular time for Kate's lesson. Sam had let slip to Greg he wasn't even sure she'd come today. Greg, as much as he liked Kate, almost hoped she wouldn't. The air around her had been poisonous since the little girl had died.

Sam braced himself. "Come in!"

He stood when Kate entered. She wore a dark blue cloth coat and a scarf over her hair. She had always worn her leather jacket and her hair in twin ponytails for her lessons. Sam and Greg exchanged a glance. In the uneasy silence, Sam said, "So, check on that…other thing, will you, Greg?"

"You bet, Boss." He and Kate traded ghosts of smiles as he passed her. She called after him, "Bye, Greg." He paused halfway through the door, turned and gave her a nod and a closed-lipped smile in reply, then shut the door behind him.

Sam gestured to the chair in front of his desk as he sat down. After an awkward silence he said, eyeing her coat and scarf, "So… looks like we're not on today. That's…"

He was going to say, 'That's OK,' but Kate silenced him with, "Sam."

It sounded like a world crashing down. He bashed on, ignoring the churning in his guts. "What about that vacation? Are you taking some time off?" even though he knew that wasn't the case.

Kate drew a breath and let it out. "Sam. I'm…I'm…" She stalled. "I'm leaving the hospital." Sam frowned. "And I have to stop taking lessons with you."

He tried to smile, with a slight shrug, as if to remind her,

'Well, we talked about that possibility, didn't we…?' but she rolled over him.

"I'm quitting my job and selling my house and moving to London."

It was a kick to his belly.

By a magnificent feat of strength she didn't burst into tears. She was *so* close to complete. If she couldn't love him romantically, she had no such deficiency of empathy, in recognizing the pain she brought him.

Sam heard the rest, more or less—but by the word "London," he'd heard all he needed to. He nodded dully as Kate, fighting tears the whole time, stumbled on about "…where she could do some good…" And, "she haunts the ward…can't bear to take myself to work…" and so on.

He tried to break in: *Yes, but what about your…our?…project with the clinics? 'Where you can do some good?'*

But Kate hurried on, faster and faster, her words mingling with her thoughts, and she wondered how she could tell him what torture it was to remain here, to remain near him. *Oh, God…look at me!* She could love a child—another's—as her own, she could love a woman the way she loved Dot, as the best of friends do. *But Sam…Sam…* She had come to realize that in all the ordinary, everyday ways she already *did* love him—only that—*so close!*—only that she couldn't—couldn't find the place inside where she could give herself, body and soul. She was a woman dying of thirst standing before a great, sparkling, life-giving fountain—but whose lips had been sealed shut and she knew—*knew*—that she would soon slip into… After all, look at the absurd tale—the lie—she'd told herself about Sally and what her recovery would mean, and her own lack, and—*Sam*. Did she need any more proof that she was soon to… *If there is a Hell, it must be quite like this.*

She finally rambled to a halt and the two sat silent and desolate.

"We'll talk," said Sam at last. "Not now…I know. But we'll talk again."

He walked her to her car and watched until she drove out of sight.

24

Jack and Laurel walked past Market Street's shops, all gaily decorated for Christmas. Laurel lingered for a moment at a newsstand, somber, scanning front-page accounts of the London blitz.

The healthful effects of her communion with the street players were beginning to fade, and she struggled to keep up with Jack. Faint shadows again lay beneath her eyes, and she'd been wracked by occasional sneezes.

Jack, moving ahead, stopped in front of a pawn shop. He stepped inside, and after a few seconds poked his head out and waved for Laurel to join him.

He stood between two tables stacked with second-hand clothing. After sizing Laurel up for a moment, he began rummaging through the old clothes. Laurel picked through them too, only mildly interested, fashion decisions being of small concern to angels.

Her attention wandered, and then she spied something that did indeed inflame her interest. She made a beeline for the back wall of the shop, which was crowded with musical instruments, among them many violins.

She at once identified the best fiddle and the best bow—which is to say only the best of a bad lot. She plucked them off the wall, tightened the bow and tuned the violin. *Now, what shall it be? Bach...but which?* She remembered the newspaper stories of the London battles, which recalled to her the terrible scenes revealed in the pool at Branch 92. She shivered and her breath halted; she closed her eyes and, after a moment of perfect stillness, drew the bow. The somber Partita in D minor, Allemanda filled the shop.

Heads turned and people gathered. A supernatural calm fell over Laurel, and the crowd grew as she spun out the stately melody. At the end of the first theme, she looked up to see a throng of grave faces surrounding her. *This won't do...*

She acknowledged the people with a nod, and then began "The First Noel." She played a chorus and a verse, and a few among the growing crowd tentatively sang along.

She segued into the "Wexford Carol," and a small, bent Irishman who had come to San Francisco in the previous century wept a little, as he always did when he heard the ancient melody. A woman who taught music admired the way the child added a stern, stepwise bass in the second verse and noted the way she suggested, as in the manner of Zen painters, the inside voices, just the well-placed note or two, to richen the music. The old teacher's practiced eye knew the fiddle for the low, pawnshop relic that it was, and marveled at the brightness and élan she heard now, so like that of the young prodigies, and the smooth, assured gravity, so like that of the older masters that she had heard, when she could afford to, in the less expensive seats high in the back of the symphony hall.

Laurel moved seamlessly to "O Holy Night." The crowd joined her, sounding finer than anyone could expect of a random gathering. Concluding the carol, she left the singers behind as she wove a handful of Christmas melodies into a shimmering tapestry, transfixing the still growing crowd.

She brought her improvisation to a triumphant climax, then reprised the individual carols. The gathering joined together with unbridled passion, sounding like virtuosi who had sung together all their days, and the dingy little space rang with their voices.

∞

In La Jolla, Kate continued to pack. She emptied the cupboards of her small kitchen, sorting everything into boxes, a small one labeled "Save," a large one marked "Give Away."

A preoccupied look, as had come over her at the time of Laurel's encounter on Lombard Street, came over her again as she began to hum the carol that Laurel now played five hundred miles to the north. Compelled, she hurried to the sunroom where she had left her drawing things.

Under her pencil a face took form on the page. Laurel— almost. She paused and studied the emerging portrait. *I can* see *her…why can't I bring her into being?*

She stared at the pencil in her hand. Her eyes widened; she leaped to her feet and rushed inside.

∞

The San Francisco pawnshop nearly burst with the crowd. More and more people flocked in from the sidewalk, listened in wonder to the extemporaneous chorus, and then joined it. At the middle of it all, Laurel, like the sun, anchored them like planets in their orbits. They were hers—but for one: a tall, pale man in a long dark coat who stood unmoving at the rear of the crowd, his face half-shadowed by the brim of his hat.

The shop's owner, a florid, heavy-set man, a man not much concerned with appearances, emerged from a back room, astonished at the spontaneous concert that had taken over his rooms. He was a man who, from long experience, could shrewdly assess what sort of price a run-of-the-mill trumpet or banjo or fiddle might bring, but there was not so much as a speck of music in his heart. He was a businessman first and last—and yet he joined this glorious, ever-enlarging celebration of Christmas that had invaded and occupied his dingy little shop. For the first time in many years, he sang.

He'd sung only a few lines, though, before the tall, pale man pinned him in his gaze. His voice halted as a sensation as of ice water pouring down his back made him gasp. The spiritual gravity of Laurel's music was powerful, however, and the heavy man found himself uncommonly stressed, as if he were a planet caught simultaneously in two mighty gravitational fields—Laurel's sun-like influence on the one hand, and that of a black hole on the other. His mouth opened and closed like that of a fish drowning in air, but he couldn't manage to produce so much as a syllable. His eyes, too, were fish-like, wide and blank under the baleful stare of the tall, pale presence across the room.

Laurel intended only the merest sliver of time between one piece and the next, but as she finished a carol, that tiny lull was all the pale man needed. In that slice of silence, as his eyes transfixed the heavy man, he raised his hand, so slightly, and made a fist.

Instantly the shop owner's mien changed from mesmerized to menacing. He spun toward Laurel as she began "Joy to the World." Stronger than ever, the joyous throng raised their voices in company with Laurel as the newly-mad man began to shove his way through them.

Near the front of the shop, Jack completed Laurel's new traveling wardrobe. He set a pair of small boots on top of a short stack of shirts, socks, coveralls, and a few other odds and ends. Then he pulled a handful of coins from his pocket and counted. *Should be enough.* He started toward the counter at the rear of the shop—and found himself, like the others, compelled to join in the singing.

Suddenly, the shop owner stood glowering before Laurel. Eyes closed, soaring on waves of glorious music, she was oblivious to the threatening bulk before her.

Lunatic fire filled the man's eyes as he roared, "Whaddya think yer doin'?" and snatched the violin and bow from Laurel's grasp. Stunned, she could only stare at this unexpected nemesis.

The crowd went silent but for a few isolated murmurs. The unhinged man waggled the bow in Laurel's face and raged, "This ain't for kids, dammit! This here's a fine old instrument! Ya keep yer little mitts…"

Laurel took a step back. The absurdity of the man's claim about the violin, which he clutched as if it were a chicken he was about to strangle for his supper, stunned her.

"*Fine?*" she said at last, cutting him off, incredulous. She leaned forward. "It's *junk!*"

The madman exploded. "You don't talk back to me, missy!"

He had gone, in mere moments, from confused to indignant to possessive to enraged to apoplectic—some of hell's proudest offerings to the human condition. His face was purple.

"You're a runaway, ain't'cha? Stolen coat ya got there, huh? Three sizes too big! Robbed a sailor, now you think yer gonna rob me too, do ya?"

Laurel took a step back. *Madhouse…*

The man raved on. "Well I'll turn ya in, see!" He took another step toward her. "I'll have ya locked up…like ya belong!"

With "locked up" he had her complete attention. She was at last wholly present, back from Music, and fully on guard.

Her mind focused. *Locked up! …Kate…go…NOW.* She shot a glance over her shoulder—and saw the way out. She took a step back. Huey's wings buzzed within her cowl.

The poor bedeviled shop owner lunged. He grabbed air as Laurel hopped backward out of reach. Huey launched out of her cowl—straight at the man's eyes—with a pulsing, menacing drone. The unexpected aerial assault broke the man's thrust, and sent him reeling backwards, hands flailing to save his eyes. Laurel turned and ran for the door.

Jack saw most of this and, overcoming his astonishment, fired a deadly look at the madman. Inspired, he overturned a long table loaded with pots, pans and other assorted metal ware. The man whirled toward the deafening, jangling crash, dithered between that chaos and the rapidly retreating waif until he was overwhelmed by another series of fast, hot hummingbird attacks.

Jack scanned the shop, saw Laurel moving fast toward him. Their eyes met and he jabbed his thumb toward the door. In less than a second she was out and racing down Market Street. Huey zoomed past Jack like a winged bullet, out the door and after Laurel. Jack sprinted out last, clutching the bundle of things he had gathered for Laurel. The three hustled down Market Street for a couple of blocks before ducking into an alley.

Catching his breath, Jack eyed Laurel with grave concern. "That's the second time you've gotten all carried away with your music. If Kate really needs you…well, you'd better try to get a grip on yourself." Laurel's gaze met his briefly, then she closed her eyes as she sank to the pavement, her head in her hands.

Jack continued, "He really could've had you locked up, you know, and as far as I can tell, you've got no help…no folks, no money, no friends. If the cops put you in the lockup, how are you gonna help Kate? See what I mean?"

She finally looked up at him, desolate.

"Let me tell you something…you want nothing to do with cops. Doesn't matter that you haven't done anything wrong. The *best* that can happen is they'll slow you down. And you don't have any time to lose, right?" She nodded. He smiled, trying to look more confident than he felt. "Well, let's go."

25

In La Jolla, Kate ransacked her purse until she found the feather that had fallen to her the day she had met Sam. She picked up a knife and fashioned the feather into a quill pen. She hurried, and in her haste, cut her finger. A trickle of blood oozed.

⟡

In the alley off Market Street, Laurel winced and clutched her hand.

"What? What is it?" demanded Jack.

She stared, puzzled, at a wound, a wound identical to Kate's so many miles away. Jack was at first perplexed—and then angry. "Did that big...?" Blood oozed from Laurel's hand.

"No. He didn't touch me. It just...just now..." She shook her head. "I don't know." She began to hum, very faintly, while gently stroking the wound with her other hand. In a few seconds, the wound was healed.

Jack looked at the place where the wound had been, where there remained not even the slightest mark or scar, then at Huey perched on Laurel's shoulder, and then long and deep into Laurel's eyes. *Who is she?* What *is she...?* Despite his youth, and despite his prodigious imagination, Jack began to question his sanity. He took a deep breath, then started to ask a question.

With the gentlest smile, Laurel shook her head, and whispered, "Don't." He continued to regard her gravely. Finally she said, "You'll understand. In time."

The moment ended. Jack closed his eyes and sighed. "All right," he said at last. He handed her the bundle he had taken from the pawnshop. "Try these on."

She unrolled the bundle—a pair of overalls, two blue cotton work shirts, two pairs of socks, boots, a couple of big red hand-kerchiefs, a knapsack and a big, floppy hat. She took off the pea coat, returned Jack's tunic to him and put on one of the shirts. Jack turned his back while she slipped into the baggy overalls and busied himself packing the other things into the knapsack.

When he finished, he handed her the big hat. "Stuff your hair in it," he said. Laurel twisted her hair into a loose coil, piled it atop her head, and pulled the hat over it. Jack appraised her and shook his head. "You're really not cut out to be a boy. But it might do long enough to get you to San Diego."

She frowned. "Did it cost a lot?"

He gave her a sly half-smile. "Not a cent."

She tilted her head, puzzled, then puzzlement gave way to alarm. She squirmed as if the new clothes burned her. "You… you *stole* these?"

He grinned broadly, perhaps a little proudly. "Think of them as a gift from that guy…to make up for the way he treated you. That was…"

"But you can't just…"

"…no way to treat a lady." Jack's anger rose as he recalled, "When he tried to grab you, well…" But Laurel's look silenced him. She flicked a glance at her clothes, then fixed Jack in her gaze again.

He sighed. "OK, tell you what…I'll go back and pay him later…" She smiled at last, heaving a relieved sigh. Jack continued, "…when I'm grown up." Her jaw dropped, and she started to protest, but he waved her to silence.

He looked at her long and earnestly, and, she thought, with a dignity and maturity that were entirely new in that moment, then he drew the broken sword from its harness and dropped it on the stained, cracked cement of the alley. He looked at the battered helmet he'd managed to hold onto through the day's ordeals, and let it fall with a clunk on the pavement.

Laurel's eyes posed a silent query. He answered, "Don't need 'em anymore. Come on. We still have a way to go." He stood, very straight, and led her from the alley.

慓

A portrait grew under the bold, fast strokes of Kate's quill, the feather that had parted from Laurel's wing when she was so spectacularly carried to Branch 92, that fell at Kate's feet, and that Kate had nearly thrown away, but instead kept for no reason she could explain.

Quickly, surely, the image developed. Long wavy hair, a heart-shaped face, lopsided wings. She paused to study her work, and then with another flurry of the quill added large eyes. She picked up a stick of chalk and made the eyes blue.

慓

Late afternoon light filtered through the beginnings of fog as Jack boosted Laurel up the fence bordering the rail yard. She was weakening again—the blocks-long trek had intensified Earth's effect—and she fell over the other side. Halfway down she managed to grab on and clung to the sheer chain link wall for a precarious second like a kitten on a curtain, then dropped to the ground in a heap.

Jack scrambled over, quick and agile. He lifted the waif to her feet and paused to look at her in wonderment yet again. "What are you made of, feathers? You don't weigh *anything!*" Before she could reply, he took her hand and led her deeper into the yard through drifting tendrils of vapor.

Dense odors of coal smoke and creosote assaulted Laurel's nostrils, while the banging of cars, clanging of bells and loco-motives' chuffing filled her ears. *I don't like this place…not even a little bit.* She shivered and drew closer to Jack. A slow series of percussive *chuffs* grew louder, distinguishing itself from the cacophony of industrial sounds, and an accompanying series of smoke puffs advanced behind a string of boxcars that stood parked in their path. As they approached the track, the locomo-tive rolled into view from behind the boxcars. Laurel clutched Jack's arm, stopped him in his tracks. She pulled back away from the smoking steel monster, her eyes wide. After she regained possession of herself—no small struggle—she wondered, *Why does that thing fill me with dread?*

The locomotive and the couple of cars attached to it rolled on, and Jack tugged Laurel back into motion. Finally, after crossing many tracks, the boy stopped beside a string of boxcars coupled to a hissing locomotive.

"This is the train for Los Angeles. Now, if only he's here…" He pulled the ever-weakening angel alongside the train, as he called out, "Tony! *Tony!* You here?" For the length of the train and back again, there was no reply.

A bell began a rhythmic clanging. The locomotive emitted two deep blasts from its whistle, then a labored *chuff* as it began to move. A series of rippling crashes followed as the behemoth took up the slack between the cars. Jack punched the air in his frustration.

Laurel watched the creeping train. She summoned all her strength, faced down her fear. *Nothing matters but Kate.* She turned to Jack. "I can manage. Boost me up."

He whirled on her. "Are you nuts? Don't even think about it!"

"It's not your decision to make."

He started to protest but faltered before the steel that was suddenly in her eyes. Still, he tried, "It's way too dangerous."

"If I go now, she might have a chance. If I wait, something terrible will happen. And you've seen me...I've already let myself get distracted. I can't stop now."

He was tormented. He knew she was right, but the sense of responsibility for her that had grown within him, together with his knowledge of the dangers she faced, made him balk. He slowly shook his head as his eyes pleaded.

But she was resolved. "Please. Help me."

They stood, a long time, eye-to-eye, her pale skin, the shadows under her eyes, signs of the relentless progress of the Earth sickness, belying an adamantine strength of spirit. Then he surrendered. He made a stirrup of his hands. Laurel smiled—more of relief than of anything like triumph. She leaned forward and kissed Jack's cheek. She stepped into his linked hands and he boosted her through the door of the creeping boxcar. He slipped her backpack from his shoulder and tossed it up to her.

He walked alongside the car, desolate, his face turned up to her as a flower turns toward the sun.

Laurel smiled down to him. "I told you."

He returned an inquisitive frown.

"That you would be different before the day was over."

He shook his head, puzzled. "Yeah? And?"

"Don't you see? You don't have to *pretend* to be a knight anymore!"

He walked faster as the train gathered speed. Then he smiled. Laurel waved and blew him a kiss. Jack stopped. He stood very straight and tall, waving until she was lost to sight.

26

After Jack disappeared from view, Laurel collapsed on the boxcar's straw-strewn floor. She had willed herself to look much better than she felt when she persuaded Jack to let her go alone. Now her breath came fast and shallow, and she was paler than ever. She fought off a sneeze for a long, heroic moment, but finally lost.

Ah-ah-*CHOO!*

A second sneeze wracked her, and she used the big red hand-kerchief that Jack had acquired for her. She crept to the forward end of the car and scraped together some loose straw to make a cheerless little bed. Her knapsack served as a pillow.

She was almost asleep when the sound of a phlegmy cough made her snap up on one arm. She peered into the darkness of the car's far end, and made out several semi-reclining figures. One of them passed something to another.

During the Great Depression, millions of men traveled the rails in search of work, if it could be found, or of charity, if no work was to be had. Dangerous, rough, dirty and illegal, freight-hopping became a way of life for many of the great army of the unemployed and dispossessed who roamed the country for a decade. Most of this great cohort were essentially decent men forced by global financial calamity into a way of life they never would have freely chosen. But inevitably, some were not of the highest virtue.

From the deepening shadows came another cough and a rough, slurring voice, "Gimme the jar 'n' go see 'bout that kid." One of the forms lifted a dark shape to his face, tilted his head back, and took a long, noisy drink. Like a snake, a hand darted and snatched the jar from his grip, and the rough voice growled, "I *said*…go have a look at that kid, Deke, ya lazy sack o'…"

Deke's answer was a resentful whine, "Awright, awright! … the hell, huh?" He struggled to his feet. He was tall and gaunt, just under six feet, and perhaps about thirty years old. He wobbled, partly due to the train's motion, partly due to his advanced state of inebriation, and staggered toward Laurel. She instinctively inched backward. Deke was a couple of yards from the retreating angel when the car filled with the metal-on-metal shriek of brakes. As the train slowed, the drunk pitched forward like a felled tree, and crashed face down in front of the horrified Laurel.

He lay still a moment, groaning, then tilted his head up and squinted into her wide eyes as blood trickled from his split lip. Laurel's nose twitched in the high-octane fumes of Deke's breath. He surveyed her, his flushed face twisted, and attempted to speak, but could manage only a grunt. He took a deep, ragged breath and rasped, "Young'un, Pete. Real young. Pretty, too."

"Pretty, is he?" replied Pete, dragging himself to his feet with the same kind of difficulty that had beset Deke. Pete wasn't as tall as Deke, but he had about thirty pounds on him. He might have been thirty-five, though between the grime and the ravages of alcohol it would've been hard to say with certainty. He navigated with exaggerated care, nearly fell when the screeching brakes further slowed the train, and finally joined Deke, who had painfully dragged himself to something like an upright position.

Pete's red, rheumy eyes rested greedily on the angel. Laurel recoiled from the stench of whiskey-laden breath and unwashed bodies as much as from their brutish expressions. An atmosphere of menace filled the slowly rolling car as the light faded. The locomotive's whistle wailed.

A third hobo, at the bottom of the car's pecking order, now crept from the far end, the whiskey jar clutched in his hand. He was slight and blond, perhaps twenty. One more figure, long and lanky, wrapped in a long, dark coat lay stretched out and inert against the wall opposite Laurel's. A hat concealed his face. He appeared to be asleep, or perhaps passed out from the whiskey.

Pete crept closer, on his hands and knees. Huey, who had been riding under the loose flap of Laurel's knapsack, buzzed out and hovered protectively above her. Pete squinted into the gloom, trying to make out the source of the low thrumming. Huey made a pass at the hobo's head, but in the fading light his aim was poor. Pete ducked and waved off the attack, muttering, "What the…?" His distraction was short-lived, and he turned again to Laurel. He squatted before her in the dim light and touched dirty knuckles to her cheek. She grimaced, and Huey made another half-blind, ineffective pass that Pete casually waved off. Laurel pressed her back against the boxcar's wall. *No…not again…*

Pete grabbed for her. She dodged sideways, barely managing to evade him but losing her hat to his lunge. A great mass of gold-white hair tumbled all around her. The hobos froze and stared. Deke gasped, "Jumpin' Judas, Pete! Look at his hair!"

"He's a girl, ya damn dummy!" Pete snarled.

By now Laurel had edged nearly to the car's corner. Pete studied her. Disappointed, he mumbled, "…can't always have your druthers."

But Deke now stood unsteadily over Pete, glowering down at him. "I'm gettin' purty fed up with the way you talk, Pete! Purty damn fed up, I tell ya. You might can have your way with Jody, but I ain't gonna take no more o' yer guff! Ain't takin' no more o' 'dummy' this, and 'dummy' that…"

Pete glanced up, his face twisted, half angry, half amused. "Izzat so?" he growled, "Well, if the shoe fits, wear it!" He hurled a final word, "Dummy!"

Deke uttered an animal sound, aimed a kick at Pete, missed, and fell flat on his back. Snarling, Pete spun clumsily, threw himself on the fallen drunk and pummeled his face. After two or three blows, he lost his balance and fell to one side. Deke took advantage of the respite. Still on the floor, he rolled and twisted and hurled a kick at Pete's face. Though his aim hadn't improved, his luck had, and his boot connected, smashing Pete's nose flat against one cheek. Pete howled and clutched his face, but before Deke could press his advantage, Pete came at him as if possessed by a demon, cursing, flailing, thrashing, slinging gouts of blood from his shattered nose.

Though the battle drifted away from Laurel, there was no relief. The smaller one, the blond boy Jody, wobbled around the others as they writhed on the floor and closed in on Laurel. He paused for another pull on the jar. Grinning, he wiped his mouth on a dirty sleeve and wove his way closer to the angel. She crept backward along the end wall to where it met the side wall—and found herself well and truly cornered. Jody dropped to his knees, and leaned toward Laurel for a closer look. He grinned, and once again, she recoiled from pungent whiskey fumes.

"I ain't like Pete. No, I ain't like Pete a-tall," said Jody, his grin widening. "See, Pete...he likes young *boys*." He set the jar down.

At the far end of the car, the formerly reclining figure, the man shrouded in the long, dark coat, was now alert. As he faced the twin confrontations opposite, a faint smile traced his thin lips. He narrowed his eyes at the diminishing distance between Jody and Laurel and extended an arm toward them. He clenched his fist.

Jody, his eyes in that instant cold and blank, thrust a hand toward the trapped angel. Laurel pressed herself hard into the corner as rough, wiry fingers closed about her neck.

Suddenly, a flying shadow and a loud *thump* froze them all in place as a duffel bag soared through the open door of the creeping boxcar. A figure vaulted through the door, a tall, imposing silhouette in the twilight. The figure's head turned in short quick arcs, and then a hand darted into the duffel bag.

A blinding glare burst from a large flashlight, pinning Jody and Laurel.

"Holy hell…the bulls!" Deke yelped.

"Move away from that child," commanded a voice from behind the light, deep and full of authority. Jody blinked stupidly into the beam. "*Move!*" said the deep voice. Jody released Laurel and scuttled backwards. The light flicked toward Pete and Deke, now huddled together. "Over there, with the others." Jody, partially mastering his shock and drunkenness, suddenly found himself in a mood to obey. He scrambled over to the older hobos.

Pete found his voice, which betrayed something like awe. "Tony! Why…we heard…"

Deke finished the sentence, "Yeah, we heard you…you caught the westbound."

"Believe everything you hear, do you?" Tony paused, sniffing the air. "What in the name of…" His light swept the car's far end, illuminating the hobos' bags, bedrolls, and several whiskey jars, then swung back to Laurel.

She squinted and averted her head as Tony held the light lower and adjusted it to an angle more comfortable for her. She looked up, studying him while he studied her.

He turned to the now subdued gaggle of drunks. "Why'n't you boys get back to your end of the car." They scrambled to obey, shuffling and stumbling to the far end, where from the darkness Deke called out, "The stranger…where'd he go?"

Tony illuminated the hobos' end of the car. The man in the long coat was indeed gone.

"Train was scarcely movin' when I got on," Tony said, "not so's any of you would've noticed. He must've jumped off when everybody was…busy." The hobos mumbled assent, then lapsed into a sullen silence.

Tony lifted his duffel and moved it closer to Laurel. He finally settled, sitting cross-legged in front of her. He placed the light between them but off to one side, the beam aimed so that it comfortably illuminated the space they shared. Laurel spoke first. "You're Tony?"

"S'my name," he replied. "And who might you be, young lady?"

"I'm Laurel. You know Jack…err…John? Sir John?"

Tony took another long look at her, then with a slow grin, he answered, "The 'Knight of Lombard Street'? Sure, sure. Seen my boy, have you? How is he?"

Laurel's relief was visible and the sudden draining away of tension left her almost limp, but she found her voice. "He's well. And kind. And generous…and brave. He told me that you'd…"

"Whoa, whoa…hang on. We talkin' bout the same kid? 'Kind,' I'll buy. 'Generous,' sure. But brave? When'd he get brave?"

"Well, he ran off two boys who were about to…umm…I'm not exactly sure what they had in mind, but I know it wasn't good."

Tony stared at her, then shook his head. "My, my…*two*, you say? Whatever could've gotten into him?"

Laurel shrugged. "I don't know, but he was magnificent." She reflected on the drama in the alley. "And now you. And them." She gestured toward the hobos. "I couldn't believe such a thing could happen twice in one day." She sat up straighter, as she suddenly remembered. "Oh! I'm sorry. I didn't thank you."

Tony nodded and touched his hat brim. "Not at all, not at all. Just glad I got here when I did. Now, Jack said I'd do what?"

"He said you could help me get to San Diego."

Huey chose that moment to drop out of the darkness onto the knapsack a little behind Laurel and wriggle under the loose flap. Tony seemed not to notice.

"I can see you through to Los Angeles, but then I'll have to head east for Albuquerque. Old friend there's not long for the world, I'm told. San Diego's not far from L.A., though. I can get you pointed right before I peel off for New Mexico."

"Oh, thank you! I'm sorry about your friend. It's good of you to go."

Tony shrugged. "Gotta do what you gotta do. Speakin' of which, what's a little gal like you doin' hoppin' freights?"

"My sister Kate's in trouble in San Diego. She needs me, and I don't have a minute to lose."

"Hmm." Tony studied her for a space. "Been thinkin' you don't look so good. When'd you eat last?"

She shook her head and yawned. "I don't remember. It's been a long day." Indeed, she wobbled with fatigue.

Tony retrieved a canteen and a bag of nuts and raisins from his duffel bag and handed them to Laurel.

As she nibbled, Tony rummaged in his bag and pulled out a small guitar, a battered survivor of countless rough boardings and exits from moving trains. After he tuned, he played a sweet melodic introduction, then the verse's melody. At the next verse, he began humming in a deep, rich baritone. Laurel settled onto her little heap of straw and closed her eyes, breathing more deeply. Her color improved under the influence of Tony's music.

She seemed to sleep, but then opened her eyes halfway. She waited for Tony to come to the end of a verse, then asked, "What is that? Sounds familiar."

He kept playing as he replied, "Oh, just an old, old thing from back home."

"It's beautiful."

He nodded his thanks, and resumed his wordless singing as Laurel again closed her eyes and drifted toward sleep. But then, half asleep, she murmured, and after a fashion began to sing— faint, fragmented, in her strange, beautiful language—wispy scraps of harmony that complemented Tony's music. He leaned toward her, his eyes narrowing, just at the moment her voice stilled and her breath deepened and she was at last sound asleep.

Tony watched her a long moment. She looked better, the circles under her eyes much diminished, her color improved. She breathed very deeply, rhythmically now, rocking a little with the train's motion.

Tony set the guitar aside and pulled from his bag some blankets with which he made two beds. He lifted Laurel onto the one nearest the end of the car and covered her. He picked up the flashlight, scanned the car's far end and satisfied himself the hobos were asleep—or passed out. He finally lay down on the other bed, so that he was between Laurel and the hobos, and turned off the flashlight. The click and rumble and sway of the train were hypnotic. The whistle sounded, distant and mournful.

08

Morning. The train rattled along at a stately clip. The whistle blew. The loud, mingled snores of the hobos filled the car. Laurel stirred. She rolled over and peeked into the knapsack. The hummer looked wilted. She frowned as she stroked his head. "Oh, Huey…you haven't eaten in…how long is it?" She sat up and looked about her, noting that Tony was awake and reading a small book. Wordless, he handed her the canteen and the bag of nuts and raisins. She shook her head. "Are we almost there?"

He chuckled. "This ain't no cannonball, Love. 'Nother day or so, depending."

She yawned and rubbed her eyes. Her health had declined somewhat in the night, the usual symptoms again in evidence.

"Huey's hungry," she said.

Tony laid the book aside and lifted an eyebrow.

She answered his silent question, "My, um…companion. I thought you saw him last night."

"Didn't want to ask…things were complicated enough," he explained, then went on, "What's he need?"

"Nectar…" She said it with a doubtful rising inflection and a furrowed brow, knowing how absurd it sounded—as if Tony were likely to have a canteen full of hummingbird flowers' sweet secretions stashed in his duffle bag. She hurried on, "And a bug or two as well, but he needs nectar for the strength to hunt for them."

Tony gave her a level look. "'Fraid we're fresh outta all that, Love." He tilted his head toward the hobos. "And I don't think the rumdums' whiskey would hold much appeal for the little feller, assumin' they'd spare him a drop. He's welcome to my water though, if it'll do him some good."

She brooded a moment, then brightened. "Say! Do you have any sugar? We could mix a little with some water. That'd hold him for a while."

Tony shook his head ruefully. "Not a speck, Love, not for the last month or so. Sorry."

Tony filled the canteen's cap and handed it to her. She opened the knapsack and offered the water to Huey. After many tongue-darting sips, he stopped, uttered a few ticking chirps, preened, settled down and slept. Laurel watched him for a moment, then gently tented the knapsack's flap over him.

"Thanks, Tony, that certainly helped. But he's going to need something more before long."

He handed her the canteen and food. "Gotta take care of yourself, too." She nibbled, sipped, and reflected. When she had finished her bird-like breakfast, she turned to Tony.

"You don't think Jack's brave."

Tony stretched his legs and considered. "Not that he ain't a good boy…just the scardiest cat I ever saw. Hidin' behind all that knight fooferaw."

Laurel thought about this, frowning a little, but as she remembered her time with Jack, she began to smile.

"How do you know him?" she asked.

"Oh, I've known Jack since he was a pup," Tony replied. "Longer. Always sorta kept an eye on him. Times I could, anyways."

He thought a while, then turned to her with a slightly incredulous look. "Beat up two bad boys, you say? Bless him." He shook his head as he chuckled. Then he grew serious, and studied Laurel for a space. "Y'know, I can see why he might've at that. Somethin' about Jack…he has a feeling for the truly good things. Boy's got a healthy gift for sorting out the good and the bad. Born with it, I'd say." Laurel gave him a shy smile.

Tony watched the scenery fly by the boxcar's open door. They entered a grove of trees so laden with white blossoms it looked as though they were covered with snow. "Glad you were there for him, Love, long as I couldn't be." He stared into the distance, not really seeing the trees and their blanket of blossoms. "Yessir. Love beats fear…if you just let it."

"I like that! Good words."

By now, though, Laurel was fading again. A sudden sneeze wracked her. She swiped at her nose with the red handkerchief, then sagged back onto the bed Tony had made for her. She looked up at him. "Would you play some more, please?" He had a long look at her, fraught with concern, then he picked up the guitar and strummed.

She watched the snow-like world pass by the big open door. Huey fluttered out of the knapsack and perched in front of her on a fold of her blanket. Laurel breathed deeply, drowsing, her color improving as Tony played, crooning wordlessly in his fine baritone.

Huey chittered and buzzed his wings. Laurel roused a little, looked at the bird, then glanced out at the acres of blossoms. "Huey..."

And then Huey was gone like a rocket, out the door and into the blossoming groves' abundance. Laurel staggered to her feet. "*Huey!*" She dashed to the door, teetered on the brink like a high wire performer about to fall. She leaned out, searching, hanging on by two fingers—then leaped.

As she tumbled through space, her ethereally small mass made her much more buoyant in the air than a human of her size would be. Still, she instinctively deployed her wings, or rather, tried to, forgetting that she had exercised the painful process of shrinking and hiding them. She arched her back and strained as she tumbled through the air, the train rattling and rumbling beside her. Her wingtips pushed against the fabric of her shirt once, twice, then ripped through only a couple of inches before they hung up in the small tear. She grimaced. Her wings burned and tingled as if they had gone to sleep and then were asked to soar.

She strained again. The rip widened and both wings unfurled through the opening, the left one out and open to its full span, but the right, weaker because of its old injury, became tangled in the straps of her overalls. Now Laurel's aerodynamic configuration was much like that of a maple seed that whirls like a little helicopter as it falls, and her formerly somersaulting arc turned into a series of wild, fast barrel rolls. Ethereal mass notwithstanding, gravity prevailed, and Laurel finally smacked onto the gravel roadbed on her butt, bounced once, tumbled through the air again, landed for good, skidded a little way, then rolled head over heels, and finally ground to a halt in a cloud of dust. A few blue-tipped feathers settled around her as the train's steel wheels clattered and rumbled by.

Seemingly out of nowhere, Huey appeared. He hovered, flashed rose and a blaze of reflected sunlight, then darted his tongue at Laurel's nose. He chittered, then dashed back into the grove where he fed ravenously, gathering the nectar of dozens of the succulent white blossoms, and harvesting a few tiny, delicious bugs—to Huey, a feast of snow crab and fine chardonnay. Still, pity the hummers, with their immense appetites and their minuscule reserves.

By the time Tony had leapt to his feet and sprinted to the door, the train had rounded a curve, obscuring his view of events. The last thing he saw before Laurel disappeared was a whirling flash of white.

Laurel scrambled unsteadily to her feet. She winced, rubbed her aching derriere, and watched Huey finish his long-deferred meal. Her left wing dangled, uninjured though the feathers were disarrayed, but the right remained snagged in the denim straps. Huey returned and circled her, examining her for injuries. Satisfied that she wasn't badly hurt, he hovered before her and uttered a long series of ticks and chirps—an apology. When his song ended, Laurel smiled and stroked his head. "It's all right. I'm just glad you finally got to eat. You look a lot better."

She squirmed to free her trapped wing as she watched the caboose dwindle in the distance. The whistle sounded—very faint.

She scanned her surroundings, turned a circle to sense her way toward Kate. *This way...* A road paralleled the tracks about a quarter mile away. She sighed and started for it.

Huey chittered.

"Oh, right," she replied. She stopped and repeated the painful task of hiding her wings. Then she realized that she had lost her hat. Remembering Jack's admonition about girls on the road, she tied her hair in a loose knot, intending to tuck it into her overalls. It immediately came undone. She knotted it again, with the same result. She sighed and continued toward the road.

B&#x3;

Kate was absorbed in her sketchbook. Again, the now familiar image of a young angel. Dissatisfied, she tore off the page and started anew, this time, the angel incognito as a girl vagabond on a country road. She began to hum fragments of Laurel's gift song as she added a hummingbird to the picture.

27

Laurel trudged along the roadside while Huey nestled in one of her pockets, resting, conserving energy. A bus sped by and its slipstream disarrayed the waif's hair. She stopped to repair it, finally managed something like a chignon, then tramped on.

A train whistle blew, low and sweet—different from the harsh blast of the slow freight she had lately ridden—and drew her eyes toward the tracks. A passenger express flew by, the Coast Daylight that Jack had mentioned, so called because it covered the the four hundred or so miles between San Francisco and Los Angeles during the daylight hours. The Daylight's signature red and orange made of it an elongated, rolling sunset. The train receded rapidly in the distance. Laurel walked on. And on.

She had no idea how long or how far she had been walking when she heard a car pull up beside her. She stopped and turned to see a tired-looking Model A pickup squeak to a stop, the bed stacked with a motley assortment of well-worn farm equipment. A pretty brunette of about eighteen called to her from the passenger-side window, "Need a lift, honey?"

By then Tony's music was many hours in the past, and Laurel again felt tired and ill, so she trudged over to the truck, a little stooped. The girl hopped out and helped her into the truck.

The girl began talking a mile a minute. "Thank heaven I got somebody to talk to, and a girl at that! Can't buy a word from George here for less'n a dollar," she said, indicating the man of twenty-two or so behind the wheel. "Oh, where *are* my manners? My name's Alma," and as sort of an afterthought, "and like I said, this here's George…we're from Santa Rosa. What's your name, sweetheart? Where you from? You been walkin' long? Why'n the world are you out here all by yourself?"

Laurel blinked into this verbal hurricane, and then sorted out her reply. "I'm Laurel. I'm going to San Diego to see my sister, Kate."

Alma's jaw dropped. "San *Diego!* Why, that's hundreds of miles! Surely you don't mean you're *walking* to San Diego?"

"Well, that wasn't the idea." She paused, considering her answer, then shrugged and continued, "I…I fell off the train."

Alma gasped, horrified. George turned for a closer look at their dusty passenger. Satisfied that she was not seriously hurt, he gave her a wry half-smile. "Musta been a pretty slow-movin' one."

Something about George's craggy but gentle face made Laurel feel at ease. She grinned. Alma, however, was not amused. She leaned across Laurel and wagged a finger in George's face. "Just like you to mock a poor, lost, injured child! Meanie!"

George closed his eyes and rubbed his temples. "I do beg your pardon, young lady, I didn't mean nothin'. I hope you're all right. We're headin' for Santa Barbara, and you're more'n welcome to tag along."

"Thanks, George. You too, Alma." Laurel sat back, the day's events catching up, weighing on her. She sniffled, got out the handkerchief, which somehow had stayed in her overall pocket during her wild exit from the boxcar.

George pulled onto the road. "Oh…and don't mind Alma. She can be a trifle excitable."

"I am *not* excitable!" Alma exploded, "The things you *say!*"

Laurel glanced at their hands. "How long have you been married?"

Silence, for an uncomfortable moment. Finally, George replied, "Three months."

Alma made a wry face. "Three eternities, seems like." The group lapsed into an awkward silence. After a long interval, Alma spoke again. "Everything was fine…when we were courtin'." She paused and smiled, remembering. "Then, after the wedding, I noticed that George enjoys a drink. Now, my mama says…"

George interrupted, "Hold on now! You never saw me enjoy more'n two, and you never will, because my daddy taught me…"

Alma cut him off, "And then, not a week after the wedding, I caught him lookin' at that flashy, red-haired Suzie Larkin!"

"A man'd have to be dead *not* to look at Suzie Larkin!" George burst in. "Anyway, I ain't sayin' it's right, but a man's made that way. A married man's gotta learn to go against nature in himself, and there ain't nothin' easy about it."

"Well, if a man's made that way, and if a married man's a unnatural thing…well…well, then maybe I don't *need* one! Mama'd be more'n happy to have me back home!"

"If I had a nickel for every time you said that, I could *buy* a home!" He glared at Alma. "Sure ain't what I bargained for in a wife…threatenin' to pack up 'n' clear out every hour!"

"Well, if you'd just *act* like a husband… Watch the road, George! You'll kill us all!"

George snapped his eyes forward. "If you'd just have a little faith, just a *speck* o' patience…"

Laurel closed her eyes, slid lower between the couple and let the tide of bitter words roll over her. She was pale, and the circles under her eyes were back. She drifted, and eventually slept, like an exhausted soldier in a trench, while angry artillery rumbled and shrieked overhead.

The sun was low in the sky by the time Laurel awakened. The battle still raged, even hotter. George shouted, "Then stop *talkin'* about it and do it! Go home to her then!"

"Well, I *will!*" Alma shrieked. "Then you can drink liquor and chase floozies to your heart's content! And what's more, mama says…"

The fury of the words tore at Laurel's nerves, and she sat bolt upright.

"*Hush up! Both of you!* George, pull over." The newlyweds, having practically forgotten their passenger's presence, were shocked to silence. George pulled over and stopped the truck. A tense silence hovered.

Laurel gave each in turn a severe look. "You two've wasted a whole day to say what takes about two seconds."

In a gently mocking tone, she said, "'George, I'm afraid you're gonna cheat on me.' 'Alma, I'm afraid you're gonna leave me all alone.'" She let her words hang in the air, shaking her head, exasperated. "You have about a hundred different ways of saying you don't trust each other."

She closed her eyes again, leaned against the hard seat back, then went on, "More to the point, you both say, 'I am afraid.' Over and over."

The couple seemed to see one another for the first time since Laurel had joined them. Again, it was Laurel who broke the silence. "George, has she ever walked out on you?"

"Well, no."

"Ever even started packing?"

"No. She ain't."

"Alma, has he ever cheated on you? And I don't mean just in your mind."

"No."

Laurel remained slumped, her eyes closed. Then, with a slow shake of her head she said, "All this worry…and pain…and hard, mean words…" Her voice trailed off. She heaved a deep sigh.

"All this agony…" Her voice was suddenly emphatic, "…over what is *NOT*." She looked left, then right, her eyes commanding. "Out! Both of you!"

Impelled by Laurel's unexpected vehemence, George and Alma scrambled out of the truck. Wisps of fog tinted by the late sunlight rolled fast over the coastal road and clouds crowded the sky. The angel took a deep breath, stood still a moment as she sought some inner reserve, and then took the two each by a hand. She led them into the sparse wood bordering the road, with a sliver of ocean view that shimmered through gaps in the fog.

They walked a while, until Laurel halted between a pair of trees that leaned toward one another to form a sunlight-dappled bower. She faced the couple. "Your marriage…it didn't take."

Alma gasped. George looked mortified.

Laurel raised her hands, palms out in a calming gesture. "Oh, don't worry…the legal part's fine." Looks of relief flooded the faces of the pair. Laurel went on, "I mean the important part. The *real* part."

George managed to find his voice. "Well…what…?

Laurel smiled. "You're in luck. I can fix it."

The couple stared at her, bemused. She continued, "Join hands. Like on your wedding day."

George and Alma joined hands. Laurel closed her eyes and intoned, "Alma, do you love George?"

"I do."

"George, do you love Alma?"

"I do."

"Will you trust each other…like you promised?" The newlyweds sneaked quick glances at each other, then stared at Laurel, frozen in doubt. The silence stretched. Laurel's serene smile faded. Her eyes popped open. "Well, *will* you?"

Something in Laurel's eyes went deep into the hearts of the

young couple, and they replied simultaneously, "I will!"

The angel's smile returned. "Then repeat after me: Love beats fear…if you just let it."

George and Alma exchanged a glance, the first in many days that held nothing other than affection. They repeated together, "Love beats fear…if you just let it."

Laurel took their hands in her own and turned her face toward the wavering, cloud-obscured sunlight. Her hair flowed in the cool breeze and she glowed in the golden light, beatific.

For a moment the fog dissipated in the ocean wind and pure sunlight flowed over the three—and between the souls of the young couple the deepest of bonds was formed. Laurel, still and reverent, whispered, "Man and wife."

She turned to them, released their hands and opened her eyes. "George, you know what to do," she said.

George grinned and kissed the bride.

Not far from the scene of the impromptu wedding, as the three got back into the truck, a tall, pale man stepped from behind one of the larger trees near the road. He watched the truck until it disappeared in the distance.

28

As George drove through the deepening dusk, his head dropped for an instant, then jerked back up. He shook off his drowsiness and focused on a white blur in the distance, which soon resolved into a sign:

SANTA MARIA FAIR

Alma and Laurel stirred as George turned onto the dirt road. "Girls," he said, "I'm all in. I need a break."

Down the road, several large tents were visible in what was left of the light. As they drew nearer, the lively sound of a string band brought Laurel fully awake.

A noisy, cheerful crowd filled the tent and couples whirled on the improvised dance floor as the band belted out western swing. Many lanterns bathed the space in a warm glow and tanged the air with the heavy spice of burnt kerosene. Laurel's color deepened as the music washed over her. She took a step toward the bandstand, but Alma put a hand on her shoulder. "Hang on a minute, honey. Let's fix you up a little."

She took a comb from her bag, stepped behind Laurel and went to work on her disarrayed hair. In a few moments, Laurel wore an expertly crafted chignon. Alma stepped back, satisfied. "There you go, Love! You're beautiful!" Laurel smiled her thanks, then turned and wove her way through the crowd to the hay wagon that served as a bandstand.

A fiddler commanded the stage, front and center, and when he took a solo Laurel's eyes locked on him and she fairly glowed. She was suddenly dragged out of her admiring fixation, however, by a hand that grabbed her arm and turned her about.

A gangly, exuberant youth dragged her to the dance floor and spun her about in a way that for a few seconds had her entirely outside herself. Within a few turns, however, Laurel attuned herself to her partner's lead as they whirled through the throng of dancers, and she almost managed to keep up. When the song ended he released her as quickly as he'd seized her. With a big smile and a "Thank you, darlin'!" he vanished into the crowd. Laurel returned to her spot in front of the fiddler and remained fixed there like a polar star until the set ended.

From the stage, the fiddler announced, "We're just gonna catch our breath for a spell, folks! Y'all stick around!" Laurel ambushed him as he stepped down from the stage.

"I love how you play! What is that music? How did you learn it?" she asked, all unselfconscious eagerness.

"Well, I'm much obliged, young lady," the fiddler replied. "Guess our kind of playing has different names…some call it western, others call it swing. My daddy got me started, and there's been many since as shown me thing or two."

"Could you show me?"

He sized her up and gave her a half-smile. "You fiddle, do you, honey?"

You bet, she would have said, had she known the local vernacular, but in the event, she simply nodded.

He gave her another half-skeptical look, then raised his violin and played a simple figure. "Can you do that?" he asked, as he handed her the instrument.

She raised the fiddle, took a breath, and repeated the passage perfectly, adding a flourish at the end.

The fiddler's eyes widened. "My, my! That wasn't bad a-tall, Love! Let's try another." He took the fiddle from her, played a longer, much more difficult passage.

Laurel absorbed the music—breathed it in. The man handed back the fiddle. She raised the bow, paused, and then blazed the passage note for perfect note. And then flew on as if she'd been playing country fiddle forever. Soon she slipped into her characteristic musical trance.

The fiddler's jaw dropped. He grinned and motioned the musicians back to the stage. Laurel shrieked in surprise and delight, but didn't miss a note, when he seized her by the waist and swung her, too, onto the stage. The fiddler grabbed a mandolin, counted aloud and led the band into a hot accompaniment of Laurel's improvisation. She played with such vigor that she broke a few bow hairs, which swayed and floated, luminous, along with a few loose strands of her own hair.

When the song ended, the fiddler counted the band straight into another, and Laurel challenged them, raising the energy still more. They met her, playing faster and hotter. Center stage and front, Laurel looked unearthly, the power of her musical presence in strange contrast to the signs of her illness.

ଔ

Hundreds of miles away, Kate tossed in her sleep. The blond girl who had lately haunted her dreams was back, playing a wild, sweet music on a violin. A blissful sense of well-being flooded her dream space, along with an urgent attraction to the radiant apparition.

ଔ

At the county fair, the players traded solos for a while, then reunited in a solid wall of sound to finish the jam.

But Laurel couldn't stop. She left the band, the crowd—the world—far behind. For a while she played Heaven's own country fiddle, then segued into a kind of music that was never heard at any country fair on Earth, nor in any royal court or presidential palace or concert hall. The crowd was transported as she played to exhaustion, theirs as well as her own. In the midst of this passion, her mind had room for one thought: *My heart swells… with joy…with gratitude…*

Then, a soaring figure and a triumphant final chord. She stopped at last, the bow aimed skyward, lips parted, eyes half closed, gazing into another world.

For a moment, the tent was silent. Then the people roared as if with one voice. The band swarmed around Laurel, and the crowd pressed.

Standing at the crowd's fringe, a tall, pale man in a long dark coat observed the crowd's appreciation. When the noisy adulation showed no sign of abating, his eyes narrowed and he took a step back. A subtle and eerie light enveloped him. He breathed deeply, raised his hands slightly—and transformed. The hollows of his cheeks filled and his ghastly pallor gave way to a sanguine glow. He swept his hands over his clothes—the dust vanished and everything became fine and new in the strange light. He smiled. He looked well, and so very nearly an ordinary human that a casual observer would not have guessed that he was anything but.

The ghostly aura disappeared, and he stepped toward the stage. Upon his approach, people grew silent and drew away. The shared passion of the music dissipated. By the time he reached the stage, the crowd had broken into small groups and the intense communal energy of a few moments earlier had faded.

The fiddler helped Laurel down from the stage as the stranger approached, smiling, but cold. With a subtle motion of his hand, he waved the fiddler away.

When Laurel and the man were alone, the coldness had left him and he said, "May I congratulate you? I've never heard the violin played so well." She remained silent, instinctively on guard. He brushed aside the moment's awkwardness, continuing, "Forgive me if I'm forward, but I believe I can help you."

"Help me? What…who are you?"

"Call me Nick. People are my business, generally. But just now I'm specifically concerned with…" His smile invited her confidence, "…those possessed of great talent."

"I don't know what you're talking ab…"

He cut her off. "Come now. You know as well as I do that you're the best."

Pleasure washed over her as for the shortest moment she warmed to his words. Then the warning instinct rose again within her. "I suppose that depends on what you mean by 'best.'"

"Don't be coy!" he exclaimed. He tilted his head back in a soundless laugh, gently mocking her. Then he looked at her directly and became serious as he continued, "You know precisely what I mean. You have an astonishing talent…this world's never seen the like. A talent that will bring you things you've never dreamed of."

"It's not like that. I play because…" She looked away. "It's like breathing."

Now he laughed aloud. "Such modesty!" He gripped her arm as he continued, serious, "You're young, a naïf. It's time you saw your gift from a new perspective. You need help channeling your abilities in practical directions. You're fortunate…we're both fortunate…that I'm here to provide that help, before you grow older, undirected, and waste your gift." His grip tightened.

Laurel pulled free, stepped back, and gave him a searching look. "You know, I'm in kind of a hurry." She turned away from him and took a step. His eyes, abruptly cold and hard, pierced her back. She halted and wavered, in the instant sapped of still more of her fading energy.

He stepped to her, his hand fell on her shoulder, and he whispered, "Of course you're in a hurry. But…to where? Watch, now…"

The hand on her shoulder tightened its grip. Laurel's eyes closed and in her mind's eye she saw herself leading the Hyde Street musicians near the cable car stop. Adoring, ecstatic faces. The image faded, giving way to scenes from the San Francisco pawnshop. Her Christmas Passion on the violin, the customers transformed into an angelic choir, their joy, their love for her. Her joy.

The hand on her shoulder relaxed, and she returned to the here and now. Nick turned her to face him. Her eyes met his, though her gaze was still far away.

"How they loved you…" He shook his head as if in wonder. Nick's tone changed: He was now businesslike and at the same time, paternal. "You're clearly unwell. And I said that I was here to help you." The Earth sickness was indeed asserting itself again—the pallor, the shadows. And the faint spot just beneath her nose—a fleck of blood?

He continued, "My people enjoy many…benefits…shall we say." Her eyes narrowed as something deep inside her struggled against his magnetic hold. "Come, don't try to deny it," he said, applying more force. "You know as well as I how ill you are. More to the point, you are dying…slowly…but dying all the same. This misguided quest of yours is killing you by inches."

She shook her head, trying to come fully to herself, but again he tightened his grip, and the trance deepened. "You know, as do I, or at least you intuit, that music…playing it, hearing it, and most of all, playing together with others…delays your approaching demise." Laurel made a little sound—assent, perhaps. The man continued, "Choose to save yourself. Join me. You will play to your heart's content, with the finest musicians of this world."

She found her voice, though it was a mere harsh whisper. "No…I won't abandon her. The Gift…"

His eyes narrowed. He was not accustomed to encountering much in the way of resistance. And, too, his confidence was high because the 20th century so far promised to be a wildly successful time for him. He sized up the little angel with a new regard as he considered his next move.

At last he whispered, "I compliment you." He regarded her a moment longer, "And I challenge you. If indeed you are a child of, and the messenger of, Love…" His mouth betrayed the smallest grimace, as if the word had a bitter taste, "…if you are that, I then challenge you to call on your Father to relieve you of your suffering. If He is Love, if you are His adored daughter, how can he refuse?" He smiled. "Perfectly reasonable, yes?"

She uttered a small sound and quivered, then again shook her head. After a moment she replied, in the same rough whisper as before, "You ask that I test my Creator." She shuddered again, then, seizing control of herself, affirmed in a clear voice, "I will not."

The man looked at her a long, silent moment. "Your loyalty is… admirable. But let me suggest that you've not considered matters as thoroughly as you should. You see your mission as a service to one woman. One speck of humanity…who pities herself and consequently is determined to take reckless chances with her life. One who may yet elude you and, who, despite your love and your sacrifice, runs headlong to her own destruction. Why should such a noble creature as you waste her substance on…a nonentity?"

He paused, all his senses alive for Laurel's reaction. She was silent and, apart from the slight weaving that betrayed her exhaustion, she stood very still. Encouraged, taking her silence as an absence of resistance, he continued, "Your gifts are wasted unless you bestow them upon the world at large. A greater public than one unhappy and self-destructive girl awaits you." Laurel remained silent. "Today's people, and those of the near future, do and will struggle under a great burden, a yearning, a great want that they don't understand or even recognize. The old ways are fast passing out of memory. Faith is decayed, and will vanish, and the people crave something to believe in. If you allow it, I will help you satisfy their hunger."

Laurel barely breathed. Her eyes remained closed and she stood apparently due only to the support of his grip on her shoulder. Her eyes flickered open for a second to dimly regard her captor.

He pressed, "For the greater glory, dedicate yourself not to one, but to the many. Watch now…"

Again, he bent her mind to his will and again images began to whirl through her inner vision:

She conducting the dove's concert upon her arrival at the Aviary.

Hyde Street. The loving singers. The Christmas caroling and the spirit of it that spread wide across the neighborhood like the sun dispersing clouds.

The pawnshop. The bystanders changed into an angelic chorus. The love that radiated from them to her and back again.

The County Fair. The crowd, captivated when the Fiddler lifted her to the stage and she played to them.

He watched her face, and his grip loosened the least bit. Pleased to see the shadow of a smile cross her face, he whispered, "How they love you! It needn't end." He reasserted his grip.

The County Fair, the crowd going wild as she leaves the band behind in her uncanny improvisation, her own ecstasy.

And now he filled Laurel's mind with the future he would give her:

A theater in a mid-sized town. A larger audience than ever she has played to on Earth. They shower her with unending applause.

A recording studio. Laurel plays a grand finish, steps back from the microphone. The man at the console is ecstatic. Her entourage swarms around her, doting.

Still further in the future, a grand theater in a great city filled to standing room only. Batteries of television cameras transmit her image—her fame—around the world.

"You claim your sacred purpose is to help Kate?" whispered the man. "Think of the help you could provide with the wealth and influence I offer you."

But something stirred in her. It felt to her as if a cord—slender but steely—were reaching back to her very beginning, her Home. And then from her Home came the command to see truly, and the power to do so, and she looked again upon the stranger's offer in a clear light.

Laurel on television—the 1950s, then the '60s, onward. Fashions change. She's ever young, but ever more ill. She's the star of television's every decade. Multitudes worship her, entranced.

A montage illustrates the disappearance of the old beloved music: *The Baroque, the Classical, the Romantic wither and vanish— the skill, the patience, the discernment, the community—the love—on which their survival depends, die. Jazz and country styles transform into ever-coarser forms of rock, and then into forms that have barely intelligible names—then those are in turn swept away in a passion of change for change's sake, of gleeful degeneracy. The Christmas songs are driven from the public places. And Laurel—as the stranger's acolyte—adapts.*

A stadium. The crowd roars, 100,000 voices combine in a harsh and brutal bellowing thunder, a sound terrifying to the remaining few in the world who are mindful of history. The music is very different now—virtuosic, but in a merely mechanical way—energetic, but dispassionate. A harsh electronic accompaniment to Laurel's violin vies with the noise of the mob's ecstatic fury. People, grotesque, so disfigured with lurid, comprehensive tattoos and fantastic mutilations as to seem a different species leap onto the stage, howling like animals, and lunge for her, but squads of armored police club them back, bloody them. Chaos. Laurel's trance as she plays is different—where before it was reverent, now it is hollow, death-like—a reflection of the prevailing emptiness.

Thus, the circuses of the 21st century's Caesars, thrown down to the people—or upon them—in deepest contempt.

The fevered vision continues: *Multiplied and amplified on colossal video displays, Laurel is a grotesque giant. The mob goes mad for her. She is sicker than ever, but none know, so fatally sick are they themselves.*

Unaware that Laurel had perceived Truth, the man caressed her shoulder, a cool caress. She half awakened, her face shadowed by the ghost of a frown. He leaned close to her and spoke in the faintest of whispers. "You are indeed Love…yet love needs love returned. Imagine, to be adored, utterly, Beloved of the World, through the ages, forever and ever. This I will give to you, if you will but be mine."

At last his grip relaxed. His eyes burned into hers, demanding her acquiescence, expecting her surrender. She returned his gaze, perfectly still, a long moment.

Then her eyes closed. His face darkened with doubt and he gripped her shoulder again. *Cease! You'll have no vision that I do not give!* But he knew he no longer controlled her.

Indeed, another stream of images flowed through Laurel's mind—and indeed, they were not given by the stranger:

A dark space that endures for only the merest instant. Then a pinpoint of brilliant light blooms.

A light-drenched Academy. Infusion of Knowledge in the companionship of others of her kind. Bathing in a fountain of music.

A sacred duty assigned.

225

A warm dark somnolence. Another soul dreams closely, very closely beside her. Flesh, alien though necessary to duty, embraces her.

An instant of agony.

Her wounded golden soul soars from bloody wreckage.

Oblivion…then…

Laurel seeking Kate, playing her violin in the clouds.

Kate, as Laurel first saw her through the waters of the pool, then as Laurel sings her to sleep.

The tiny sun cradled in her hands.

Laurel returned to the present. She opened her eyes, met the stranger's, deeply, and whispered, "Leave me. I serve Love alone."

At that moment a fine, rich baritone came to them, faint at first but growing ever stronger, singing a melody Laurel knew… The man, filled with angry urgency, grabbed her arm. "You can have it *all!*"

Tony stepped into the tent, crooning his old song from back home, his duffle and Laurel's knapsack slung over his shoulder. He stopped and calmly regarded the pair.

The man, pale and gaunt again, eyes full of hot hatred, whirled on Tony, who ceased his song. Cool and strong, he met the man's malevolent glare. To Laurel he said, "Come on, Love. We'll miss our train."

Laurel, finally fully awake and present, yanked free of the man's hand and turned a fiery look on his hate-filled face.

The pale man roared, "Go then, and throw yourself down for her sake! Court your death chasing her to the ends of my kingdom and be damned! Your beloved angels won't save you!"

"Liar!" she hissed, evading his last attempt to seize her as she ran to Tony.

Gathering her under his arm, he looked down at her with a smile—faint, but warm. "Y'done good," he said.

She looked up at him, then back over her shoulder. Where

the pale man had stood, there was only empty space. She looked back to Tony, silently questioning. He said, "When folks choose right, he's gone…" He snapped his fingers in a dismissive gesture, "…like that."

After a searching look at her, he continued, "You look hungry." He put down the duffle, rummaged and came up with the bag of nuts and dried fruit and the canteen. She nibbled, and took a sip of water.

As they headed for the exit, Tony paused to reach into a hip pocket and came up with a small, slightly crushed wildflower bouquet. Laurel's face lit up when he handed it to her, but Tony said, "Hold on now, these ain't for you, strictly. They're supper for your bird. Don't need any more surprise exits."

Music and the happy noise of the crowd again filled the tent of the county fair.

29

Steel wheels clattered on the rails as dawn's light chased off the shadows in the boxcar. The coast road flowed by the open door, and dimly visible surf edged the beach beyond the road.

Laurel stirred, then sat up. Before she could speak, she was wracked by a huge sneeze.

"Bless you," Tony greeted. He regarded her with concern, noting her pallor. He handed her the food and water, which she barely touched.

Recalling her harrowing experience earlier in the same surroundings, she looked about and was relieved to see that she and Tony were alone in the car. "What happened with the…" she began.

"The rumdums? Oh, what usually happens, mostly. They whined about how tough things are, then ran off to try their old foolishness in new places. I told 'em…I said, 'Yes, times are tough, but however that is, you're carrying your own Great Depression around with you in them damn liquor jars.' 'Scuse my language, Love. Told 'em I had half a mind to do 'em a favor and toss their hooch overboard. 'Spose that's why they got off next chance."

"It's sad."

Tony nodded. "Uh-huh. But there's one one thing you'll like. Jody, the young one?"

She nodded.

"Seems you had an effect on him. After you bailed out, he

kept his distance from the other two. Then he lingered a while after they jumped. Sobered up, he felt just terrible about what he'd done…or almost did."

Her eyes softened. Tony continued, "Said he'd do anything to make amends, but since you were gone, next best thing he could think of was to go back home and help his folks with the farm, like he should have been anyway."

She smiled a little.

"Told him that'd please you."

Her smile widened.

"Hope you don't mind…my speakin' for you like that."

She shook her head.

"You did that, changed the boy, you know." Tony said. He studied her a long time.

She returned his scrutiny, then asked, "How did you know?"

"How'd I know what?"

"You know perfectly well what. How did you know I was at the fair? And why would you come for me, anyway?"

"They have a sayin' down here: 'Takes one to know one.'"

Laurel's eyes widened as Tony continued, "I had a notion you and I were of a kind when I first set eyes on you…"

She interrupted, "So *that's* how you know Jack!"

"Yep. And you remembered the old song in your sleep…sang it in the old words. That was pretty strong, though some, a few down here, get it without really knowin' they do. And you're the *first* one I've seen whose road buddy's a wild bird." His eyes flicked to Huey, who was making breakfast of the wildflower bouquet. "When you bailed out, I was pretty sure I saw a bit of wing…hard to tell, though, train goin' around the bend as it was."

He paused, his gaze resting on Laurel. "Gotta be a good reason you're down here, regardin' your…sister, I presumed, so I figured I oughta do whatever."

She watched the scenery sail by as the burgeoning light brought color back to the world. Tony resumed reading.

After a space, she asked, "You don't get sick down here?"

Eyes still on his book, he shook his head. "I'm assigned here." Then he looked over the book and met her eyes. "I'm guessin' you ain't, strictly speakin'." They held each others' gaze a moment, then together looked out the door just as a billboard ad displaying Kate's look-alike glided by.

Laurel's composure cracked. "I'm afraid...I might not last long enough to find her. Music helps, for a while..." She sank down on the bed of blankets Tony had made for her. "...but...I don't know." She heaved a sigh and yawned, so hard that it hurt.

Tony laid his book aside and regarded her and, they being what they were, her suffering became his. He reached for the guitar, tuned it and played. A new song, for their time together—a ballad, a complement to Laurel's wild solo at the fair—characteristic of their common Home's music, but slow and sweet, a lullaby. Laurel smiled her thanks, closed her eyes, breathed deeply. When she was well asleep Tony paused to arrange the ragged blanket over her and then resumed their song.

◌

The locomotive's bell clanged a slow rhythm and the whistle blew a couple of short blasts as the train crept through a large rail yard. The characteristic railway smells of coal smoke and creosote filled the air. Laurel opened her eyes to the late afternoon sunlight that flooded the car.

She rolled to face Tony, to breathe in the music he played still, that he had played and sung all the while she slept—a day and a night and more—sweet melodies, gentle rhythms, graceful rhymes in the ancient language. Words celebrating love and brotherhood and community, and words celebrating strength and endurance in dark times and, of course, the Source of all these things. Her color had improved a good deal though faint shadows remained beneath her eyes.

Brakes squealed and the train ground to a halt. Tony laid the guitar down. "We're here, Love."

⁓

Laurel and Tony walked among strings of freight cars in the great Los Angeles rail yard. He carried her knapsack along with his duffle, and maintained a slow gait so that she could keep up. Though she was much improved by Tony's music, the relentless Earth sickness, as Aurora had predicted, worked faster the longer the exposure.

They crossed a wide, largely empty area and came to a yard of a different kind—the boarding area of Los Angeles Union Station. Rather than endless chains of road-worn freight cars lying in the open, here there were short strings of clean, attractive passenger coaches resting next to boarding platforms sheltered by long awnings. Tony led Laurel past several platforms then turned onto one. He led her to the middle of the string of coaches, set down his duffle and dug in his pocket. Laurel looked up at the coach, puzzled, then turned to Tony. "What…?"

"Think I was gonna put you on a slow freight all by yourself? This baby'll get you there in three, four hours or so." He took her hand, pressed some bills into it. "That'll get your ticket, with a little left over." Her eyes welled. He continued, with mock sternness. "Oh, knock it off…the office'll make it good." He smiled wryly, then turned sincere. "You're paid up, anyway, Love. You were there for my boy Jack when I couldn't be."

He offered his hand, but she lunged, embraced him in a great bear hug. He stroked her hair and gazed down the line past the cars into the far distance.

A bell began a rhythmic clanging and a locomotive's whistle sang a couple of sweet, short chords. Laurel released Tony and stepped back. He unslung her knapsack from his shoulder and put it on hers. She swiped at her eyes once, then she was brave.

"Bye, Tony."

"Be seein' you, Love." He helped her up into the coach and waited until she appeared at a window and waved. Tony returned her wave, then ambled off.

ᙒ

Golden light from the setting sun flooded the coach as the train clipped along the water's edge. Laurel slumped against the window and watched the sun sink into the Pacific.

30

A brisk ocean breeze washed over Kate as she sat at the easel on her patio. With every mile Laurel had covered on her way to San Diego, as her spiritual nearness increased, Kate's impression of her had strengthened. Her sketches became more uncannily accurate and detailed until now, with Laurel arrived in the city, Kate had nearly completed a magnificent portrait of the angel.

She had created the outlines and shadows with the fallen feather that she had made into a pen, then had finished in water colors. Laurel's expression was joyous, caught at the instant her gaze left the viewer's to look upward. Her open hand extended in front of her, palm up.

Kate seemed not to notice a knock on the gate, absorbed as she was in adding fine detail to the portrait. Startled at the second knock, which was accompanied by a "Hey…" she turned to see Sam looking over the gate. She rose, stepped to the gate and opened it.

"Sam! This is a surprise."

His smile concealed his inner agitation. "Well…in fact, it's a business call."

She frowned and gave him a questioning look.

"I think you should reconsider. The more I think about your project, the more I like it. Our knowledge and experience, and inclinations…it couldn't be a better match. Your vision and medical experience, my life in aviation, my contacts…my resources… It's a perfect fit, and I think we'd be making a mistake if we didn't…" He trailed off, his expression all at once haunted.

He continued, his tone urgent. "You know…I have a bad feeling about this London business."

At this her guard went up, and Sam shifted back to his pitch. "I thought we could name your outfit for Sally… 'Sally's Shelter'… something like that. You'd know best, of course…"

Pain filled her face at the mention of Sally's name and brought Sam up short. He regretted his words.

Kate recovered and replied, "I'm sorry. I'm so sorry…but my mind's made up."

Sam's eyes pleaded, but she was unmoved. Surrendering for the moment, he drifted to the easel. He studied Laurel's image for a long time.

"This is very good. Who is she?"

Kate joined him and stared at her work. With a slight shake of her head, she replied, "If only I knew. She haunts me."

He lingered over the joyous, ethereal image a long while, then whirled on her. "Marry me, Kate," he pleaded. "You'll learn to love me. I promise."

She turned away and gazed at the restless, darkening sea. At last she replied, "It wouldn't be right. It's so generous of you… and I'm so grateful…but it would be so wrong of me to accept." A heavy silence hung long between them.

Sam spoke first. "Then let me wish you good luck. And Merry Christmas." He held out his hand and she grasped it. But when a single tear escaped she pulled her hand back to swipe at it.

Again, she fought to compose herself. Finally, she replied, "Goodbye, Sam. Merry Christmas."

31

Early light filtered through a clerestory window of the baggage room in San Diego's Santa Fe Station, casting a thin, mote-dusted beam upon a dusty tarpaulin in an otherwise shadowy corner. A small hand emerged from under the rough cloth, then another, then Laurel's eyes appeared and she scanned as much of the room as she could without moving. Tony had confirmed Jack's warning about the police—had told her that it wouldn't do at all for her to be found sleeping in the station—so when she had arrived in San Diego the evening before, she took care to conceal herself before she collapsed, exhausted. Now, again taking care to remain unobserved, she arose and made her way to the station's exit, her knapsack slung over her shoulder. Huey peeked out from his shelter under the flap.

On the sidewalk, she half closed her eyes and turned a full circle, alert for any sense of Kate's direction. But the ether was turbulent and obscure at the moment, so she decided as much on whim as on spirit sense and headed toward downtown San Diego.

After only a few steps, she stopped, wracked by a great shudder, and an enormous sneeze. She fished out the red handkerchief to dab a bit of blood from her nose and trudged on.

Some blocks further, Laurel paused, distracted by faint music. Her pace quickened. The music, Christmas carols played by an off-key brass band, grew louder, until she turned a corner where the full awfulness of a very spirited but very amateur brass band confronted her. Even as poor as it was, the music restored her a bit. And, as always, her musical magnetism improved the band in return, though Heaven knew there was little help for them, as limited as their resources were.

As she watched, a few people, despite the meager times, dropped coins into the bucket suspended from a tripod in front of the band. She recalled the money Tony had given her and the change the conductor returned with her ticket on the train from Los Angeles. She dipped into her pocket for some coins and dropped them in the bucket.

Through the morning and into the early afternoon, she trudged through the city. Several times when she saw a billboard with Kate's image, Laurel stopped passersby, pointed, and asked if they knew the beautiful young woman in the ad. No one did.

Belatedly, it occurred to her to sing Kate's song. *What am I thinking? If I can't feel where she is or find someone who knows where she is, maybe I can call her to me with her song.* Once, she sang out loud in her native tongue, but when this attracted puzzled stares she decided simply to hum the melody. She recalled Jack's and Tony's warnings about the trouble the police could give her and reminded herself to keep a low profile.

By early afternoon the symptoms were back—the pallor, the weakness. Her nose had bled—a couple of times in the morning and more heavily around noon after a great sneeze.

She heaved a sigh and stopped to rest, lost and dazed. When at last she moved on, she realized that what little sense of Kate's direction she had, or thought she had, was gone. She stopped to turn a wobbly circle as she was halfway across a residential street.

A couple of hundred yards away a gray-haired, school-marmish woman drove along the street. Though usually as meticulously careful a driver as her prim and tidy appearance suggested, she was just then distracted, rummaging in her purse for a note she had put there. After a brief search she located the elusive paper, looked back to the road—and shrieked and stood on the brake.

The tires screeched and the car came to a halt just as its bumper touched the pale young girl who stood in the middle of the street. Eerily calm, as much due to her exhaustion as her native demeanor, Laurel looked down at the chrome bumper just touching her leg, then looked up through the windshield to the driver, who by then was as pale and wide-eyed as Laurel.

For her part, the gray-haired driver was transfixed by huge blue eyes that held her gaze but for a couple of weary blinks. After an odd, frozen moment, she came to her senses, scrambled out of the car and hurried to Laurel.

"Oh, child! Are you hurt?"

Laurel stared dumbly for a second, her only reply a weak smile and a shake of her head. The woman fussed and fluttered, then, forcing herself to be calm, held Laurel gently by her shoulders and examined her. Finally the pallor, the shadows, the exhaustion registered, and she decided. "We'll get you some help. Come." She bundled Laurel into the car.

"I'm Clementine, dear," the woman said as she put the car in gear and drove on, "But everyone calls me Clem." She turned a sweet smile on Laurel. "I'm so relieved you're not hurt, and I'm *so* sorry to give you such a scare, poor thing."

"I'm Laurel," said the waif, returning about half a smile. Off her feet now, weariness overcame her, and she slumped back in the car's seat and drifted toward sleep—sleep denied by her rescuer's relentless questioning: "Where are you from?" and, "Where were you going?" and, "Who are your people? Where are your parents? Why is a young girl like you out in the streets, alone?"

Laurel, drowsing, fading, replied in dreamy non-sequiturs, mostly alluding to her "sister," and yet more vaguely, to her mission. Before long, Clem gave up trying to make sense of Laurel's sleepy ramblings. She turned inward and wondered at a world that could simultaneously contain beauty and grandeur and lost children, and the old anger returned. *When will something be* done…? She turned on the radio, and for a while, Brahms washed over them.

For many years Clementine had kept a small, quaint music shop in a nearby neighborhood. She parked the car in the alley behind her shop and roused her peculiar passenger.

As Clem guided Laurel to the back door, Huey darted out of the knapsack to an abundant wall of trellised trumpet vines.

The shop's rear entrance led into a small and cramped room that served several purposes: office, kitchen, repair shop. On the wall opposite the entry, a calendar displayed the date: December 24, 1940. A table draped with a red-and-white-checkered cloth stood under a window to the right, and a narrow counter held a sink and a miniature refrigerator. Also crammed into the space was a rack containing small boxes of odds and ends. Close under a window that allowed light from the alley stood a small workbench.

Laurel's eyes widened when they alighted on a half-assembled violin resting on the workbench. A few luthier's tools were scattered around it and more hung on a pegboard attached to the side of the rack.

Laurel turned to ask Clem how it was that she had a violin maker's workshop, but her hostess had already disappeared through the door that led to the shop's front room. Laurel slipped off her knapsack, hung it on the back of a chair beside the dining table, and followed Clem.

The front room was in deep shadows, Clem having drawn the blinds when she left on the errands that had led her to an encounter with an angel. When she opened the blinds and flooded the shop with light, Laurel gasped, struck speechless at the treasure of violins, violas, cellos and bows hanging in tiered rows that covered a good part of three walls. Her expert eye at once recognized their quality.

A miracle! Now…*I will bring her…* The only interruptions in the back wall were the doorway to the rear of the shop, and a large portrait with a brass placard below it on which was engraved, "President Franklin D. Roosevelt," and below that, on a card, in a feminine hand, "Our Leader."

Laurel whirled on Clem, a request on her lips, but Clem had slipped away again. After reopening the public part of the shop she had returned to the private back room.

Laurel turned to the rows of violins. She ranged along the wall, all her senses alive to the signs violins give to those who love them. What she did not notice, in her absorption, was Clem's silent, stealthy peek around the doorframe and her subsequent retreat.

In the back room, Clem picked up the phone, taking care to muffle the dial's whirring. She glanced again into the front room as she waited for an answer, then spoke in a hushed voice, nearly a whisper, "Children's Bureau, please."

After a moment, she continued, her voice still low, "Hello… yes, I've come across a young girl…Just today…Fourth Avenue, just north of Kalmia."

She listened briefly, then went on, "Yes, she's with me…I brought her home. She's a lovely child, but ill, I'm afraid, and, well…confused. I tried to explain to her that she needs medical attention…clearly she does…but she didn't seem to understand, or even care. She hardly seems to hear me. She just goes on, obsessively…when she was awake, I mean, in the car…she could barely stay awake, you see… Yes. Well, anyway, she just kept on incoherently about a sister she says lives in town, but she has no idea of the sister's address, or even the neighborhood. The whole thing has me confused…worried and confused. She's a dear thing, but she needs help."

Clem peeked into the front room as she listened, then whispered, "Oh, could you…that soon? I'd be so relieved… Yes, I'll keep her here."

Satisfied that she had done her duty, Clem returned to the front room to find Laurel examining the finest violin in the shop, one of 18th century Italian make and a recent acquisition for which Clem had thanked her stars—and had nearly exhausted her cash reserves. Laurel turned the fiddle casually, carelessly, one might have thought, this way and that in her one hand, while the shop's finest bow, a very good 19th century French piece, dangled from the little finger of her other. The pale dusty waif, absorbed with the fine old fiddle, oblivious to Clem's presence, plucked a string and tweaked a peg to bring it into perfect tune.

With a struggle, Clem recovered her voice and stammered as her hands fluttered, "Oh!…dear… That…that's for grownups! Let me…"

Laurel ignored her. She tucked the violin under her chin, raised the bow, dived into a fiery rendition of the E Major Partita, Preludio, and instantly silenced Clem, who stared for a stunned moment, then sagged into the chair that, fortunately, happened to be just behind her.

08

At the same time, a few miles away, Kate watched a neatly dressed middle-aged man uproot a FOR SALE sign from her front yard and tuck it under his arm. "Thanks for the fast work," she said, as the realtor took her proffered hand, "It certainly helps."

He smiled. "Oh, the ones by the water usually go quickly… even in times like these. And this is an especially nice one."

Kate didn't hear his remark, however, because her attention had gone to some distant place. Music had begun to play in her head, fast, insistent, impossible to ignore.

With Laurel physically so near, and in possession of a fine instrument that, as it happened, resonated especially well with the musical element of Kate's spirit, she could only yield. She turned toward the south, toward Clem's shop and Laurel, and squinted as if looking for something, or someone, in the distance.

The mystified realtor stood by until the moment reached the limits of politeness, then cleared his throat and said, "Well… ahh…goodbye then. Good luck in London."

⋈

When Laurel finally ceased playing, Clem could only stare. She began to speak, but before she could make a sound, Laurel launched into a theme of Paganini's, very fast. Clem slumped back in her chair, again overwhelmed.

After a long while, silence filled the little shop as Laurel returned to the world and laid the violin down. Clem finally found her voice. "I've never heard…such…such…" She shook her head, stood, continued, "And so young! How could you possibly…your Bach! I've heard the best play him…but never, never… Who taught you?"

The question caught Laurel off guard, and her eyes flickered as they did when memories from her lost years tried to bubble up. A picture of a suave, mustached figure flashed before her and vanished. She frowned, tried to recall, shook her head, and replied, "A friend showed me…a little while back."

"'A little while?' How can that possibly…?" Clem stopped, her thoughts turning to a distant past.

"What?" Laurel asked.

Clem remained silent a while. Then, "Oh…this just calls my mother to mind. Near the end, I'd play Kreisler's Bach records, the slower ones, to get her to sleep."

Laurel echoed, "Kreisler?" Her eyes flickered.

241

Clem stared at the tablecloth a long time, then finally looked at Laurel. "I couldn't ever get her to listen to the modern things. She hated new things. I could hardly wait to get away from... from all that backwardness. You need to be in a *city* for music, and certainly to meet progressive, right-thinking people. But mother was crazy as a coot..."

"No! Really?" Laurel interrupted, sympathetic.

"Hah! One time she said she saw an angel...with a black eye! Is that crazy enough for you?"

Laurel's eyes fluttered again, briefly.

Clem shook her head as she remembered. "It seems as if I spent half my life hunting her down, tramping the countryside back in Illinois. She'd just disappear...for hours sometimes..."

Her voice trailed off. The waif's gaze went distant. *Illinois...* Her eyes narrowed, and she shivered.

Clem continued, "The only way I could get her to sleep was to play those old Bach records...the slow parts."

Laurel pondered the sound of that word...*Illinois.*

Clem started out of her reverie. "Oh! Look at the time! I'm famished, aren't you?"

Clem led Laurel, still clutching the violin and bow, to the little back room, seated her at the table with the red-and-white-checkered cloth, and busied herself preparing lunch. She clattered plates and silverware, sliced bread and stooped down to the little 'fridge for chicken and mayonnaise. She interrupted herself to place a tall glass of milk and a napkin in front of Laurel, who continued to admire the violin, examining it from all angles as her smile gradually widened.

Laurel finally looked up, noticed the milk and took a sip. Her eyebrows rose in approval, and she took a bigger swallow. She saw a flicker at the window and looked out to spy Huey hovering, eyeing her. She gave him a milk-mustachioed smile. Though the glass muffled his chittering response, Laurel understood: she picked up the napkin, dabbed away the milk and smiled her thanks. The hummer zipped off.

Looking at the violin again, she observed, "This is a really good fiddle." She turned earnest eyes on Clem. "Would you mind if I used it for a little while?"

Clem averted her eyes, stared out the window, glanced at the phone, and finally replied, still failing to meet Laurel's gaze, "Let's talk about that after lunch, dear." She finished making the meal and set two plates with sandwiches on the table. Laurel nibbled hers as Clem sat, her face carefully composed as she gazed over the top of her guest's head.

Then, forcing a smile and a cheerful tone, she announced, "I have good news! Some people are coming to see you." Laurel put down her sandwich and gravely studied Clem, thinking that her good cheer seemed a little off-key. "They…they want to help you. They'll give you medicine for your…your cold. And…" She was starting to sound strained. "…they'll help you find your sister!"

Laurel sat up straight, eager smile and wide eyes. "They will?"

Relieved by Laurel's change of mien, Clem plunged ahead, "Oh, I'm sure of it! I just know they'll do everything they can to help you find her once they get you settled."

Laurel's eyes returned to their normal size. "Settled?"

"Ahh…into your new home."

"New home?" Her dimming excitement veered into apprehension. "What new home?"

By now flushed and fluttering, Clementine babbled on. "Oh, I wish you could stay here, Love, with all my heart, I do. But it's just not that simple. We don't know where your people are… oh, you talk about your sister, but where is she, really? These are hard times and people, especially children, have been known to…well, make things up. Not because they're dishonest, I don't mean anything of the kind, but because times are so hard, they need a little make-believe, to get by."

Laurel looked as if she'd bitten into something bitter.

Clem continued, her voice rising in inverse proportion to her vanishing confidence. "And you need medical attention, too. It…it's, well…pretty plain that you're ill…" She dithered as she suddenly noticed that Laurel actually looked quite a bit better than she had earlier, still benefiting as she was from her session with the old violin. "Or…you were, or, well… Anyway, there are laws…laws to protect young girls. A girl your age can't just… ah… ah… And of course, you should be in school…children need to be, um, managed… By experts!" She thrust a finger in the air to emphasize "experts."

But grave doubts had begun to assail her. Laurel's Bach and Paganini sang through her memory. And that hard, level look the waif was giving her was anything but waif-like. *Perhaps she's… not what she seems…*

Clem opened her mouth to speak again, but by now, Laurel's apprehension had curdled into steely-eyed suspicion, and she leaned forward and preempted, "These people…they're friends of yours?"

"Oh, no, Love. They're not friends. They're the government."

Laurel blinked twice, then her eyes narrowed as she spoke, slowly. "I don't like the sound of it."

The door chime rang as someone entered the shop's front entrance, rescuing Clem, for the moment at least, from the pincers of her guilty conscience and Laurel's fervidly distrustful eyes. She fled the room.

Laurel's expression cooled, her eyes went far away. *Isn't anything simple down here?*

Clem entered the front room and came face-to-face with a very large, florid, middle-aged police officer and a shorter, younger one. Something inside her shrank away from the larger man. The exaggerated sternness? Something in the eyes? Before she could greet them, Pat, the larger officer, boomed, "You the owner? Brats' Bureau says you picked up a sick kid."

In the back room, Pat's harsh voice rocked Laurel out of her reverie. Her head snapped around. She leaned toward the door to catch Clem's stammering reply, "Ah…ah…that's right, officer."

Everything Jack and Tony had said about the police flooded back to her. She glanced about, found a scrap of paper and a pen, and scrawled a note:

Clementine,
I really, really need the violin for a little while.
Hope you don't mind. Thanks!
Laurel

She left the note on the workbench, found a case and stashed the violin and bow into it, then grabbed her knapsack off the back of the chair and dashed out the back door. The breeze of her leaving caught the note—whisked it off the table and onto the floor where it glided beneath the rack of violin parts.

Laurel eased the door shut, then whirled and whispered, "Huey! Let's go!" The hummer was beside her in an instant and the two zipped off down the alley.

In the shop's front room, Pat towered over Clem and demanded, "So, where's the kid?" Clem remained frozen in the man's forbidding gaze as Frank, the younger officer stood at a distance and scanned the shop. "*Well?*" Pat insisted.

Clem stuttered, "I…I'll go get her!"

She fled to the back room where she glanced about, blinking, quivering. Laurel was gone. She emitted a little moan and crept back to face the menacing policemen.

When she returned to the front room, alone, Pat leaned over her. "This some kind of game, lady?" he growled.

Clem shook her head and shrugged, palms up, helpless. The big cop glanced around, almost casually, and then nailed Clem in his iron gaze again. "Everything here that's 'sposed to be here? These runaways got sticky fingers, often as not."

Frank interjected, "Over there, Pat…" Clem darted a nervous look in the direction he indicated, to an empty space in the violin rack, the space lately occupied by the fine old Italian violin.

The big cop challenged Clem, "One o' them fiddles missing?"

Clem wilted. The day's disorder. Laurel's accusing eyes. The rough treatment by the police. And now, her treasure—gone. After a moment's miserable reflection she turned weary eyes back to Pat.

The big cop made disgusted grunt as he pulled a notebook from a pocket. "OK. What's the kid look like?"

Down the street from the shop, Laurel peeked around a corner, followed a second later by Huey, who hovered beside her. They watched until the policemen left Clem's shop and drove away. The waif and the hummer dashed off in the opposite direction.

Part 3

The Gift

32

In the 1930s and early '40s, Americans welcomed Christmas more gratefully than they had in better times. The present was squeezed between a past haunted by the specter of the Depression, and a future that loomed black with the threat of war, so the spirit of Peace on Earth, Goodwill toward Men resonated more deeply than it had during times in which security was more easily taken for granted. So despite the anxiety that beset daily life, San Diego, in the Christmas Season of 1940, carried on, donned its holiday livery, and showed the world a cheerful face.

In much the same way, Laurel carried on, putting one foot in front of the other, ignoring, to the extent she could, her relentless physical decline, and pressed her search for a safe harbor from where to play the borrowed violin in the hope of drawing Kate near, so that she might, at last, bestow the Gift.

Laurel's wandering led her to the downtown district where strings of colored lights, wreaths, and garlands of evergreen transformed the storefronts, and the sound of carols filled the streets. The strains of "O Holy Night" drew her to a shop where a gaily decorated Christmas tree glittered in the window. She sank down on the display window's wide sill, leaned back on the plate glass and breathed in the healing music. After a bit, somewhat restored, she stood and turned a circle. Nothing.

She can't be so very far…I must be fading pretty fast.

Another sound caught her attention: a ringing that reminded

her of the bells of the locomotives she'd heard during her travels on the rails linking San Francisco, Los Angeles, and San Diego. She followed the sound, finally turning a corner to discover a red-nosed Santa Claus resignedly clanging away beside his collection bucket, which, despite obviously having seen better days, was made festive with some sprigs of holly and a red ribbon. Laurel watched as a passerby clinked a coin into the battered but gaily decorated vessel.

When the traffic thinned for a moment, the old fellow darted a look this way and that, slipped a flask from his pocket, and took a nip, missing not a stroke of the bell. As Laurel's eyes caught his, he jammed the flask back into his pocket in one quick motion, and winked.

Laurel regarded him a moment, the parchment skin, the rheumy eyes, the grog-blossom nose. She remembered, with a tremor of apprehension, the "rumdums," as Tony had called them, on the train from San Francisco. But recognizing the old man's weariness, and—with a remnant of her fraying angelic sensitivity—feeling his essential good nature, her fear fell away.

"Merry Christmas!" she called to him.

"Merry Christmas, yourself, sweetheart!" replied Santa, with a smile that was disarming in such a rough-looking old fellow.

"You look tired," she said. "Why don't you take a rest?"

With a wry grin, he replied, "Strikes me as a fine idea, Love, but if I wanna fill the bucket, I gotta make the racket."

"Let me, then," said Laurel, setting the violin case on the pavement and undoing the latches. Santa watched her tweak the pegs and tighten the bow. He ceased ringing when she began to play Jesu, Joy of Man's Desiring. He smiled and sat on the beat-up little box in which he carried his bucket and bell. Caught up in the Christmas spirit, passersby stopped to listen and to drop a little something into Santa's bucket. A few coins landed in the violin case, too.

The Lowlands of Heaven

❧

While daylight remained, Kate took a last tour of her little yard atop the cliff overlooking the Pacific. The ocean was calm, and waves whispered on the cobblestones at the foot of the cliff. In disharmony with the soothing murmur from below, dark clouds crowded the offing, and still darker curtains of rain squalls shadowed the horizon here and there. A small pod of dolphins broke the surface no more than sixty yards offshore and ambled southward, their dorsal fins making lazy arcs in and out of the small waves.

When the dolphins had passed from view Kate walked to the garden that edged the sunward side of the house and watched a hummingbird at the trumpet vine trellised there. When she'd bought the house, the yard was nothing more than a threadbare carpet of grass. She remembered the hours, the days she had worked to create her gardens. *No...not* my *gardens anymore.*

She opened the door beside the trellis and stepped into the sun room. The house was bare but for the easel and portrait of Laurel in this "conservatory," as Kate ironically thought of the room when she considered the house's modest size. She'd started to pack these last things several times but for no reason she could name, did not. She reached toward the portrait, then halted, frozen.

She tilted her head, listening, and stepped back to gaze at Laurel's image. After a time, she turned away from the picture and glanced about, eyes narrowed, as if trying to locate the source of the music that played in her head—the strange, lovely filigree of Jesu, Joy of Man's Desiring.

33

Pat drove the police cruiser in a steadily widening pattern centered on Clem's shop, his hard eyes scanning the streets with practiced thoroughness. His young partner Frank likewise kept on the lookout for a little blond girl dressed in blue coveralls and toting a knapsack and a violin case. The officers remained silent for some time, intent on their search, but as the time wore on Frank became distracted, sneaking the occasional sideways glance at Pat. Finally, he asked, "What's eatin' ya, Pat? Seem kinda tense."

Pat continued his scan a moment longer, then replied, "I know this kid we're lookin' for…bet my life on it." Frank shot him an inquiring look. Pat continued, tight-jawed, "Description fits her to a T."

ೞ

Laurel concluded Jesu to enthusiastic applause and, as she segued into "O Come All Ye Faithful," the crowd joined in singing. As the crowd grew, so did the reach of their sound and their spirit, which drew yet more people. New arrivals would feed Santa's bucket or Laurel's violin case, or both, and then add their voices to the choir.

At the back of this large and ever-growing crowd, a young girl jumped up and down, trying vainly to see who it was that could do such lovely things with a violin. Susan had wavy blond hair, wore a blue jumpsuit, and clutched a violin case under one arm.

ය

As Pat and Frank pressed their hunt for the little blond violin thief, the older officer expanded on his theory about their quarry. "Strictly pro, they were. Little 'Betty' and 'Mother'…best short change artists you ever seen. Kid was six then. Later on they had her workin' catch in a pigeon drop scam…you know…the one where they have a phony lost wallet or purse? They get the mark thinkin' he's gonna share a big chunk of dough, then the cons switch the wad and dump the pigeon." He paused, slowing the car to look up an alley. "Guess they got a new game now."

Frank shook his head, disgusted. "The hell's a matter with people, use a little girl like that?" He scanned his side of the street for a while. "So how'd you get onto her? You never said nothin' about working bunco."

The silence grew long, then heavy. Frank slowly smiled. "Say… the cop that got burned on that pigeon drop… That was…"

"Awright, awright! Don't rub it in, eh?"

As Pat's fury and humiliation filled the car like sulphur fumes, Frank looked straight ahead and bit his lip. He considered his short partnership with Pat. *He's always been a blowhard…but I didn't figure him for…*

But now Frank's attention was caught by a large crowd spilling off the sidewalk and onto the street. "Hey, what's all that going on over there?"

Pat followed Frank's direction—and focused like a radar beam on one person alone. A blond girl of about twelve, in blue coveralls, half-concealed by the last row of the crowd, was jumping up and down trying to see over the heads of the people in

253

front of her. She landed awkwardly after one leap and stumbled backward out of the crowd. Pat fixed on the violin case under her arm. He pulled over—so hard that he ran the car up on the curb—and leaped out and ran heavily toward the gathering.

೫

Laurel, remembering her purpose, brought the concert to a close. The crowd watched, mystified as, eyes closed, she turned a slow circle in the hope that the music might have restored some of her ethereal sense. She did in fact experience a stirring as she came around to face toward La Jolla. Her eyes snapped open. "Kate?" she called, her face aglow. "Kate, are you here?"

Though she had recovered a portion of her directional sense, she had no sense of distance. As far as Laurel could tell, Kate might have been three feet in front of her or somewhere in Alaska or anywhere in between. "Kate! I'm here!"

Those who heard began to trade glances—a pity that the wonderfully gifted stranger was, apparently, a little unhinged. A pity…so young.

Finally, Laurel gave up. She began to put the violin away, and was astonished to find the case half-filled with coins—and even a few bills, a kind of generosity scarcely heard of in those hard days. She stared at the jackpot for a second, then with an air of decision, picked up the case and tilted it over Santa's bucket. The crowd cheered as the coins jingled and the bills fluttered—even if Laurel's act, in their eyes, removed any lingering doubts that she was a bit demented.

The crowd's puzzlement over Laurel's doings ended abruptly when a piercing shriek rang out, followed by a hoarse shout, "Game's up, Betty!" Pat had rushed Susan from behind and seized her arm with one hand and the violin case with the other. In his single-minded focus on the girl, he failed to notice the large

254

man who stood a few feet behind her. Though Pat was himself a large man, the bystander was half a head taller, proportionately heavier and still looked every inch the All-American halfback he had been fifteen years earlier.

At Susan's cry for help, it took the big man little more than an instant to cover the distance and seize her captor's arms in a steel grip. Pat instantly released the girl. The former All-American whirled the stunned cop around to face him. "What the hell do you think you're doing?" he bellowed.

Shocked by the civilian's interference, Pat took a moment to recover. He jerked free of the big man, thrust his chin up at him and bellowed back, "That fiddle's stolen property! And I'm an officer of the law, if you couldn't tell! And I'm gonna run *you* in too, along with this little thief!"

The big man's face turned a deeper shade of red. He leaned into Pat and roared, "Your 'little thief' is my daughter! And I bought that violin brand new a half hour ago and it hasn't been out of my sight since! And furthermore…"

At that moment Frank spotted Laurel through a rift that had developed in the crowd as it dispersed. But as his eyes locked onto her, another pair of eyes locked onto him.

Their small size notwithstanding, hummingbirds are utterly ferocious when defending their territory, and Huey's territory was any ground on which Laurel stood—now more than ever with her so weak and a threat so close. The young cop was a step and a half into his pursuit of the weary angel when Huey launched himself like a rocket.

Frank suddenly was disoriented by a shadow that grew—very fast—out of nowhere, accompanied by a low and menacing thrumming, the more threatening in that its source was indiscernible and that its volume swelled with dreadful speed. Far worse, the hurtling shadow turned out to be possessed of a needle that drove into the outer corner of his left eye. Frank's agonized scream rose over the noise of the crowd, as his hands shot to his stricken eye.

The thing was gone even quicker than it had arrived, well before Frank's scream was spent. His eyelid snapped back and a rivulet of blood ran down his cheek and over his fingers. He noticed dimly that he was aware of light and his mind emptied itself of any and all thoughts about little blond thieves or violins or Pat or anything else but a deep gratitude that he apparently hadn't lost his sight, or at least not all of it.

To the startled bystanders, Huey's attack was a spectacular demonstration of the physics of flight gone awry. Though determined to protect Laurel, he nonetheless knew that the high-speed impact with the aiming point would have dire effects on his aerodynamics. Indeed, his bill's snag in Frank's eyelid—while the rest of him obeyed Newton's First Law of Motion and continued upon the original trajectory—threw him violently sideways and made him roll until he was fully inverted. His thrashing wings no longer bit into the air at an angle to provide lift and thrust, though they made an impressive amount of noise as, for a tiny fraction of a second, he traveled upside-down and backwards, still under full power.

Momentum carried the bird onward where, whirling like a discus, he smacked into a bystander, caromed off her like a buzzing, feathered pinball and collided, still tumbling, with a couple more of the crowd before he resumed controlled flight about an inch above the pavement.

His mission accomplished—and nearly spent—Huey darted back to Laurel and frantically chittered to her as she finished packing up the fiddle. Apprised of the potential danger (Huey couldn't know with certainty the outcome of his attack), the angel ducked into the nearest alley and trotted off toward the other end. Exhausted, Huey zipped under the flap of the knapsack and went instantly to sleep.

A half-block away Susan's father was concluding matters with Pat. "...and furthermore, do you mean to say you don't recognize your own Deputy Police Commissioner, *jackass?*"

The blood drained from Pat's face, and after an agonized moment, he managed to stammer, "I...I'm sorry, sir!" He darted a look at Susan. "And...and you, too, young lady!" Susan huddled under her father's arm, clutching her violin case, pouting at Pat.

The Deputy Commissioner mercifully put an end to the miserable spectacle. He held up his hand to silence Pat, heaved a sigh, then took in the whole of the surroundings—the holiday crowd, happy, if a bit bemused by the events of the last few minutes, the abounding Christmas decorations, a bright and cheerful carol from some distant source. He turned back to Pat, his expression much eased, though not what anyone would call friendly. "Hell, man...get about your business. If it weren't Christmas Eve, I'd have your badge. Now go on...and for God's sake, watch what you're about."

By now Frank had rejoined Pat. He touched his cap to the Deputy Commissioner and his daughter, and then took Pat's arm and led him back to the patrol car.

34

By the time Laurel had run three blocks, she could hardly pick up her feet and her gait had become a kind of shambling trot. Though the musical interludes had had a healthful influence, the overall effect was "one step forward, two steps back." She was losing ground and the rate of loss was accelerating. She sank down on a bus stop bench, fished out the handkerchief and dabbed at her nose. She tried not to notice that the bleeding had gotten heavier.

Huey awakened at the change of rhythm and fluttered out of the knapsack to perch on Laurel's shoulder.

She wobbled and fell back against the bench, and after a few labored breaths spoke in a hoarse whisper, as much to herself as to the hummer, "We'd better find her pretty soon."

Huey lifted off, hovered before her, sang a long, detailed chitter.

Laurel nodded as she considered. "Yes, the connection *was* a lot stronger with the band at the fair. I felt her, too…even that far away. Helped me more, too, when there were good players."

"Chp…chp, chp."

"True, but I can't imagine where we're going to find a band now…" She interrupted herself with a great yawn. "…so I guess I'll just keep playing as long as I can and hope for the best."

Huey perched on her shoulder and nuzzled against her neck. After a few minutes' rest, she took out the violin, stood and started to play her Christmas medley. As always, a crowd gathered, and the people began to sing. And too, as always, their voices helped ease her, but—she couldn't help but notice—not as much as on earlier such occasions.

ↀ

As he had told Kate, Ted and Dot the day he met Kate, Sam had put together a band to take part in a Christmas Eve concert. At the same time Laurel was raising yet another impromptu choir, Sam was rehearsing his band for the evening's performance. As it happened, both Sam and Laurel convened their musical events on the same city block.

In a large room on the vacant second floor of a sparsely occupied office building, Sam handed out sheet music to the band. He whistled for attention, meaning to let the group know that their violinist had suddenly been called away, that they would have to make a few changes in the arrangements to cover his absence. But as the room grew silent he paused and listened. Outside in the street a choir sang—and a violin wove a bright descant over them. Sam strode to the window and scanned the gathering on the sidewalk.

"Hang tight, guys. Back in a minute."

On the sidewalk Sam watched and listened, bemused, as the motley crowd wove lovely harmonies. When the song ended he worked his way through them, searching for the violinist.

When he spied Laurel, he thought, *Her? That's the fiddler? Never heard the like...not from anyone that age, anyway.*

She stood very still, eyes closed, breathing deeply, but as Sam reached the front of the crowd her eyes opened and met his—and in that moment an odd shift moved through both of their minds: Something in her strained forward to apprehend—what, she couldn't say—only that here, there was a flavor of a tantalizing

259

familiarity. At the same time, for an instant Sam thought that he knew her, but that impression was cast out by the next one: *She's not well…* This too registered only fleetingly as, pressed by his need for a substitute musician, Sam smiled at the unlikely violinist and said, "You sound great, kid. Are you busy the next little while?"

She looked up, dimly. The music had restored her somewhat, but all in all she was failing fast. "I have to…find my sister." The natural and charming shadow of hoarseness in her voice had by now become a rasping whisper.

Sam stifled a laugh. "Well. You have a funny way of looking for her." Laurel responded with a shrug and a weak grin. Sam continued, "Anyway, my band's got a show in a couple of hours and I just lost my fiddler."

Her mind instantly cleared and her eyes widened. "Band?"

Sam continued, "Can you read?" She nodded. "Would it be OK with your folks?" She nodded again. "We'll be done early. And of course I'll pay you triple scale…for the holiday."

"How many people in the band?"

"With you, twenty. Want the job?" Before Sam finished speaking, Laurel was packing up the violin. When she finished she stood, mute, her big eyes locked on him. She wobbled a little, and his eyes narrowed.

"You OK?" he asked.

"Uh huh." A wheezing croak.

"Hm. Oh…and uh, do you have any decent clothes?"

"Uh huh." She indicated her knapsack with a tilt of her head.

Sam eyed her dusty coveralls, the pale golden hair half fallen out of its chignon, then at her wan face. *She* does *look sick. I'd swear she's turned whiter just in the time we've been talking.*

She dabbed her nose with the red handkerchief. He began to wonder if this was such a good idea after all.

Laurel broke the silence. "So…where's the band?"

He held her eyes a half-second longer, then decided. "Come on." They introduced themselves and Sam explained the situation as he led her up the stairs.

Sam showed her the ladies' room in the hallway between the stairs and the rehearsal room, and told her how to find him when she was ready. She emptied the knapsack and found a brush that Jack had slipped into it. She brushed her hair through its full length for the first time since the county fair, when Alma had shown her how to make a chignon. She changed clothes and before she left had the foresight to stash her handkerchief up her sleeve—the bleeding was becoming more and more frequent.

When she entered, the band ceased randomly riffing and chattering. She stood before them in her angelic robe and cowl— wings still hidden—long, wavy hair falling to her waist but for the strands in front she'd tied back to keep it from her face when she played. Dusky shadows beneath her eyes marked her pallor.

Her battered, dusty knapsack, now a jarring contrast to her clothing, hung by a strap from her shoulder. The violin case dangled casually from two fingers.

The musicians stared, and Sam eyed her critically. *Wouldn't have thought…Very classy, even if she still looks pretty peaked.* He made a courtly gesture toward her and announced, "Guys, we're in luck. This is Laurel. She's going to fill in for Sascha tonight."

The band was ambivalent. On one hand, every man's heart was drawn to Laurel, to her fragile beauty, now the more haunting in the shadow of her illness, but more because she reminded each of a daughter or a younger sister. She evoked sympathy and the urge to protect.

On the other hand, in their professional view, Sam had just said that this waif, this child, was to take the place of a seasoned professional musician in a public performance that was sure to be well attended. *Sam's judgment has always been sound...but...*

Before Laurel could acknowledge their greetings, her enormous sneeze drew a chorus of "Bless you!" Some of the players exchanged dubious looks. *Not only young and inexperienced, but sick, too.*

Sam moved them past the awkward moment. "We don't have all night. Let's get started."

To Laurel, he whispered, "Just take it easy and read until you're comfortable. Any questions, give me a wave."

She watched him as he returned to the piano, and covertly dabbed her nose with the hankerchief. *Please, please hold it back. I won't be able to stop it when I'm playing.*

Sam counted off the first piece.

When the first chord rang out, Laurel eased back in her chair, breathing deeply, inhaling the music, the healing.

Ahh...this could do it...this could bring her...

The band jammed on, smooth and tight, as Laurel breathed in and clung to the lifeline of sound, and began to dare to hope. About halfway through the piece, she opened her eyes and looked at the music on the stand. She raised the violin and began to softly bounce the bow on the strings, tight with the piano and guitar.

When the band was warmed up, Sam brought them to the theme of the evening's program, the traditional carols. Laurel knew these well enough, and the band's apprehension eased as they heard her ease confidently into the arrangements.

When the Christmas pieces were polished to Sam's satisfaction, he took the band back to their accustomed ground, and counted off "Brother, Can You Spare a Dime." Laurel had the melody in the introduction. Perhaps her days on Earth had prepared her, perhaps it was simply her heritage—for whatever reason, she played the sentimental minor-key melody with a lyrical conviction that finally and utterly won the band's confidence.

Sam took them through their repertoire of standards, "Stardust," "Moonlight Serenade," "Frenesi." With as little effort as she had when she had played with the band at the fair, Laurel made a new-found music her own.

❧

The bungalow was starkly empty, all of Kate's things by now sold, given away, or packed for her journey. She had spread her travel documents out on the kitchen counter for a final review and had assured herself that all was in order.

The itinerary was the last to go back in the folder. Once again she read the line near the top, "Depart San Diego, Calif. December 25, 1940."

She'd put the paper halfway back into the folder when she stopped and looked up. She started to hum, without really intending to, "When You Wish Upon a Star." For no apparent reason, and without any destination in mind, she picked up her purse and coat. She stood, bemused, another second or two, then hurried out. She barely noticed that it had started to rain.

❧

In the pause before Sam called the last tune, the band was startled to hear rain drumming on the windows. It would be a wet trip to the theater.

Sam counted off "Sing, Sing, Sing"—high energy and a chance for everyone to stretch out with a solo. After a verse and chorus, he nodded to the players one at a time, the signal to "take a ride."

As Sam took his solo he realized that he'd neglected to cue Laurel, unaccustomed to thinking of her as part of the band, so when he wrapped up, he raised an eyebrow in her direction. She smiled. Then she stood and dived into the racing,

263

throbbing music. She began with a syncopated figure on the G-string, echoing the pulsing drums that made the song so recognizable and compelling.

After her eight bars, Sam took eight of his own, then nodded to Laurel again. She played the theme—with subtle variations— still in the violin's lowest range. Eight bars of it and she tilted her head to Sam. He played a variation on her theme, then nodded back. Laurel put Sam's take of the melody into double stops, an octave higher. Eyes locked, they laughed.

Back and forth they went in a musical game of catch, the energy rising with every turn, until he gave it up, surrendered to her, and stood aside.

Her passion was contagious. A musical storm broke to challenge the storm brewing outside, and the band slipped into a fine kind of madness as they backed her. She swayed, eyes closed, breathing deeply. Somewhere in a far corner of her mind, a thought penetrated. *She* must *hear…she* must *be coming…*

At last, Sam glanced at his watch, and was startled. He tried to get Laurel's attention, but she was in another place altogether. He watched her for a while longer and, just as he reached to bring her back, she opened her eyes. He saw that she was far, far removed, but gradually she focused, and finally she saw him and subsided, and then knew again where she was, and Sam brought the piece to a close.

For a few seconds, the room was silent but for the rain's hammering on the rehearsal room's windows, punctuated now by fierce gusts of wind. Then the band erupted into cheers, and the players flocked around Laurel to welcome her to their ranks. Sam whistled for attention. "An hour 'til show time! Let's hit the road."

35

Pat and Frank's luck was consistent, if nothing else. Since the one's encounter with the Deputy Commissioner and the other's run-in with an apparently homicidal hummingbird, their search had taken them near to Laurel, then far from her, then near again, but never near enough to allow them to put their eyes on her. Pat took out his rage and humiliation on the car. He drove wild and fast, with violent starts and stops.

Frank grew more and more uneasy. After a while he blurted, "Slow down, why don'cha, huh? You're makin' me nervous."

Pat's head snapped around to fix a murderous look on the younger cop. Frank shivered and turned back to his search. He hardly recognized his partner. He absently touched the throbbing flesh at the corner of his eye, then had to abruptly brace himself as Pat hurled the car around a corner.

"Pat! Slow down, for cryin' out loud! You wanna kill somebody on Christmas Eve?" Frank was on the border between nervous and downright scared. The more the rain intensified, the more aggressively Pat drove. The longer they searched without a sign of Laurel—or "Betty" as Pat still believed their quarry to be—the hotter his rage burned.

Pat took a corner at a speed that made his partner suck in his breath and hang on. "I'll slow down when I have that damn brat in the lockup!"

On the coast road between La Jolla and San Diego where a light drizzle driven by a freshening wind polished the pavement, another car barreled along dangerously fast. As she drove, Kate hummed or sang, compelled to try to express the crazy, insistent music that possessed her.

She reached downtown San Diego by the time the band started "Sing, Sing, Sing." So intense was the pull on her when Laurel began to develop her solo in earnest—amplified by the band's searing energy and the ever-decreasing physical distance between them—that Kate nearly ran onto the sidewalk. She willed herself to focus on the road. The rain grew heavier.

ᔕ

Fox Theater housed a capacity crowd. By the time the band had arrived at the elegant building and made their way to their green room, the first group, a choir, was already performing. Echoes of layered voices wafted into the room where Sam and Laurel sat. He eyed her with concern as she dabbed her nose. "You gonna be OK?"

She essayed a smile and nodded. Unconvinced, he continued to study her. She turned her eyes to his. "What?" she asked.

He considered his reply. "I keep thinking that..."

An inquisitive tilt of her head.

"I keep thinking we've met before."

She held his eyes a long time, and again something inside reached in pursuit of an elusive...not a memory...what, then?

"I know what you mean," she replied at last. "But I'm sure we haven't. I would've remembered." She changed the subject. "Do you know Clementine?"

"With the violin shop? Sure, we all know Clem."

Laurel nodded, fading even as Sam watched her. She gestured

toward the violin case. "This violin…it's hers. Will you do me a favor?" He nodded. "If anything happens, will you see that she gets it back?"

Sam was puzzled. "Sure, but, 'happens'? What's going to happen?"

She yawned and shrugged as she shook her head. Sam watched her for a second longer, before leaving to see to the details of the band's entrance. Laurel, somber, drifted into slumber and dreamed of Kate, and in her dream, willed her to come before it was too late.

❧

Kate's car roared up the street where Laurel had gathered her last impromptu choir. The music in her head had stopped a little while before, but she plunged ahead with a will. When she reached the place where a little while ago common passersby, strangers of no distinguished talent, had gathered around an ill and dusty waif and together made glorious music, she hit the brakes and skidded and nearly rode over the curb—here at the last place Laurel had made music, and where Sam had recruited her into the band—the last place from where the angel's attraction had captivated Kate.

Her arrival threw a sheet of water over the sidewalk—the rain was increasing and water ran in the gutters. She jumped out, left the motor running, looked up and down the street. She couldn't have said what she was looking for, but something deep inside assured her that she would know when she saw it. Then she looked up, to the window of Sam's rehearsal room. A single light burned there, limning the drops that fell past the window. She looked at the light for a long space, careless of the rain. Then the music began again.

She jumped back into the car, revved the engine and roared off in a skidding, splashing u-turn.

36

Gerard sat silent, slumped over the still, dark water of the pool. Aurora, Ambriel, and Abel stood behind him, peering over his shoulder, exhaustion written in their faces. Gerard's hand rested limply on the knurled stone. An occasional random image flickered in the water but none relevant to the elders' dayslong, fruitless search for Laurel.

Gerard yawned, stretched, then spoke. "When I can get anything at all, there's no time to discover a context. A flash of Laurel here, a glimpse of Kate there, but never a thread to follow. What troubles me, though…there's more and more of London in it."

Ambriel nodded. "There would be. Since Kate has decided on London, it's to be expected the pool would seek the place."

"There's little enough of clarity," Gerard continued, "but some of what I've made out suggests that something like three thousand will die in an air raid there on the 29th. All but the least sensitive feel it coming, and they're jamming the ether with their worry. Laurel just gets lost in the turbulence."

Aurora broke out of her brown study. "Look at us…" she exclaimed. A moment passed.

Gerard urged her, "And?"

"The entire time since she left we've been taking turns at the water. Gerard when he can steal time from the Aviary. Abel's turned the library inside out while I've turned the lab inside down, Ambriel has meditated without cease. But always…each of us…alone."

"What are you getting at, Aurora?" asked Abel.

She held their eyes. "For where two or three come together in My name…' What have we been thinking?"

Understanding dawned. The four spread out around the pool and, by a shared impulse, they whispered together, "Laurel" as they touched the knurled stones, and in that instant a blaze of light burst from the water's surface.

As the radiance faded, the elders leaned over the water, where they saw, as from high above, a city on a seacoast glittering in the night. The image expanded as the point of view quickly descended. Ambriel exclaimed, "That's San Diego, Kate's town! Do you suppose Laurel's…?" The three leaned over the shimmering picture—just as it blurred and threatened to dissolve.

They calmed themselves and touched the stones again. When clarity returned they found themselves viewing a concert hall— Fox Theater—and Sam's band on stage just as Laurel stood.

"They'll be together for Christmas!" Aurora exclaimed.

☙

Some time before the elders of Branch 92 finally found Laurel, the band had finished the Christmas songs and had moved on to the swing pieces. As the angels watched the scene in the water, Laurel and Sam traded solos as they had done at rehearsal. The energy rose as the audience felt the electricity between the two.

Meanwhile, Kate had been steadily homing in on Laurel. She rushed through the dark, the attraction that drove her ever-increasing, like the wind and the rain. She pulled the car to the curb, stepped out into the driving downpour and looked about, trying to orient herself. Controlled, utterly, by Laurel's attraction, she had no idea where she was. Peering through the rain,

269

she recognized the rear of the Fox Theater down the block and across the street. The magnetic pull on her eased as Sam and Laurel finished their piece.

☙

Laurel struggled with the forces that pulled her in different directions—the sickness, threatening to overtake her at last, the music's healing energy, which, intense as it was, still only barely kept her upright, and the giddy sense of Kate's nearness. She felt her nose begin to bleed as she sat down after the jam and covertly dabbed with her handkerchief. There was more blood than before, and dread again encroached. *Oh, please come! I know you hear me...*

And in that moment, Kate's nearness broke through the fog of the Earth sickness. Laurel stopped hoping and at last knew. Knew that Kate was in fact nearer than she'd ever been. Knew that the fulfillment of her quest was at hand.

She drew herself up, her eyes wide. *Oh, yes... you're very, very near.* When she rose and walked to the front of the stage, the lingering applause ceased. Sam and the players stared, bemused— this was not a part of the set. She raised the violin, and with all of the grace she brought from her distant home, she began to play the melody of Kate's song. Peace, repose, and an otherworldly sense of well-being touched every soul in the theater.

Sam gestured to the stage manager, and the lights dimmed but for a single spotlight illuminating Laurel. She played one verse, then, as the band took over the accompaniment, lowered the violin and began to sing in her ancient native tongue.

☙

Not far away, Pat drove the patrol car as if he were possessed by the very demon of rage. Frank was beside himself. "For Pete's

270

sake, Pat, knock it off! She's not gonna be out in this weather, anyway!"

If Pat heard him, he gave no sign of it. He yanked the wheel, and the car skidded squealing around a corner.

In the street behind the theater, Kate paused, motionless as Laurel began her song and the attraction reasserted itself, stronger than ever before. She began to walk toward the theater, then to run as Laurel began to sing "her" song—as the angelic music penetrated and filled her mind.

So absorbed was she, Kate hardly noticed the squeal of tires as a car careened around the corner at the end of the block. The music possessed her, negated the rest of the world.

Neither Kate nor Pat, at the wheel of the speeding patrol car, saw the tall, pale man in the long dark coat who stood, very still, in a sunken stairway in the middle of the block. No one saw him look right to Kate, left to Pat and then raise both arms, fists clenched so hard they trembled.

Nearly out of control, the car swerved madly as Kate drew even with the theater. Now, closer to Laurel than she had ever been, the pull overwhelmed her and she dashed into the rain-drenched street. Frank lunged for the wheel—too late.

37

Laurel froze. Her face was a study in horror as she collapsed to her hands and knees, ashen, deathly. Blood dripped from her nose, thick red drops that ran together on the boards, and a red rivulet flowed from the corner of her mouth. With the handkerchief, and a great act of will, she stanched the flow.

The audience was stunned to silence.

Laurel staggered to her feet and stumbled forward a couple of steps, her hands wide before her, a supplication. "What's happened? Where are you?" Though only a hoarse whisper, her voice filled the cavernous hall.

Reeling, eyes closed, she turned a circle. This time the direction was unmistakable. She gathered the last of her strength, leaped off the stage to the center aisle, and ran weaving toward the exit. Wrenching open the door, she rushed out into the rainstorm.

Sam and a few others followed in Laurel's wake but halted, confused, when they emerged from the theater and saw no sign of her. As they looked about for her, the dismal wail of a siren swelled in the distance.

On the other side of the theater, Laurel stumbled and fell. Everything was crashing down on her—the sickness, her empathetic reaction to Kate's injuries, her sheer exhaustion from the days on the harsh and cruel Earth.

Huey had, of course, concealed himself during the concert.

272

But now he hovered before Laurel, and with all his heart he sang, to give her heart, to will her into motion.

She rose to her knees and cupped her hands. Nothing—only darkness and rain. She uttered a little moan, clapped her hands together and cupped them again. At last the little golden sphere appeared, but it was dull, with none of its former luster. It flickered, dimmed. Laurel staggered to her feet and pressed on.

After a fruitless search of the alley beside the theater, Sam encountered a throng of people spilling over the street behind the building, clustering about a police car half-on, half-off the sidewalk at a crazy angle, doors hanging wide open, one front fender crushed. A large policeman sat dazed on the curb, rocking and moaning.

A red light pulsed and as Sam approached he saw attendants lift a gurney into an ambulance. The doors closed, the siren resumed its wail, and the ambulance disappeared into the rain-lashed darkness.

Laurel, bleeding and dizzy with exhaustion, had made her way to the street behind the theater where she heard the siren's rising wail and watched the throbbing red light of the ambulance vanish around a corner. Numb with grief—for the last shred of her angelic empathy told her the worst had happened—she staggered through the slowly dispersing crowd, to where Kate had lain, and collapsed. Blood—Laurel's and Kate's commingled—chased by the rain, spilled over the curb into the gutter.

Sam saw her fall and raced to her. He lifted her and looked about, frantic, until he spotted a policeman in the patrol car, tense, talking on the radio. "You, officer!" he shouted.

Frank looked up, took in the man and the limp, bloody waif he held in his arms and gestured for Sam to put her in the car. He jumped behind the wheel, and again a mournful siren penetrated the rainy night.

Balboa Naval Hospital's emergency entrance was bathed in red light as attendants removed the gurney from the ambulance and rushed it inside. Rain hammered on the portico and sheets of water poured off the roof. The emergency room team, alerted by the approaching siren, were prepared and waiting.

Shocked to realize the broken body on the gurney was Kate's, Ted, the ER chief that evening, pulled himself together and marshaled the team to do what could be done. But Kate's decline was inexorable; her heart rate, blood pressure, and respiration sank in grim unison.

At last, Ted looked up at the eyes above the masks and shook his head. As he left, one nurse drew a curtain around the space and another disconnected the IVs and instruments.

Her shift in pediatrics over, Dot approached the ER, hoping the night was a slow one so that Ted could leave before midnight. She smiled as she anticipated another Christmas together.

Her smile vanished when their eyes met as she caught up with him at the admitting station. Silently, he guided her into an empty room and closed the door.

38

The last of the emergency team had left Kate and so, even had any of them possessed second sight, none was there to witness the translucent blue sphere that rose from the still, sheet-draped form on the gurney. The light rose a few feet above the body and stopped.

Kate's consciousness, spirit, soul—whatever its right name—rolled to look down on the gurney, tried to understand. As she watched, an attendant came in, adjusted the sheet covering the still form, and then wheeled the gurney out into the hallway. She drifted, disoriented and uneasy in the empty, sterile space, rising to the ceiling—and through it. Up, up, through the higher floors she soared, faster and faster and out into the wet night sky.

❧

Alerted by the sound of another siren arriving, Ted and Dot stepped into the hallway just as a young police officer threw open the door and stood aside for a man who carried in his arms a young, ashen-faced, blood-stained girl.

With a jolt of recognition, Ted exclaimed, "Sam! How did you…?"

As they stood in shocked silence, the strains of "O Holy Night" emanated faintly from a radio at the receiving station.

Suddenly, words tumbled from Sam, "She's in bad shape, Ted…"

A nurse cut him off. "This way," she said, indicating one of the emergency room cubicles. "Let's see what we have."

Sam tenderly placed Laurel on the gurney and faced Ted. "She just collapsed on the stage…" he began.

Ted took Sam's arm and led him aside, wordless, grim.

"What? What is it?" demanded Sam.

Restored somewhat by the radio's faint music, Laurel had wriggled off the gurney in the cubicle and made her painful way to Sam. She hung on his arm and answered for Ted. "It's Kate."

Ted turned to her, astonished. He confirmed her declaration with a slight nod.

Sam resisted the darkness, the dread that was creeping into his mind. Ted held Sam's eyes. "We couldn't help her. I'm sorry."

Laurel drew a shuddering breath and began to weep. Both Ted and Dot reached for her, offering comfort even as they wondered who this strange child might be and how she might be connected to Kate and to Sam, and stranger still, how it was that they felt certain she belonged here.

But Laurel didn't want comfort now. She recoiled from them, and in a broken voice cried, "Where *is* she?" The force of her demand belied her frailness and took them aback. An awkward silence lingered for a moment, until Ted gestured and led them down the hall.

They rounded a corner and saw the gurney resting by the wall. Laurel hobbled to it and threw herself upon the draped form, sobbing.

"I'm sorry. I'm sorry…"

Sam followed and laid a hand on her quaking shoulder, his breath quickening as he fought the fear and nausea of early grief. Ted and Dot joined Sam and Laurel around the gurney to form a wretched little knot of grieving, the desolate silence punctuated by Laurel's sobs.

39

Gerard, Aurora, Abel and Ambriel had lost sight of Laurel when she ran from the theater. A kaleidoscope of images whirled in the water as they struggled to find her again.

Then, who could say for what reason—the love of the elders above, the grief of the survivors on Earth below—the flaring, wheeling motion slowed and stopped and resolved into the image of Ted and Dot, Sam and Laurel, and the draped form in the hallway.

"No!" cried Aurora. "It can't be!" The others stared, struck silent by the import of the image. Then, as it so often did, the water seemed to express a will of its own. The edges of the tragic scene began to dissolve; colors swam and shifted, forming a swirling palette beside the image. Gradually, the formless colors coalesced, transmuting into a blue sphere that seemed somehow to hurtle through a dark space—a luminous blue comet, its energetic trajectory a startling contrast to the desolation of the tableau in the hospital corridor.

The elders understood that they were witnessing the departure of Kate's soul from the Earthly plane—ordinarily an occasion of joy from Heavenly perspectives—but in this instance, they watched with sinking hearts as they absorbed the meaning of the twin images. A gloom unknown to this place, halfway to Heaven, settled upon them, and their minds darkened in a manner almost Earthly.

In spite of the encroaching darkness that threatened to paralyze, Gerard's mind reached, and sought. He pondered, and recalled recent, madly busy times at the Aviary the uncounted numbers of birds… He raised his head and exclaimed, "It might… it just *might* work!" He leaped to his feet and raced off. After a stunned moment, the others followed.

CR

Kate's spirit soared through a dark vault. Iridescent filaments, so fine as to be nearly invisible, danced and wove on the "walls" around her, seeming a kind of living artwork to soothe her passage, while music, as pleasing as the gentle colors, reached her from some far source. Yet despite the soothing sights and sounds, an oppressive undertone haunted her.

After some indeterminate time—though in this realm "time" was quite flexible—the sense of tremendous speed slackened, the space around her began to brighten, and the aspect of her surroundings to change, so that soon it seemed to Kate as if she were walking through a grove suffused with drifting banks of mist that glowed a pale butterscotch, permeated as it was by what seemed like bright sunlight from above—though "walking" hardly did justice to the motion she experienced. And still, though the environment evinced an Elysian loveliness, an indefinable weight dragged on her spirit.

A dim form loomed in the distance. As she drew nearer, it became a silhouette of vaguely human aspect, then—nearer still and less obscured by the glowing mist—Kate saw that the form was in fact two figures somewhat to the side of the path she traveled. At last the figures resolved into two young girls just on the verge of womanhood. Both had green eyes and blond hair, and both wore expressions of happiness mingled with concern. That they were identically similar struck Kate simultaneously with a strange sense of familiarity. Then it struck her—Sally! And her twin sister, Suzanne, no longer children as they had been when they had passed from Earthly life, but now at a heavenly ideal age. None of the three communicated in any direct way, but a mood radiated from the girls—of love and joy upon seeing Kate, and of Sally's gratitude for Kate's love and care—but also of regret that she had left Earth unfulfilled. There was no time for anything more, though. Their fingertips brushed as Kate continued on, swept along by some urgent, unseen current. The sisters seemed wordlessly to wish her well as they faded in the golden mist.

A bright point of light appeared before her. It grew as she approached it and soon it was a great brilliant globe. Sam's story about his experience flashed through her memory as the sphere hovered before her, radiating celestial light. And though she rested in a serenity the like of which she had never in her life known, still, a bare shadow of misgiving remained.

Then a voice "spoke" to her—not an audible sound—rather, a voice inside her.

"Welcome, Kate…" The voice expressed a perfect confluence of strength and gentleness. A beam of the great glowing sphere separated, began to transform, and became an angel of a surpassing beauty, floating between Kate and the great sphere of celestial light. Her serenity deepened in the presence. The angel spoke. "Observe now, your Earthly life."

The angel gestured, and before Kate appeared a window or mirror, in which an image began to take shape.

A train's whistle sounded. At the same time, the sound of an antique automobile swelled. The image began to clarify. The warm serenity faded, and the bud of apprehension in her mind began to open—and threatened to burst.

Below in the corridor, Laurel had regained control of herself, and stood as still as a statue before Kate's body. And then something stirred within—the fine and supernal sense that had led her from her Heavenly home to Earth and back, and back again, always and unerringly toward Kate. She stepped away from the gurney, to the middle of the hallway and looked up at the skylight and the hammering rain.

ᘓ

Aurora and Ambriel, along with Abel, and the young ones, Benedict and Kaira, Victor and Emelia, who had joined them on the way, finally caught up with Gerard in the Aviary's control room. He was seated at one of the large consoles, eyes intent on the display, hands flying over the controls. They saw the images of Kate and the Angel in the part of the display labeled "Destination." Gerard shifted the focus to the hospital corridor, the gurney, the bereaved—then narrowed it to Laurel. He touched a control, and the label, "Source" appeared over the image. He muttered under his breath, "Steady, Love…steady…"

ᘓ

Below, Laurel arched and strained at the painful bundle of her wings that she had borne on her back for the long, aching sojourn on Earth. Huey zoomed out of her cowl and hovered beside her. A wing tip edged with blue appeared, then another, and then both wings burst out and spread wide to their full span.

I will go to her.

Dot turned away from the gurney to see where Laurel had gone. Sam and Ted whirled at the sound of her gasp, and the three stared dumbstruck at the vision before them.

Oblivious to the others, Laurel stared straight up at the skylight, spread her wings and gave them a great, whooshing beat. She rose a couple of feet, then fell back, stumbling as she landed. She crouched, breathed deeply, and spread her wings again, wider. Another beat. She managed to rise only about a foot, then dropped—hard—to the floor again. For the first time, doubt clouded her face, but she gathered the bit of strength that remained to her, spread her trembling wings as best she could and gave one more beat.

She rose only to the balls of her feet, and sank to her knees, bowed, worn out. Her nose began to bleed. Scarlet drops spattered on the terrazzo floor. She weaved, and for a moment her mind swam, and she began to collapse.

This is what it's like to die.

With the last of her strength, she raised her face and her hands toward the black, rain-drenched skylight and cried, "Help me! Oh, please help me!"

 C⒔

Far above, Gerard gripped the controls. In the display, a glowing box surrounded Laurel as she pleaded. Gerard, his eyes riveted on the pitiful figure, made a final adjustment. The glowing box blinked and chimed. He smiled, so slightly, as he hit the domed button.

And nothing happened.

He hammered the button again. Nothing. He slapped the side of the console, and still there was no brilliant beam to transport Laurel from Earth to the place Kate now inhabited.

Suddenly, the image twisted grotesquely, and then the screen went black.

Kate stared at the astral window, aghast at the image of the gurney in the dim corridor, surrounded by those who had loved her in life. The picture shimmered, then vanished, giving way to a formless opalescent light. She spun to face the Angel. "But it wasn't supposed to be like that! It couldn't have been! So I never was complete…what does it matter? There's still so much I could do on Earth!"

The Angel's eyes were sympathetic, but the smile was sad. Kate continued, growing desperate, "Are there…are there *no* second chances?"

The angel regarded Kate with fathomless sympathy, and at last replied, "Some…a very few…may return. As when some great thing is left undone…or when some great love is left unfulfilled. But there must be love…a love complete."

oʒ

Gerard slumped, then struck the domed button so hard he nearly broke it, but it was no use. Laurel was lost to him. His head dropped to his chest. The others stood silent, sharing his grief.

And then time halted—a deep golden hue suffused Branch 92, and peace settled over all. The elder angels recognized the onset of a *Shift*, the harbinger of momentous change. For a space, all rested in the tranquility that stole over them. Then, Benedict and Kaira, Victor and Emelia lifted their heads and their eyes met as one inspiration visited them all. Three ran from the Aviary, and Kaira remained only long enough to cry, "Come on, Gerard! All of you! The Old Way!"

Benedict was the first to reach the campanile, and at a dead run he seized the tenor bell's rope. He swung on it twice before he regained his feet and then rang the bell as if he were announcing the end of the world—or the beginning of a new one.

The Lowlands of Heaven

All came—from the village, from the outlying hills, from the cliffs above the sea. Every angel came and the circle formed as the golden moon graced the western horizon, and the silver moon sailed overhead, and the sun broke above the eastern mountains.

Chains of hands were forged, and all hearts turned to Laurel, and to Kate, and to a common purpose. All came as one, all knew what was needed.

Gerard was the last to join. He gave one hand to Aurora, the other to Kaira, and the circle was complete.

And then, as they had through the ages, angelic minds stilled, and sought, and in the ancient way, descended interweaving, from the lowlands of Heaven toward the dark, aching Earth.

ლ

In the dim grief-sunken corridor far below, the skylight began to glow, and fast brightened, until the space was filled with a brilliance far greater than daylight. Shifting, weaving light embraced Laurel and, in an instant, she was restored to the radiant well-being she had known before she had first come to Earth. She glowed in the celestial light, and rose to her feet.

Sam stepped to her, shielding his eyes. She smiled, and extended her hand. He took it in his as she turned her eyes upward to the skylight—and in that instant, she was the very image of Kate's portrait of her. Sam cried, "My God! You're Kate's angel!"

A thin white beam darted from above and touched her forehead. She released his hand, and with a great beat of her wings, vanished in a flare of celestial light. Sam, Dot, and Ted stood in silence as the light faded. So dazzled were they, none noticed the blue-tipped feather that skittered across the floor in the wake of Laurel's leaving; so stunned, they barely noticed the faint scent of jasmine.

40

Laurel, freed from the prison of Earth, and from the cruel illness it had brought upon her, beat powerfully through a dark labyrinth. Iridescent, living filaments raced by and disappeared behind, and the ever-faithful hummingbird kept pace at her side. She paused for a moment, hovering, to turn a complete circle. Her perception was clear and certain, and she cried, "*This way!*" as she resumed her flight through the ether.

Laurel began to sing Kate's song, words in the ancient tongue pouring forth in joyful rhyme. Far ahead, a dim glow appeared. As she approached it, it resolved into something like a window. She remembered the first time she had visited Kate, by way of the pool, the thin place between Earth and Branch 92. She held her hands before her and the golden sphere burst into being, brighter than ever before.

છ

At this same time, the Angel took Kate's hand and began to lead her toward a distant, brightening Light. Kate looked back longingly, downward, toward Earth.

And then she heard, very faintly, music, "her song," sung by a familiar voice. She pulled her hand free of the Angel's, stopped and listened. As she turned to the window the song grew louder, closer, as the light pouring from the pane grew brighter.

The Lowlands of Heaven

❧

Laurel flew faster and faster, giddy with anticipation. Finally, she arrived before the glowing portal and peered into it, searching, wings spread wide. And then she saw Kate. She extended her cupped hands, and the golden sphere glowed ever brighter.

To Kate, the window became a living portrait of Laurel. She and the Angel stared, enchanted. Then Laurel burst through to hover before Kate, beatific. Their auras bloomed all around them, Laurel's gold, Kate's blue.

Kate cried, "It's…it's *her!* Oh, is there *any* way…?"

The great Angel turned, eyes closed, head bowed, toward the great Light in the distance as Laurel and Kate looked on, hushed.

All was calm—then the distant Light brightened. The Angel turned back to them, smiled, and said, "Merry Christmas, Kate."

Laurel glided closer to Kate, and offered the incandescent sphere. Their auras brightened, touched, pulled apart. Kate looked at the gift, then back to Laurel. Laurel smiled and nodded.

Kate extended her cupped hands and Laurel passed to her the Gift. Kate cradled it in her hands, then pressed it to her heart. Instantly, a new aura bloomed all around her, mingled gold and blue, the colors blending in a pale green glow. She extended her arms to Laurel and they embraced, Laurel enfolded Kate in her wings, laid her head on her shoulder and whispered, "Merry Christmas, Love."

A great burst of white light enveloped them.

41

The hospital corridor was dim again, and silent—the rain had slackened and no longer hammered on the skylight. Then—terrible irony—the clock at the nurses' station chimed twelve times. It was Christmas.

Sam, Dot, and Ted hardly noticed, but stood still, stunned by all they had seen. A faint moan brought them back to themselves. They turned, still numb, toward the gurney—apparently, if incomprehensibly—the sound's source. Sam rushed to it and pulled the sheet from Kate's face.

She was bruised and pale, but now she breathed. Her eyes flickered open and wandered a moment, then found Sam. He leaned to her, and embraced her. At last he released her and straightened so that he could see her eyes. She whispered, "Are you... Are you still looking for that...partner?" He sank to his knees beside her, and took her hand.

And so as Christmas Eve became Christmas Day, Laurel, young yet ancient, found Kate at last, and bestowed upon her the Gift that made her complete.

Epilogue

High above, the circle had broken and the angels had gone back to their various pursuits. The elders, and the young ones who had prompted the saving exercise of the Old Way, had drifted back to the Aviary, where to everyone's surprise, the capricious console was operational again, and the great light of Kate and Laurel's reunion was fading in it.

Only Laurel and the great Angel remained in view, and as the elders and the young ones watched, rapt, the two each extended a hand and touched fingertips. Then they drew apart. Faster, faster the great Angel drew away, fading, diminishing to a point of light. Laurel watched until the light vanished.

Huey zoomed into view, hovering. With a chirp, he perched on Laurel's shoulder. A moment passed. Aurora whispered, "Gerard, bring them home."

∝

A bird, or say, a spirit, roaming thereabout might notice at this moment a slender, winged figure, an angel, floating in the void, in deep repose. A closer examination reveals that one wing droops, that she gazes into a far distance. A little bird rests on her shoulder. The angel's eyes flicker, and she yawns.

Light blooms high above and fast brightens. As the firmament pours white-gold radiance over the winged pair, the angel closes her eyes and turns her face skyward. Her smile blossoms.

My heart swells…

A brilliant flash.

One blue-tipped feather spirals Earthward.

9 780615 376226